The Quanta Chronicles

Book I: Quanta Jones and the Awakening

By: Garrett Shanafelt

Published by Awakened Minds Press
Pittsburgh, Pennsylvania

ISBN: 979-8-218-76417-3
First Edition, January 2025

frequency, coherent states, and the quantum field of consciousness draw from research in neuroscience, quantum biology, and consciousness studies. Readers interested in exploring these concepts should conduct their own research and consult qualified practitioners. The author does not claim that the specific outcomes depicted in this fictional story will occur for readers who practice these techniques.

The references to systemic consciousness suppression, elite manipulation through media and education, and frequency prison dynamics represent a fictionalized exploration of how institutional systems may inadvertently (or intentionally) limit human potential and consciousness development. These narrative elements are designed to provoke critical thinking about social conditioning rather than to make specific factual claims about coordinated conspiracies.

The consciousness education concepts—including the 1% effect, morphic resonance, consciousness contagion, and collective field dynamics—are based on research by scientists including Rupert Sheldrake, studies on group meditation effects, and social tipping point theory, though their specific applications in this story are fictionalized for narrative purposes.

The books referenced in the story—including works by Eckhart Tolle (*The Power of Now*), Dean Radin (*The Conscious Universe*), Michael Talbot (*The Holographic Universe*), and Michael Singer (*The Untethered Soul*)—are real published works exploring consciousness, quantum physics, and spiritual development. Readers are encouraged to explore these and similar resources for deeper understanding.

This work draws inspiration from publicly available scientific research, consciousness studies, and spiritual teachings discussed by various authors, researchers, scientists, and spiritual leaders. Any mention of or similarity to the work of real individuals is for illustrative and educational purposes only. The interpretations and integrations of these concepts represent the author's original synthesis within a fictional narrative. This book is not affiliated with, endorsed by, or representative of the views of any real individual, organization, or institution whose work may be referenced or conceptually aligned.

Tesla's principles about energy, frequency, and vibration are based on the historical scientist's documented work and writings, though the specific applications demonstrated by the characters represent fictional extensions for narrative purposes.

The progression of consciousness awakening depicted—from initial "glitch" experiences through systematic development of awareness and reality creation abilities—represents a narrative framework drawn from spiritual awakening literature, mystical traditions, and consciousness development teachings rather than a scientifically validated developmental model.

The author's intent is to present authentic consciousness education principles and inspire personal growth through an engaging fictional framework, while clearly distinguishing between established scientific concepts, documented spiritual wisdom, and speculative fictional applications. This story explores what might be possible when young people discover their consciousness capabilities early—not as a prediction, but as an invitation to question limiting beliefs and explore human potential with curiosity and discernment.

MEDICAL AND MENTAL HEALTH DISCLAIMER: The consciousness techniques, breathing exercises, meditation practices, and mental exercises described in this book are for educational and entertainment purposes only within a fictional context. They are not intended to diagnose, treat, cure, or prevent any disease, medical condition, or mental health disorder. These techniques should not replace professional medical advice, diagnosis, or treatment. If you are experiencing anxiety, depression, panic attacks, or other mental health concerns, please consult a qualified healthcare professional, licensed therapist, or psychiatrist. If you are under medical care or taking medication, consult your healthcare provider before attempting any consciousness practices or breathing exercises. The author and publisher assume no responsibility or liability for any consequences resulting from the use of any information, techniques, or practices described in this book.

A Note from the Author

For nearly three decades, I climbed the corporate ladder. I earned an undergraduate degree and MBA from two of America's top universities, plus multiple industry certifications. I landed the prestigious titles and the six-figure salary—everything society promised would bring success and fulfillment. But despite checking every box, something fundamental was missing.

In my mid-forties, I began exploring consciousness, quantum physics, spirituality, and cosmology—fields that revealed truths no conventional education had ever mentioned. The deeper I went, the more clearly I saw what I'd been missing. And one realization hit harder than all the rest: *I wish I had known all of this sooner—it would have saved me years of struggle and searching.*

As a father of three, I couldn't stop thinking: What if my kids could learn these truths now? What if an entire generation could discover their true capabilities before the world convinced them they were powerless?

That question became this book.

Quanta Jones and the Awakening is fiction, but the principles within it are not. The consciousness techniques, the quantum physics, the universal laws—they're real, documented, and accessible. Some of what you'll encounter may challenge beliefs you've held your entire life. That's by design. I'm inviting you—whether you're young and just beginning to question reality, or older and finally ready to see beyond the illusions—to think critically, stay curious, and explore what's possible.

The systems around us work best when we remain unconscious, when we accept our limitations without question, when we forget what we're truly capable of. But what if those limitations were always an illusion? Funny how people trust radio signals and wi-fi, but doubt energy, vibration, and frequency.

This is the first book in *The Quanta Chronicles* trilogy—a journey designed to help you wake up and recognize the power you've always had.

The tools are real. The science is sound. The only question is: are you ready to remember who you really are?

— Garrett Shanafelt

Contents

Chapter 1: The Glitch

The fluorescent lights in Mr. Rike's classroom flickered like always, buzzing just enough to be annoying. Quanta Jones sat in his usual seat—third row, second from the window—half-listening, half-counting the dust specks drifting in the sunlight sneaking through the blinds. It was November, but it felt colder than that. Or maybe that was just him.

The flat-screen monitor mounted above the whiteboard came to life, displaying the South Ridge High logo with its pixelated red and white hawk that looked more outdated than intimidating. Principal McWreath's voice crackled through the wall-mounted speaker, carrying that familiar edge of someone who'd given the same speech so many times the words had lost all meaning.

"Hello, South Ridge Eagles. Happy Monday. Remember, what you choose to do today will shape who you become tomorrow. Make it count."

The announcement ended with a soft click, leaving behind the usual mixture of shifting papers, muffled conversations, and the steady tick of the wall clock. Quanta stared at the now-dark monitor, feeling that familiar knot of anxiety tighten in his stomach. *Make it count.* As if any of them had real choices about how they spent their days. As if sitting in these plastic chairs, memorizing information they'd forget by summer, was somehow shaping them into the people they were meant to become.

He glanced around the room at his classmates—twenty-three other freshmen who seemed perfectly content to go through the motions. Jessica Martinez was already taking notes even though Mr. Rike hadn't started teaching yet. Tyler Chen was discreetly checking his phone under his desk. Sarah Williams was braiding and unbraiding the same strand of hair, a nervous habit she'd had since elementary school.

Everyone looked so... settled. So accepting of this routine they'd all been dropped into. It made Quanta feel like he was watching a movie where everyone else had been given a script except him.

Mr. Rike stood at the front of the classroom, a man who seemed frozen in time. Quanta estimated he'd been teaching for at least thirty years, maybe more. His mostly-bald head caught the glare of the fluorescent lights, with a graying comb-over that didn't fool anyone. His thick-rimmed black glasses were so far out of style they'd actually come back in—but he clearly hadn't gotten the memo. Fashion wasn't his concern. He wore them slightly tilted, doubling as makeshift readers, like he'd figured out one trick years ago and just stuck with it.

"All right, people," Mr. Rike announced, his voice carrying that particular tone teachers used when they were about to say something they considered profound. "Let's dive into the order of operations. I know we've covered this before, but repetition is the mother of learning."

Quanta resisted the urge to groan. They'd covered the order of operations last week. And the week before that. Mr. Rike seemed to believe that mathematical concepts could only be truly understood through endless repetition, as if PPMDAS was some kind of sacred mantra that required constant chanting.

"Remember," Mr. Rike continued, turning to write on the whiteboard with an Expo marker that squeaked against the surface, "Pretty Please My Dear Aunt Sally. Parentheses, Powers, Multiplication, Division, Addition, Subtraction. In that order, always in that order."

The marker squeaked again, and Quanta felt his teeth clench. Everything about this place—the sounds, the smells, the routine—felt designed to numb their minds. He'd tried explaining this feeling to his parents once, this sense that school was less about learning and more about conditioning them to accept boredom as normal. His mom had just smiled and told him that everyone goes through phases of not liking school. His dad had given him a more thoughtful look but hadn't said much.

Quanta shifted in his chair, and the familiar clunk of the uneven leg against the tile floor reminded him that nothing in this building worked quite right. The heater that was either too hot or too cold. The windows that wouldn't open properly. The internet that cut out at random times throughout the day. Even the clocks didn't all show the same time.

At fourteen, Quanta was one of the younger freshmen, having skipped kindergarten and started first grade early. His parents had thought he was "intellectually ready," but sometimes he wondered if being younger than his classmates contributed to his feeling of disconnection. Or maybe it was something else entirely.

His name certainly didn't help him blend in. *Quanta*. He'd been explaining it his entire life. Teachers would pause when they reached his name during roll call, eyebrows raised in confusion or amusement. "Like quantum physics?" they'd eventually ask, and he'd nod and mumble something about his dad being a college science professor.

Quantum physics is the branch of science that explores how matter and energy behave at the smallest levels— atoms and subatomic particles—where the ordinary rules of physics no longer apply. It seeks to uncover the invisible building blocks of reality and the hidden forces that shape how everything in the universe interacts and comes into being.

What he never mentioned during those explanations was how the name made him feel—like he was supposed to be something more than just another kid going through the motions of school, like there was some significance to carrying a word that meant the fundamental unit of energy.

"It means you're meant to be powerful," his dad had told him once when he was eight and complaining about the weird looks his name got. "Quanta are the smallest particles that still carry energy. Small but essential. Without them, nothing else exists."

At eight, that had sounded cool. At fourteen, not so much.

The pressure of school was constant and it consumed most of his waking hours. While his parents had never explicitly demanded straight A's, Quanta had somehow internalized the belief that his grades were the most important thing in his life. He spent countless hours in his room studying, probably too much, sacrificing social time and relaxation in pursuit of academic perfection. During the week, he rarely hung out with friends outside of football practice, convinced that every moment not spent studying was a moment wasted.

His rationale had always been clear: good grades in high school would lead to a good college, which would lead to graduate school, which would ultimately land him a high-paying job. He looked at the successful adults around him—his parents, his teachers, his neighbors—and saw that they all seemed to make good money and have nice things by following this traditional path. That's what he wanted too. At least, that's what he'd always thought he wanted.

But lately, the pressure was eating at him. The anxiety that came with every test, every homework assignment, every report card. The way his stomach would knot up when he thought about going off to college, about choosing the right major, about competing with thousands of other students for spots at the best schools. There had to be more to life than this structured pattern that everyone seemed to follow without question, right?

Mr. Rike was writing another equation on the board: $3 + 4 \times 2 - 1$. "Now, who can tell me how to solve this using proper order of operations?"

Half a dozen hands shot up. Quanta kept his down, not because he didn't know the answer—multiplication first, then addition and subtraction from left to right, final answer ten—but because participating felt like agreeing that this was a worthwhile use of their time.

"Jessica?"

"First you do four times two, which is eight. Then you add three to get eleven. Then you subtract one to get ten."

"Exactly," Mr. Rike said, nodding as he turned back to the board. "Multiplication comes first, so four times two gives us eight. Then we go left to right—add three to get eleven, subtract one, and we land on ten."

He wrote it out as he spoke: $3 + 4 \times 2 - 1 = 3 + 8 - 1 = 11 - 1 = 10$.

"Nice work following the order of operations."

Quanta looked out the window, watching a maintenance worker rake leaves in the courtyard. The man moved with steady, practiced motions, gathering the orange and gold leaves into neat piles. There was something peaceful about the repetitive action, something honest about being outside and doing physical work that had a clear beginning, middle, and end.

The courtyard was one of the few beautiful parts of South Ridge High. When the school had been built fifteen years ago, someone had decided to include a small outdoor space surrounded by classrooms, complete with benches and a few mature trees that had been saved from the farmland that used to occupy this spot. In spring, the trees and flowers bloomed which filled the air with a fresh scent that drifted through the open windows. In fall, like now, the trees turned brilliant shades of orange and yellow that looked bright against the dull November sky.

Quanta's hometown, located twenty miles south of Pittsburgh, Pennsylvania had once been all farmland—rolling hills dotted with red barns and fields of corn and soybeans. His parents had moved here when he was five, drawn by the good schools and the promise of a safe, suburban community. What they'd found was a place caught between its rural past and its suburban future. Old farming families sold their land to developers who built neighborhoods with names like "Stratford Manor" and "Meadowbrook Estates"—places that tried to capture some sense of history while erasing the actual history that had existed there.

The result was a patchwork community where kids like Quanta lived in large houses with three-car garages and manicured lawns, going to a school that served students from both the new developments and the remaining rural areas. To outsiders, they were all "rich kids from South Ridge," but Quanta knew the reality was more complicated. His parents both worked long hours—his mom on her feet all day at one of the most upscale salons in the area, his dad buried in research and teaching at Carnegie Mellon University. They lived in a nice house, sure, but "rich" wasn't the word he'd use to describe their family.

The label bothered him, especially when he heard it on the football field. Opposing teams would mutter it after plays: "Soft rich kids from South Ridge." As if having a nice house somehow made you less tough, less determined, less worthy of respect. Quanta had learned not to respond to the taunts, but they still stung.

Football was another complication in his life. At six feet tall and 200 pounds as a freshman, with broad shoulders and thick legs, he looked exactly like what he was—an offensive lineman. He'd started playing in middle school, partly because he enjoyed it and partly because everyone simply expected him to. His father, Justin, had played Division I football in college, and while he'd never explicitly pressured Quanta to follow in his footsteps, the expectation hung in the air like morning fog.

"You play football?" was always the first question people asked when they met him. Not "What do you like to do?" or "What are you interested in?" Just the automatic assumption that his body type determined his identity.

And the truth was, he did enjoy football. He liked the strategic aspect of it, the way plays developed like complex puzzles. He loved the camaraderie with his teammates, the shared struggle of conditioning and practice. The overnight camps, the long bus rides to away games. He especially liked the moments of perfect clarity that sometimes came during games, when time seemed to slow and he could read the defense like a book.

But he also knew that football wasn't going to be his life. He had other interests, other questions that seemed bigger and more urgent than anything they covered in school or sports. Questions about reality and the strange feeling he sometimes got that there was more to existence than what everyone else seemed to accept as normal. Questions about whether the path he'd mapped out for himself—the grades, the college, the career—was really going to lead to the kind of life he wanted, or if it was just another form of the same routine that seemed to trap everyone around him.

These weren't the kind of questions he could discuss with his teammates or most of his classmates. Andy Callahan, his closest friend and a fellow lineman, was a good guy who took life as it came. He never seemed troubled by deeper questions about meaning or purpose. For Andy, high school was just something to get through on the way to whatever came next.

"Mr. Jones?"

Quanta snapped back to attention. Mr. Rike was standing directly in front of his desk, looking down at him with raised eyebrows.

"I asked you a question," Mr. Rike said.

"Sorry, I was—"

"Daydreaming, apparently. This is exactly why we need to review these fundamentals. You can't build complex mathematical understanding on a foundation of inattention."

A few students chuckled, and Quanta felt his cheeks warm. "What was the question?"

Mr. Rike sighed and returned to the front of the classroom. "The question was about the importance of following rules in mathematics. Rules that apply whether we feel like following them or not. Rules that create order from chaos."

He turned back to the whiteboard and began writing another equation, his marker squeaking against the surface with each stroke. The sound seemed louder than usual, more irritating. Quanta found himself focusing on it, the way it cut through the low hum of the heating system and the distant sound of traffic from the main road.

Everything in the room seemed to have its own frequency—the buzz of the lights, the tick of the clock, the rustle of papers, the soft sound of breathing from a bunch of teenagers trying to stay awake. Usually, these sounds blended into a familiar background noise that Quanta barely noticed. But today, for some reason, each sound seemed distinct and sharp.

He looked around the classroom again, studying his classmates more carefully. Jessica was still taking notes, her pen moving across the paper in neat, careful strokes. Tyler had given up pretending to pay attention and was openly scrolling through his phone. Sarah had moved on from braiding her hair and was now doodling in the margins of her notebook—tiny flowers and stars that she drew without looking down at the paper.

They all seemed so far away, like he was watching them through thick glass. The feeling reminded him of swimming underwater in the community pool during summer, how sounds became muffled and movements slowed and everything took on a dreamlike quality.

What if we're all underwater? The thought came from nowhere, surprising him with its intensity. *What if we're all moving through something thick and heavy, and we just don't realize it because we've never experienced anything else?*

Mr. Rike had moved on to another problem: $2 \times (3 + 4) \div 2 - 1$. He was explaining the importance of parentheses, how they changed the order of operations, how following the rules led to the correct answer.

"Rules create order," he repeated, underlining the phrase on the board. "Without rules, we have chaos. Without order, we have confusion. Mathematics teaches us that there is always a correct way to solve any problem, as long as we follow the proper sequence."

Quanta stared at the equation, but instead of numbers and symbols, he began to see something else. Patterns. Relationships. The way the parentheses created a boundary, a space where normal rules were suspended and different operations took precedence. It was like... like stepping outside of normal time.

The thought made him dizzy. He blinked hard and tried to refocus on the board, but the numbers seemed to shimmer and dance. The lights above him flickered once, twice, then settled back into their usual steady glow.

"Now," Mr. Rike continued, "let's work through this step by step. First, we solve what's inside the parentheses..."

His voice seemed to be coming from very far away, even though he was only standing ten feet from Quanta's desk.

Quanta's heartbeat started to quicken, a steady beating in his chest that seemed too loud, too fast.

Something was wrong. Or maybe something was very, very right.

The room felt different now, charged with an energy that hadn't been there moments before. The air seemed thicker, more substantial. Colors appeared more vivid— the blue of Jessica's sweater, the white of the marker board, the orange leaves visible through the window. Even the harsh fluorescent lighting seemed softer, more natural.

Quanta glanced at the clock on the wall: 12:29 PM. In one minute, they'd move on to fifth period. In one minute, the carefully ordered world of Mr. Rike's mathematics classroom would dissolve, and everyone would shuffle through the hallways to their next class.

But something told him that the next minute was going to be different.

12:30 arrived with the usual bell that marked the end of each period. But instead of the familiar rustle of papers and scraping of chairs, something impossible happened.

Everything stopped.

Not slowly, not gradually, but instantly and completely. Mr. Rike froze mid-sentence, his mouth slightly open, his hand holding the marker halfway to the board. Jessica's pen halted in the middle of a word. Tyler's thumb hovered motionless above his phone screen. Sarah's hand was suspended in the air, a pencil gripped between her fingers.

The clock stopped ticking. The fluorescent lights stopped buzzing. The heating system stopped humming. Even the dust particles visible in the sunlight hung motionless in the air, as if time itself had suddenly forgotten how to move forward.

Quanta sat perfectly still, afraid that any movement might shatter whatever had just happened. His heart was still beating—he could feel it pounding inside his chest—but everything else in the world was frozen in place.

There was no sound at all. Not just quiet, but empty of sound in a way that felt impossible. He'd never experienced anything like it, hadn't even known such silence could exist. It was like being inside a photograph, surrounded by total stillness.

Then, from somewhere deep inside his mind—or maybe from somewhere far beyond it—came a voice. Not spoken out loud, not even really heard, but somehow received directly into his consciousness.

Remember.

The word arrived with the force of a lightning strike, filling his entire body with electric awareness. The hairs on his arms and the back of his neck stood straight up. It wasn't a request or a suggestion. It was a command, an imperative that reached into the core of who he was and demanded a response.

But remember what? Remember when? The questions formed in his mind, but before he could even fully articulate them, images began to flash behind his eyes.

Himself as a small child, maybe five years old, sitting in the backyard of their house and talking to someone who wasn't visible. His mother finding him there, asking who he was talking to. "My friend," he'd said. "The one who knows about the light." His mother had smiled and ruffled his hair, dismissing it as childhood imagination.

But it hadn't felt like imagination. It had felt like memory.

More images came, faster now. Dreams he had throughout his childhood, dreams of floating in space filled with bright colors and sounds that had no earthly equivalent. Moments when he'd felt suddenly, inexplicably certain that he was much more than his physical body, that his awareness extended far beyond the boundaries of his skin.

These memories had faded as he'd grown older, pushed aside by the demands of school and sports and the general business of becoming a teenager. But they hadn't disappeared. They'd been waiting, buried beneath layers of routine, expectation, and the gradual acceptance that normal life was the only life available to him.

Remember.

The voice came again, softer this time but just as urgent. And suddenly, Quanta understood. He wasn't supposed to remember a specific event or moment. He was supposed to remember who he was. Who he really was, beneath all the roles and labels and assumptions that had accumulated around him over the years.

He was supposed to remember that he was more than just a fourteen-year-old kid sitting in a classroom bored out of his mind. More than a football player or a good student or the son of hard-working parents who lived in a nice house in the suburbs.

He was supposed to remember that he was awareness itself, the part of him that could observe his thoughts and feelings without being trapped by them. The part that had always been there, watching, knowing, understanding things that his thinking mind couldn't grasp. His dad always talked about consciousness, but Quanta never really understood what it truly meant until now. It was this awareness that was observing.

Consciousness was so much more than he'd ever imagined. It was like Wi-Fi for his soul—an invisible field of awareness that his brain could tap into, not something his brain created, but something it received, like a radio picking up waves that already existed in the air. His physical body and personality were like a character or avatar in an advanced VR game, walking around and experiencing this physical world. But his true self—his "higher self"—was the player holding the controller, the eternal awareness experiencing the game but never actually being the character on screen.

Most of the time he forgot this and got completely absorbed in being the character, identifying totally with his body, thoughts, problems, and story. That's what felt so suffocating—feeling separate from everything else, trapped in the drama of his personal identity. But in this moment, he remembered he was the player, not just the character, and that the same consciousness experiencing life through his eyes was the same consciousness experiencing life through everyone else's eyes.

This awareness wasn't limited by his physical brain or body—it was non-local, connecting instantly across any distance, part of an invisible field of "Infinite Intelligence" that existed everywhere at once. He wasn't a physical body having a spiritual experience; he was consciousness itself having a physical experience.

Consciousness—that's what this was. The silent witness inside him, the part that was always awake and aware, no matter what was happening. Not the voice in his head that was always chattering, but the part of him that could hear that voice talking. It was like being a mirror, he realized. The mirror reflected everything—happy faces, sad faces, beautiful scenes, ugly scenes—but the mirror itself was never changed by what it reflected. He was the mirror, not the reflections.

The realization hit him so hard that he gasped—and the sound of his own breathing shattered the frozen moment like glass.

Instantly, everything resumed. Mr. Rike's marker squeaked against the board as he finished his sentence. Jessica's pen completed the word she'd been writing. Tyler's thumb scrolled to the next post on his phone. Sarah added another petal to the flower she was drawing.

The clock resumed its ticking: 12:30:01, 12:30:02, 12:30:03.

No one else seemed to notice that anything had happened. They continued with their activities as if the world hadn't just stopped and restarted, as if reality hadn't just revealed one of its deepest secrets to a confused freshman in the third row.

But Quanta knew. He knew that something fundamental had shifted, not just in his understanding but in his very being. The word—*Remember*—continued to echo in his consciousness, a word that couldn't be unheard.

He looked around the classroom with new eyes. His classmates were still there, but they seemed different now. Or maybe he was the one who was different. Maybe he was finally seeing clearly for the first time in his life.

Everyone gathered their books and papers, closed their laptops and started to walk out of the classroom. Quanta sat motionless for a moment longer, trying to process what had just happened. Then he slowly packed his things and joined the stream of students flowing into the hallway.

The main hall was filled with the usual chaos of passing periods—lockers slamming, sneakers screeching against the polished floor, conversations overlapping into a constant buzz of teenage voices. But beneath it all, Quanta could sense something else. A deeper current, a flow of energy that connected everything and everyone in ways that couldn't be seen but could somehow be felt.

He made his way to his locker, moving carefully as if he were carrying something fragile. Which, in a way, he was. He was carrying the memory of what had just happened, the knowledge that reality was far more mysterious than anyone wanted to admit.

"Yo, Q!"

Andy Callahan appeared beside him, slightly out of breath from hurrying across the school. "You okay, man? You look like you've seen a ghost."

Quanta turned to look at his friend, this good-natured kid who'd known him since elementary school, who'd never seemed troubled by questions about the nature of existence. How could he possibly explain what had just happened?

"I'm fine," he said finally. "Just thinking about something."

"Must be some deep thinking," Andy said with a grin. "You've got that look you get when Coach is explaining a play that's way too complicated."

They walked together toward the cafeteria, Andy talking about football practice and weekend plans and all the normal concerns of teenage life. Quanta listened with part of his attention while the rest of his mind remained focused on the echo of that impossible word: *Remember.*

The rest of the school day passed in a strange blur. He sat through Spanish class with Miss Clark, who tried to teach them proper pronunciation while half the class stared at their phones. He endured social studies with Mrs. Koon, who lectured about the Industrial Revolution as if it were ancient history instead of the foundation of the world they still lived in. He struggled through English with Mr. Suzinski, who wanted them to analyze the symbolism in Lord of the Flies without acknowledging that maybe the symbolism was less important than the story's warning about what humans were capable of. The only class that might have interested him today was science with Mr. Wagner, his favorite teacher, but unfortunately that wasn't until tomorrow.

In each class, Quanta found himself studying his teachers and classmates with new attention. They all seemed to be sleepwalking through their days, going through motions they'd been taught without questioning why those motions mattered. Even the teachers, who supposedly were there to help students learn and grow, appeared to be trapped in the same cycle of routine and expectation.

What if we're all asleep? he wondered. *What if this whole place—this whole system—is designed to keep us asleep?*

The thought should have been disturbing, but instead it felt liberating. If everyone was asleep, then maybe waking up was possible. Maybe what had happened in Mr. Rike's classroom wasn't a one-time event but the beginning of something larger.

By the time the final bell rang at 2:30, Quanta felt like he was moving through a different world than the one he'd woken up in that morning. The hallways looked the same, the students sounded the same, but everything felt charged with possibility.

He gathered his things from his locker and stepped outside into the crisp November air. The sky was a dull gray, heavy with clouds that promised rain before evening. A few yellow leaves drifted down from the trees that lined the parking lot, and somewhere in the distance he could smell smoke from someone's fireplace.

Fall had always been his favorite season. There was something about the changing colors, the cooling air, the sense of time slowing down that made him feel more connected to the natural world. Today, that feeling was stronger than ever. He could sense the life flowing through the trees, the subtle shift in energy that came with the approaching winter, the way everything in nature moved in cycles of growth and rest and renewal.

As he walked home through the familiar streets of his neighborhood, Quanta was noticing details he'd never seen before. The way afternoon light slanted through the remaining leaves. The pattern of shadows on the sidewalk. The sound of wind moving through the trees, like a conversation in a language he couldn't quite understand but somehow knew was important.

When he reached his house—a modern rustic home with a blend of wood, brick, and natural stone, complete with a covered front porch that his mom had decorated with pumpkins and cornstalks—he paused for a moment before going inside. Something told him that crossing that threshold would mark another transition, another step away from who he'd been this morning and toward who he was becoming.

He opened the front door, and Sol came barreling out to greet him—his little blue French bulldog full of energy and enthusiasm, spinning in circles and letting out a single bark to welcome his best friend home. Sol's tail was short, as all French bulldogs' tails were, but what he lacked in tail length he made up for in his whole-body wiggle of excitement.

"Hey, buddy," Quanta said, kneeling down to scratch behind Sol's ears. "Did you have a good day?"

Sol looked up at him with his intelligent amber eyes, and for a moment, Quanta could have sworn he saw recognition there. Not just the normal recognition of a pet greeting his owner, but something deeper. Something that suggested Sol knew exactly what had happened at school today.

"You felt it too, didn't you?" Quanta whispered.

Sol tilted his head and then sat down directly in front of Quanta, staring at him with an intensity that seemed to acknowledge the shift that had just occurred. It was as if the dog could sense that Quanta had awakened to something beyond normal awareness—the way animals naturally perceive energy that humans had forgotten how to notice.

"Sol?" Quanta said. "What is it?"

The dog stood up to return inside, then turned back to look at Quanta. The message was clear: *Follow me.*

Inside the house, Sol led him down the hallway that connected the front of the house to the back. There, he sat down again and looked up at Quanta expectantly.

Quanta had walked through this hallway thousands of times in the nine years his family had lived here. It was just a corridor with hardwood floors and family photos on the walls—pictures from vacations, school events, birthday parties. Nothing special or unusual about it.

But now, standing there with Sol at his feet, he felt the same shift in energy he'd experienced in Mr. Rike's classroom. His skin tingled with heightened awareness. Every detail around him stood out with unusual clarity. And beneath the normal sounds of the house settling, he could sense that same deeper current, that flow of energy that connected everything.

Sol barked once—a short, sharp sound that seemed to say *Pay attention*—and then trotted into the living room.

Quanta followed, and immediately understood why Sol had brought him here. The living room felt different. Not visibly—everything was exactly where it should be. His mom's decorative pillows were arranged precisely on the couch. His dad's reading chair was positioned at its usual angle to catch the afternoon light. The coffee table still held the same stack of magazines and books it always did.

But the energy in the room was alive in a way he'd never noticed before. It pulsed gently, like a slow heartbeat, and Quanta realized that what he was sensing wasn't coming from any particular object or location. It was coming from the space itself, from an invisible field that seemed to connect everything.

This is what he meant, Quanta thought suddenly. *This is what Dad was talking about when he said energy is everywhere—maybe part of that field he mentioned, the one that connects everything somehow.*

His father, Justin, was a quantum physics professor at Carnegie Mellon, though he hadn't always been interested in the more mysterious aspects of this science. During his undergraduate and graduate studies, he'd been grounded in classical Newtonian physics—the solid, predictable world of forces and motion that could be calculated and understood. That's what he'd been trained in, what he'd built his early career on.

But somewhere along the way, the questions had gotten bigger. The neat equations of Newton couldn't explain everything he was encountering in his research. Quantum physics had started to make more sense than the mechanical universe he'd been taught to believe in. That explained all the books that were always scattered around the house—quantum physics texts on the coffee table next to his mom's fashion magazines, theoretical works about the nature of reality mixed in with suburban family life.

"Energy can neither be created nor destroyed," his dad had told him once. "It can only change form. And maybe consciousness—our awareness that can observe our own thoughts and feelings—is actually the most basic form of energy in the universe."

At the time, Quanta had filed that information away with all the other interesting but ultimately confusing and abstract things his father talked about. Now, standing in his own living room and feeling the energy that pulsed through everything, those words took on new meaning.

His classroom awakening had shown him what consciousness was—that infinite field of awareness he could tap into. But this moment was different. This was about recognizing that same consciousness flowing through his everyday environment. His familiar living room had become a visible demonstration of what his father had been trying to explain all along.

The questions came naturally now: What if individual minds were just points of contact with something infinite and eternal? What if everything was connected through this same field? What if awareness wasn't produced by the brain, as most people assumed, but was the energy field itself—the invisible foundation that made everything else possible?

The invisible foundation wasn't just a concept anymore—it was something he could sense.

The word *Remember* echoed again in his thoughts, and the understanding from the classroom felt even clearer now. He was awareness itself—not his thoughts, not his emotions, not his roles, but the observer of all those things. That's what had happened in the classroom. For just a moment, he had stepped outside the normal flow of time and accessed that deeper awareness directly.

As the understanding settled in, Quanta felt something else stirring—a sense that this awakening wasn't meant to stay private. There was a knowing, quiet but persistent, that what he'd discovered was meant to be shared. Not pushed on anyone, but offered to those who might be ready to remember their own true nature as well.

The front door opened, and he heard his mother's voice calling from the entryway.

"Quanta? Are you home?"

"In here, Mom," he called back, his voice sounding strange to his own ears.

Anne Jones appeared in the doorway of the living room, still wearing her work clothes—black slacks and a burgundy blouse that complemented her professional salon appearance. Her hair was styled in loose waves, and her makeup was perfect despite having spent the day on her feet in high heels cutting and coloring hair for the upscale clientele at Geno Levi's salon.

She worked hard, his mom. She'd built her reputation one client at a time, developing relationships with both men and women who trusted her with their appearance and often their personal problems as well. She was good at her job, genuinely loved making people feel beautiful and confident. She'd chosen this career because she was naturally social, the extrovert in a marriage with someone who was more comfortable with books and theories than small talk. While Justin could spend hours absorbed in abstract concepts, Anne came alive when she was connecting with people, making them laugh, helping them feel good about themselves.

"How was school?" she asked, the automatic question that parents asked and teenagers answered without much thought.

"Different," Quanta said, then immediately regretted being so honest.

Anne raised her eyebrows. She'd been expecting the typical teenage response—"good" or "fine" or maybe just a grunt—not something that actually required follow-up. "Different how?"

He looked at her—really looked at her—and for a moment he saw past the role of "mom" to the person underneath. She was forty-three years old, had grown up in a small town in Central PA, had married his father when she was twenty-five and moved to a place where she knew no one. She'd built a new life from scratch, had learned to navigate the politics of suburban parenting and professional networking.

She was also, he realized, someone who'd probably never experienced what had happened to him today. Someone who'd learned to find satisfaction in routine and security, who'd never been visited by impossible voices or felt the world stop and restart around her.

How could he possibly explain?

"Just... thinking about stuff," he said finally. "You know how school is."

She studied his face for a moment, and he could see her weighing whether to push for more information. But Anne Jones had learned over the years that teenage boys didn't always want to share their inner lives, and that sometimes the best approach was to let them process things on their own.

"Well," she said, "I'm glad you're thinking. That's what school is for, right?"

She smiled and headed toward the kitchen to start dinner. Quanta remained in the living room, still feeling the pulse of energy around him, still processing everything that had changed the past few hours.

Sol had settled onto his favorite spot on the rug, but his ears remained alert and his eyes stayed focused on Quanta. It was as if the dog were keeping watch, making sure that whatever had awakened in his human companion continued to grow rather than being forgotten or dismissed.

Remember.

The word echoed again in Quanta's consciousness, softer now but no less significant. He understood that this was just the beginning. Whatever had happened in Mr. Rike's classroom, whatever shift in awareness had occurred, it wasn't going to simply fade away. It was going to continue unfolding, continue changing him in ways he couldn't yet imagine.

And somehow, he wasn't afraid. For the first time in his life, Quanta Jones felt like he was exactly where he was supposed to be, doing exactly what he was supposed to be doing.

He was remembering who he really was.

And that was only the beginning.

Chapter 2: Nova Ray

The next morning arrived with the kind of heavy November sky that pressed down on everything. Quanta had barely slept, his mind cycling through what had happened in Mr. Rike's classroom, turning it over and over like a puzzle piece that didn't fit anywhere in his understanding of how the world worked.

Remember.

The word had followed him into his dreams, repeating through strange, colorful scenes that felt both familiar and completely foreign. He'd woken three times during the night, each time finding Sol sitting at the foot of his bed like a guard dog, his eyes watching him with an intensity that felt almost human.

Now, walking to school forty minutes earlier than usual, Quanta hoped the extra time might help him shake off the restless energy that had been coursing through him since yesterday. The familiar streets of his neighborhood looked different in the early morning light—sharper somehow, more vivid. Colors seemed more intense, shadows more defined. Even the air felt different against his skin.

At fourteen, Quanta was caught in that awkward phase between childhood and whatever came next. Too young to drive, too old to be driven everywhere by his parents, he'd become familiar with these sidewalks and street corners through countless walks to and from school. But today, the route felt different.

Lost in these thoughts, Quanta almost missed the big moving truck parked three houses down from his own. The logo was faded, and two men in work clothes were unloading boxes and furniture. A pile of cardboard boxes sat on the driveway, each one labeled in neat handwriting that he couldn't quite make out from this distance, though one box clearly had "Journals" written in larger letters across the side.

He slowed his pace, curious to see who was moving in. New families were rare in their neighborhood. Most of the houses had been occupied by the same people for years. He'd heard his mom mention at dinner that someone was moving into the Peterson house, but he hadn't paid much attention.

That's when he saw her.

She was sitting on the front porch steps, legs crossed, with a book balanced on her knees. Her dark hair fell in waves past her shoulders, and she wore the kind of layered outfit that suggested someone who put thought into how she presented herself to the world—a long cardigan over a vintage band t-shirt, dark jeans, and boots that looked like they'd collected stories from multiple states. Even from across the street, there was something about her presence that made Quanta stop walking entirely.

She looked up from her book as if sensing his attention, and their eyes met. The moment stretched longer than it should have, filled with the kind of recognition that doesn't make logical sense. Quanta had never seen her before—he was certain of that—but something about her felt familiar.

She smiled then, not the polite, automatic expression most people wore when they noticed a stranger staring at them, but something genuine and slightly amused.

"You must be the neighborhood welcoming committee," she called out, closing her book and standing up.

Quanta felt heat rise in his cheeks. "Sorry, I didn't mean to stare. I was just—"

"Curious about the new girl?" She walked down the porch steps and across the small front yard, stopping at the edge of the sidewalk. "I'm Nova."

"Quanta," he said automatically, then braced himself for the usual confusion, the questions about spelling and pronunciation, the inevitable comparison to quantum physics.

Instead, her smile widened, and something lit up in her dark eyes. "Seriously? That's incredible."

"Incredible?" The response was so unexpected that it took him a moment to process. He was used to confusion, sometimes teasing, occasionally interest from science teachers, but never genuine amazement.

"Think about it," she said, crossing her arms. "Nova—a star that suddenly burns brighter than everything around it, releasing more energy in a few moments than our sun will produce in its entire lifetime. And Quanta—particles of light and energy, the fundamental building blocks of everything that exists. We're basically neighbors in the universe."

Quanta blinked. In all the years of explaining his name to teachers, classmates, and random adults, no one had ever made that connection. Most people barely understood what quantum physics even was, let alone what quanta actually meant.

"I can't believe you know what quanta means," he said, still processing her response.

"I've been reading a lot about energy and consciousness lately," Nova said, glancing back toward the house where the movers were attempting to get a couch through the front door. "My grandmother was really into that kind of thing before she passed away a few months ago. She left me this whole library of books and personal journals about science and spirituality and how they're all connected."

Quanta felt a jolt of recognition at the word "consciousness," but something held him back from responding immediately. Yesterday's experience was still so fresh, so profound. How could he even begin to explain what had happened?

"I'm sorry," Quanta said, and meant it. There was something in the way she mentioned her grandmother—

not exactly sadness, but a sense of profound loss mixed with gratitude. "About your grandmother."

"Thanks. She was..." Nova paused, searching for the right words. "She was the kind of person who saw magic in everything. Science, nature, spirituality, the universe, human relationships—she believed it was all part of this bigger pattern that most people just don't notice."

"She sounds like a wonderful person."

"She was. Her name was Alma. I loved her very much. She actually prepared us for her death, which sounds weird, but it wasn't morbid or scary. It's almost as if she knew it was coming. She said death shouldn't be viewed as an ending, but as a transition to something new. Like energy changing form, you know? She called it 'returning to source.'"

Nova's voice carried a maturity that seemed older than sixteen, the kind of depth that came from grappling with concepts most teenagers never had to consider. Quanta found himself studying her face, noting the way her eyes seemed to hold questions and answers.

"She was very spiritual," Nova continued, "but not religious in the traditional sense. There's a difference, though most people don't understand it."

"What is the difference?" Quanta asked. "I never really understood that. Aren't spirituality and religion the same thing?"

Nova's expression grew thoughtful. "The way my grandmother always explained it was that religion is for people afraid of hell, and spirituality is for people who have already been to hell. That always helped me understand the distinction."

"That... actually makes a lot of sense," Quanta said slowly. "Like religion is about following rules to avoid punishment, but spirituality is about finding meaning after you've already been through something difficult?"

"Exactly," Nova continued, her voice taking on the quality of someone sharing deep wisdom. "How to recognize the difference between inherited beliefs and personal experience. She taught me that the most valuable skill is trusting your own instincts while keeping your mind open to new possibilities."

Before Quanta could respond, a woman appeared in the doorway of the house. She was tall and lean with the same dark hair as Nova, but pulled back in a practical ponytail. She wore a navy-blue dress and had the slightly exhausted look of someone who'd been up late dealing with moving logistics.

"Nova, honey," the woman called, "I'm heading to work. Can you help the movers with the boxes marked 'fragile'? And remember, you start school tomorrow."

"Got it, Mom," Nova called back, then turned to Quanta looking slightly annoyed. "That's my mom, Mickey. She works in IT. We move around a lot for her work, but she thinks this job might be more permanent."

"How much is a lot?" Quanta asked.

"This is our fourth state in five years," Nova said matter-of-factly, though something in her voice suggested she was tired of always being the new person. "Moving used to bother me more, but I've kind of gotten used to it."

"What grade are you in?"

"Sophomore. You?"

"Freshman. I'm only fourteen, so I'm one of the younger kids in my class." Quanta hesitated, then added, "I'll be fifteen in February."

"I just turned sixteen last month," Nova said. "October 13th."

"Friday the 13th? That's actually pretty cool."

"My grandmother thought so too. She said I was born on a day when the veil between worlds is thinnest, whatever that means." Nova's smile took on a slightly mysterious quality. "She was always saying things I didn't quite understand."

"I know what you mean," Quanta said. "My dad's always saying stuff about physics that goes right over my head. Sounds like your grandmother's spiritual stuff and my dad's science stuff might not be that different though."

"I think you might be right," Nova replied with a slight smile. "My grandmother said science and spirituality were just different languages describing the same truth. She left me all these journals and notes, some of which I understand and some of which seem like riddles I'm supposed to solve."

Nova glanced at the book in her hand—Quanta could now see it was *The Power of Now* by Eckhart Tolle. "This was one of her favorites. It's about being present, about how the mind creates suffering by living in the past or future when reality only exists in the now."

"That sounds incredibly deep for..." Quanta caught himself before finishing the sentence.

"For a sixteen-year-old?" Nova's eyes sparkled with amusement. "Yeah, I get that a lot. But after moving around so much, after losing my grandmother, after spending time with her books and ideas... I guess I've had to think about bigger questions than most people my age."

"I'm with ya on that," Quanta said, surprising himself with the admission. "I've always felt like there were these important questions that no one else seemed interested in asking. Like everyone's just going through the motions of school and social stuff, but there's this whole other layer of reality that we're all ignoring."

Nova studied his face with the kind of attention that made him feel like she was seeing something beyond his surface appearance. "What kind of questions?"

"Like... what if our thoughts and awareness actually influence what happens around us? What if consciousness isn't separate from reality but somehow participates in creating it?" The words spilled out before he could stop them, ideas that had taken on profound new meaning since yesterday's experience.

"Yes!" Nova's response was immediate and enthusiastic. "That's exactly what my grandmother believed. We don't just observe the universe—we help create it just by being aware of it."

A chill ran down Quanta's spine. The idea of helping to create reality carried extra weight after yesterday's experience in Mr. Rike's classroom. "Did you ever... I mean, have you ever experienced anything that seemed impossible? Like reality behaving in ways that shouldn't be possible?"

Nova tilted her head, studying him with those dark eyes that seemed to see more than they should. "Why do you ask?"

Quanta hesitated. How could he explain what had happened without sounding completely crazy? "Yesterday, something weird happened to me. At school. It was like... like time stopped, but only for me. And I heard this voice that said 'Remember.' I think I understand what it meant, but it's still confusing."

Instead of looking at him like he'd lost his mind, Nova's expression grew more serious and interested. "What time yesterday?"

"Around 12:30. Right at the end of math class."

Nova's eyes widened slightly. "That's... that's really interesting."

"Why?"

"Because yesterday, at almost exactly that time, I was unpacking boxes in my room, and I suddenly had this overwhelming feeling that someone was waking up. Someone important. I literally stopped what I was doing and looked out the window, like I was expecting to see something or someone, but there was nothing there."

"You felt someone waking up?" Quanta's heart began to beat faster.

"Not physically waking up. More like... spiritually waking up. Like someone was remembering something they'd forgotten." Nova paused, then added quietly, "And now I meet you, and your name is literally about particles of light and energy, and you're telling me about hearing voices telling you to remember things..."

They stared at each other for a moment, both processing the implications of what they were discussing. A car drove by, and somewhere in the distance a dog barked, but the normal sounds of the suburban morning felt muted and distant.

"Nova!" One of the movers was calling from the porch. "Where do you want this box marked 'fragile'?"

The spell broke, and Nova blinked as if remembering where she was. "I should probably help them," she said, but she didn't move immediately. "Would you maybe want to hang out later? After school? I know this probably sounds crazy, but I feel like we're supposed to talk more about this stuff."

"I have football practice until five," Quanta said quickly, "but after that, yeah. Definitely. There's a park about ten minutes that way if you want to meet somewhere quiet."

"Actually, I'd love to see the park. Nature is where you can hear the universe most clearly."

"Did your grandmother say that?"

Nova laughed, a sound that seemed to lighten the heavy November air. "You know what? That one's mine. But she taught me to trust what feels true, even if I can't explain why."

"Nova!" The mover called again, this time with more urgency.

"I really do need to help them," she said, taking a step back toward the house. "Just know that what happened to you in that classroom—that was just the beginning. There are techniques, practices, even sciences that can help you develop what you've awakened to. My grandmother left behind more than just books about spirituality. She left behind a complete system for consciousness development."

"Really?" Quanta asked with keen interest. "Let's meet back up at 5:30."

As he walked away, he could feel her watching him. When he glanced back at the corner, she was still standing in her front yard, one hand raised in a small wave. For the first time since the glitch, he felt like maybe he wasn't losing his mind. Maybe he was just finding something he'd lost.

The rest of the walk to school passed in a strange blur. His mind kept circling back to the conversation, to the way Nova had understood things he'd never been able to explain to anyone else. The connection between their names, the timing of their shared experience, the way she'd talked about consciousness and reality as if they were living, breathing things rather than abstract concepts.

By the time he reached South Ridge High, the building was starting to show signs of life. A few early buses had arrived, and students were beginning to trickle through the main entrance. The familiar sight of his school—red brick, large windows, the banner announcing the upcoming winter dance—should have grounded him in normalcy, but instead it felt like he was looking at a stage set, artificial and temporary.

"Hey, Q!" Andy's voice cut through his thoughts as his friend jogged up beside him. "You're here early. Couldn't sleep?"

"Something like that," Quanta said, working his familiar locker combination while his mind stayed focused on the morning's conversation.

"You still acting weird about whatever happened yesterday?" Andy asked, leaning against the neighboring locker. "What's going on with you?"

Quanta looked at his friend—really looked at him. Andy was a good guy, loyal and straightforward, but Andy would think he was crazy if he tried to explain what was really going on. Actually, none of his friends would be able to comprehend his recent thoughts about reality. That's what made Nova so special. She seemed to get it right away. He therefore kept the conversation high level.

"Andy," he said slowly, "do you ever feel like you're supposed to be doing something important, but you have no idea what it is?"

"Dude, I'm a high school freshman. The most important thing I'm supposed to be doing is talking to girls," Andy replied with a grin. "Why? What's got you thinking about important things?"

"I don't know. It's just... what if there's more to life than school and sports and all the stuff we're supposed to care about? What if we're missing something really big because we're too busy following the script everyone's handed us?"

Andy stared at him for a long moment. "Okay, seriously, what happened yesterday? Because you're starting to sound like you're having some kind of early-life crisis."

The warning bell rang, cutting off any chance of deeper explanation. Quanta was relieved. Students began hurrying toward their first period classrooms, and Quanta realized he was going to be late if he didn't move.

"I'll explain later," he said, grabbing his books.

"You better," Andy called after him. "You got me curious."

The day crawled by with painful slowness. In each class, Quanta once again found himself studying his teachers and classmates, wondering if any of them ever questioned the routine they were all trapped in.

At lunch, Quanta sat with his usual group—Andy, a few other guys from the football team, some girls from their grade—and listened to conversations about weekend plans, social media drama, and complaints about upcoming tests. Normal stuff. The kind of stuff that had made up his entire world just twenty-four hours ago.

But now it felt hollow, like everyone was reading lines from a script they'd memorized without understanding what the play was about.

"Earth to Quanta," Jessica Martinez was saying. "Are you okay? You look like you're in another dimension."

"Just thinking," he said.

"About what?"

The question hung in the air, and Quanta realized he had a choice. He could give the expected answer—homework, football, something normal—or he could try to bridge the gap between what he was experiencing and what his friends might be able to understand.

"Have you ever heard of the observer effect?" he asked, the words coming out before he could second-guess himself.

The table went quiet. Andy raised an eyebrow. "The what now?"

"It's a physics thing. The idea that just by observing something, you change it. Like, reality isn't fixed—it's responsive to consciousness."

"Okay," Jessica said slowly. "And you're thinking about this because...?"

"Because what if it's true? What if we're not just passive observers of our lives? What if we're actively participating in creating our reality just by being aware of it?"

The silence was deafening. Finally, someone laughed—not meanly, but in the way people laugh when they're trying to lighten a mood that's gotten too serious too quickly.

"Dude," Andy said, "did you get hit in the head too hard last practice?"

"Never mind. It's just quantum physics stuff," Quanta said quietly.

"Quantum… what?" Tyler Chen muttered, and a few people chuckled.

The conversation moved on to safer topics, but Quanta felt more isolated than ever. These were his friends, people he'd known for years, but suddenly it felt like they were speaking different languages. The gap between what he was experiencing and what they were willing to consider seemed unbridgeable.

The rest of the day passed in a similar haze of disconnection. In gym class with Mr. Cunningham, while they ran laps around the track, Quanta found himself thinking about energy and movement and the way consciousness seemed to flow through physical form. In social studies with Mrs. Koon, while she lectured about the Cold War, he wondered about the forces that really shaped human history—not just politics and economics, but the deeper currents of awareness and belief that drove human behavior.

By the time football practice arrived, he was desperate for something physical and immediate to focus on. He yearned for the camaraderie with his teammates that he so thoroughly enjoyed. But even here, in this space that had always felt like home, Quanta noticed things differently. The way confidence affected performance. The way doubt created hesitation that led to missed blocks and blown assignments. The way the team's collective energy could shift based on Coach Cathell's mood and the way he communicated with them.

"Jones!" the coach shouted during a blocking drill. "Where's your head today? You're playing like you're half asleep."

"Sorry, Coach," Quanta called back, forcing himself to focus on the immediate task of moving the player across from him back off the ball.

But even as he threw himself into the physical demands of practice, part of his mind remained elsewhere, counting down the minutes until 5:30, when he would sit with Nova in the park and try to make sense of everything that was changing in his world.

Practice ended at five, and Quanta hurried through his post-practice routine. Usually, he was one of the last to leave, taking his time in the shower and chatting with teammates about the upcoming game. But today he was dressed and out the door within ten minutes, his hair still damp and his backpack slung over his shoulder.

The walk to Riverside Park took exactly twelve minutes at his usual pace, but today he found himself moving faster, driven by an anticipation he couldn't fully explain. The sun was already low in the sky, casting long shadows across the suburban streets and painting everything in the golden light that came just before dusk in November.

Riverside Park wasn't much to look at—roughly thirty acres of grass and trees, some old playground equipment, and a walking path that followed the creek for about a half mile before looping back on itself. But it was quiet, away from the main roads, and it had always been a place where Quanta could think without interruption.

He found Nova sitting on a bench near the creek, reading the same Eckhart Tolle book she had that morning. She looked up as he approached, and her smile was like a light turning on in the gathering dusk.

"You came," she said.

"Did you think I wouldn't?"

"I hoped you would. But I know how weird all this must seem."

Quanta sat down beside her, close enough to smell her shampoo—something that reminded him of vanilla and sandalwood. "Actually, it's the first thing that's made sense in a long time."

They sat in comfortable silence for a moment, watching the water flow past. The creek was shallow this time of year, barely more than a trickle, but the sound was soothing. Somewhere in the distance, a car door slammed, and a dog barked once before falling quiet.

"Can I ask you something?" Nova said.

"Yeah."

"This morning, when you told me about what happened in your math class, about hearing that voice... can you tell me more about what that felt like?"

Quanta took a deep breath and began to talk. He told her everything—the way time had stopped, the complete silence that had filled the classroom, the voice that had spoken directly into his consciousness without using words, the sense of remembering something he couldn't initially grasp. He told her about Sol's strange behavior afterward, about the way his house had felt different when he got home, about the dreams that had followed him through the night.

Nova listened without interruption, her expression growing more thoughtful with each detail. When he finished, she was quiet for a long time.

"Unreal," she finally said. "And it explains so much."

"Explains what?"

Nova reached into her backpack and pulled out a leather journal, worn soft with age and handling. "This was my grandmother's. She left me dozens of them, but this one is special. She wrote in it almost every day for the last year of her life."

She flipped through pages covered in neat handwriting until she found what she was looking for. "She wrote this about six months before she died."

Quanta leaned closer to read the passage she was pointing to:

"'The one who sees the field will awaken in the place of learning, surrounded by those who sleep. His name carries the essence of light itself, and he will know the truth of observation. When the girl arrives, she will carry the keys to remembering. Together, they will begin to heal the dream.'"

"The place of learning," Quanta said slowly. "School."

"And his name carries the essence of light," Nova added. "Quanta. Particles of light and energy."

"But how could she have known? How could she have written about me specifically?"

"I don't know. But there's more." Nova flipped to another page. "Listen to this: *'The awakening will begin when the veil grows thin and the old systems start to crack. Those*

*who remember will find each other through resonance, like
tuning forks that vibrate at the same frequency.'"*

"Resonance," Quanta repeated. "My dad talks about that.
He says everything in the universe is vibrating at different
frequencies, and things that vibrate at similar frequencies
tend to amplify each other."

"Your dad sounds like he knows more than most people
about this kind of thing."

"He does. He's a physics professor and is always reading
books about quantum physics and consciousness, talking
about how they might be connected. Sometimes I catch
him looking at me like he's waiting for something, but I
never know what."

"Maybe he was waiting for this. For you to start waking
up."

Nova closed the journal and turned to face him fully.
"Quanta, I need to tell you something else. The feeling I
had yesterday, about someone waking up? It wasn't the
first time. I've been having dreams and... experiences... for
months now. Ever since my grandmother died. Like she's
still trying to teach me things, still trying to prepare me for
something."

"Prepare you for what?"

"I think for meeting you. For helping you remember."

"Remember what? That I'm awareness?" Quanta asked.

"Perhaps it's more than that. Maybe how to live from that awareness? Knowing it is one thing, applying it is another. This is what we need to figure out together."

The sun had disappeared behind the trees, and the park was growing darker. Street lamps were beginning to flicker on in the distance, and Nova gathered her backpack.

"I should probably head home," she said reluctantly. "My mom's still nervous about me being out after dark in a new place."

"I understand," Quanta said, though he was reluctant to end the conversation.

They walked back toward the neighborhood together, the evening air crisp and clean. At the corner where their paths diverged, they paused.

"Thank you," Nova said. "For trusting me enough to tell me what happened. For not thinking I was crazy when I told you about my grandmother's journals."

"Thank you for moving here," Quanta said. "I was starting to think I was losing my mind."

"Maybe you're finding it instead."

As they went their separate ways, Quanta felt lighter than he had in months. The anxiety and confusion that had been his constant companions since he could remember seemed to have lifted, replaced by something that felt like hope. Like possibility.

For the first time in his life, he felt like he wasn't alone in asking the big questions. And more than that, he felt like he might actually find some answers.

Sol was waiting at the front door when he arrived home as always. Inside, the house was warm and bright, filled with the smell of dinner cooking and the sound of his parents' voices from the kitchen.

"Quanta?" his mom called. "Is that you?"

"Yeah, I'm home."

When he entered the kitchen, both his parents looked up from their dinner preparations. His mom was stirring something on the stove, while his dad was setting the table.

"You look better," his mom observed. "Less... I don't know, less troubled than you have lately."

"I feel better."

His dad studied him with those sharp eyes that seemed to see more than they let on. "Good day at school?"

"Actually, yeah. I met someone new. A girl named Nova. She just moved into the Peterson house."

"Nova," his mom repeated. "That's an unusual name."

"She's an unusual person," Quanta said, and realized it was true in the best possible way.

"Is she in your grade?" his dad asked.

"She's a sophomore. Really intelligent. She knows a lot about consciousness and spirituality and how they might connect to science."

Justin's eyebrows rose. "That's... refreshing. Most kids your age don't think about those kinds of things."

"She's not most kids. Her grandmother left her this whole library of books and journals about spirituality, energy and awareness, and the nature of reality. Nova's been working through them, trying to understand what her grandmother was trying to teach her."

"Sounds like a wise grandmother," his dad said thoughtfully.

"Yeah, she passed away a few months ago, which is one of the reasons Nova ended up moving here. That, and her mom got a new job."

"I'm sorry to hear that," Anne said gently. "It sounds like she was an important person in Nova's life."

"She was. And the weird thing is, some of the stuff Nova told me about... it connects to things you've said, Dad. About consciousness and quantum physics and how observation might affect reality."

Justin paused in his table-setting, and Quanta caught something in his expression—not surprise, exactly, but something that looked almost like relief.

"What kind of things?" his dad asked carefully.

"Like the observer effect. Like the idea that consciousness might not be produced by the brain, but might be this fundamental energy field that everything else emerges from."

"And what do you think about that?"

Quanta looked at his father, this man who'd spent his career studying the deepest mysteries of the universe, and suddenly understood that this conversation was more important than it appeared on the surface.

"I think," he said slowly, "that maybe there's a lot more to reality than what we learn in school. And maybe some people are starting to wake up to that."

Justin nodded, and Quanta could see him weighing his words carefully. "You know, son, there's a lot of research being done right now about the connection between consciousness and quantum physics. Things that suggest the universe might be far more mysterious—and far more responsive to awareness—than most people realize."

"Like what?"

"Well, there's the double-slit experiment, where particles seem to behave differently depending on whether they're being observed. There's quantum entanglement, where particles separated by vast distances seem to communicate instantaneously. There's Schrödinger's cat, which demonstrates how observation seems to collapse multiple possibilities into a single reality."

"But what does that mean for regular people? For how we live our lives?"

"It might mean," Justin said carefully, "that consciousness is much more powerful than we've been taught to believe. That our thoughts, our attention, our awareness itself might actually influence what happens around us."

"Justin," Anne said from the stove, her voice carrying a note of warning. "Don't fill his head with too much of that stuff."

"I'm not filling his head with anything," Justin replied calmly. "I'm just sharing what the science is showing us. And encouraging him to think for himself."

"Dinner's ready," Anne announced, clearly wanting to change the subject.

As they sat down to eat, Quanta found himself thinking about the conversation. His parents had always approached life differently—his mom practical and grounded in conventional wisdom, his dad more inclined toward abstract thinking and theoretical possibilities. But lately, the gap between their worldviews seemed to be widening.

After dinner, he helped clear the table and then headed upstairs to his room. Sol followed him, settling onto the bed with a contented sigh. Quanta pulled out his phone and found a text from an unknown number.

"Hey, it's Nova. Found your contact info in the student directory on the school district's website. Hope that's okay."

He typed back: *"Definitely okay. How's the unpacking going?"*

"Slow but steady. Found something else interesting in one of my grandmother's boxes though."

"What kind of interesting?"

"The kind that might help us understand what's happening. Want to see it tomorrow?"

"Absolutely," he replied. *"Should we meet at the park again?"*

Her response came quickly. *"Actually, would you want to come over after school? My mom's working late, and I think you should see this."*

Quanta hesitated. Going to Nova's house felt like crossing some kind of threshold, stepping more fully into whatever was unfolding between them. But then again, maybe that was exactly what needed to happen.

He typed: *"Sure. I'll walk you home from school."*

"Perfect. And Quanta? Thanks again for today. For listening. For believing."

"No problem. Thank you for helping me feel less crazy."

"You're not crazy. You're just waking up."

He set the phone down and lay back on his bed, staring at the ceiling where shadows from the window created shifting patterns in the lamplight.

Tomorrow, he would see what Nova had found in her grandmother's boxes. Tomorrow, he would take another step into the mystery that was unfolding around him.

He was ready to remember.

Wednesday morning felt different from the moment Quanta opened his eyes. His standard anxiety replaced by something that felt almost like excitement. He'd slept better than he had in weeks, and even his dreams had been different—less chaotic, more purposeful.

Sol was already awake, sitting by the bedroom window and watching the street with that intense focus that had become more pronounced since Monday's experience. When Quanta sat up, the dog turned and gave him a look that seemed to say *About time.*

"Morning, buddy," Quanta said, scratching Sol's belly. "Good dreams?"

Sol tilted his head and did that thing where he seemed to be listening to something Quanta couldn't hear. Then he trotted to the bedroom door and looked back as if waiting for him to follow.

Downstairs, his parents were already in their morning routine. His mom was packing lunches while his dad sat at the kitchen table with his coffee and another one of his quantum physics books. This one was called *The Divine Matrix* by Gregg Braden, and Quanta could see yellow sticky notes marking dozens of pages.

"Morning," his dad said, with the kind of expression that suggested he'd been waiting for this conversation. "How are you feeling today?"

"Better," Quanta said, pouring himself a glass of orange juice. "A lot better, actually."

"That's good to hear," his mom added from the counter. "You seemed more relaxed last night after spending time with your new friend."

"Nova," Quanta said. "Her name is Nova."

"Right. Are you planning to see her again today?"

"Actually, yeah. I'm walking her home from school. She wanted to show me something her grandmother left her."

Justin's eyebrows rose slightly. "Something related to what you two were discussing yesterday?"

Quanta nodded, then found himself asking, "Dad, you know Tesla, right?"

Justin's expression shifted to something that looked almost like surprise. "You're asking about Nikola Tesla?"

"Yeah. I was googling energy and frequency stuff last night, and his name kept coming up. I honestly didn't even realize Tesla was a person before it was an electric car company."

"Ah." His father closed his book and gave Quanta his full attention. "Well, Nikola Tesla was one of the most brilliant inventors in history. He's probably best known for developing our modern electrical system—AC power, wireless technology, things we use every day. But what made him really special was how he thought about energy."

"What do you mean? I know we've discussed energy before, but not in this regard."

"Tesla understood something that most people in his time—and even today—don't really grasp. He believed that if you want to understand the universe, you have to think in terms of energy, frequency, and vibration. Everything, at its most fundamental level, is energy vibrating at different frequencies."

"So Tesla said that?" Quanta asked. "About energy, frequency, and vibration?"

"That's what people say. Whether or not he actually said the exact words, it captures the essence of what he believed. He was way ahead of his time."

"What did he mean by that?"

"Well," Justin said, setting down his coffee mug, "Tesla understood that everything in the universe is energy, regardless of what it may look like to the human eye. The chair you're sitting on, the books you carry to school, the juice you're drinking, even your thoughts—it's all energy vibrating at different frequencies. People tend to think solid objects are only matter, but deep down, everything is energy. Modern physics has actually proven Tesla was right through something called string theory. Scientists have discovered that at the most fundamental level, everything in the universe—every particle, every atom, every form of matter and energy—is made of tiny vibrating strings. Think of it like rubber bands. When you stretch a rubber band and pluck it gently, it vibrates slowly in long waves. Stretch it tighter and pluck it harder, and you get faster, tighter vibrations. String theory shows us that these cosmic strings work the same way—they vibrate at different frequencies to create electrons, protons, photons, all the building blocks of reality. So, when Tesla said everything is energy, frequency and vibration, he was literally describing what string theory has now proven to be the foundation of existence itself. And here's the really mind-blowing part—consciousness isn't separate from this vibrational reality. It's directly interfacing with these fundamental frequency patterns that string theory describes. In other words, your thoughts and awareness are actually interacting with the same vibrational strings that create physical matter. That's why consciousness can influence reality—because at the deepest level, consciousness and matter are both made of the same vibrating energy."

Quanta felt that familiar chill run down his spine. "Thoughts are energy too?"

"Absolutely. Your brain generates electrical activity. Every thought, every emotion, creates measurable electromagnetic frequencies. It's like your mind is a radio transmitter, constantly broadcasting signals. And just like radio stations, you're always broadcasting whether you realize it or not. The question is: what station are you playing? Are you broadcasting worry and stress, or confidence and curiosity? Other people and situations naturally tune into whatever frequency you're consistently transmitting."

Anne turned from the counter with a slight frown. "Justin, don't you think that's a bit much for breakfast conversation?"

"He asked," Justin replied mildly. "And it's not speculation—it's measurable science."

Quanta leaned forward. "So if thoughts are energy, and they're transmitting frequencies..."

"Then they can interact with other energy fields," his dad finished. "They can influence things around you in ways most people never consider."

"Like what kind of things?"

Justin glanced at Anne, who was giving him a warning look, then back at Quanta. "Well, think about your phone. It sends invisible signals through the air to cell towers, right? You can't see those signals, but they're real and they affect things—they carry information, connect you to other people, make things happen in the world."

"Right."

"Your thoughts work similarly. They're electromagnetic signals that can interact with the energy fields around you.

Most people don't realize this because the effects are usually subtle. But sometimes..." He paused. "Sometimes, when someone is in a heightened state of awareness, the effects can be more dramatic."

Quanta's heart started beating faster. "What kind of heightened state?"

"The kind you might experience during a moment of deep presence. When you're completely in the now and not thinking about the past or future, when your usual mental chatter stops, when you're purely observing without judgment. This is usually experienced during meditation." Justin's eyes met his son's. "The kind of state where time might seem to... shift."

The words hung in the air between them. Quanta knew his father was talking about what had happened in Mr. Rike's classroom, although they never discussed that experience directly.

"Boys," Anne said firmly, "this conversation is getting way too weird for a school morning. Quanta, you need to get going or you'll be late."

"She's right," Justin said, but he was still watching Quanta with those sharp eyes. "We can continue this conversation later if you want."

Quanta nodded, grabbed his backpack, and headed for the door. But as he was slipping on his shoes, his dad appeared beside him.

"Son," Justin said quietly, "if you're starting to experience things that seem impossible, just remember—impossible is often just another word for 'not yet understood.' The universe is far stranger and more responsive than most people realize."

"Okay," Quanta said, though he wasn't sure it was okay at all.

"And if you need to talk about anything—anything at all—I'm here."

Quanta looked at his father, this man who seemed to understand things that most adults wouldn't even consider, and felt a surge of gratitude. "Thanks, Dad."

Instead of the restless energy that had driven him to leave early for school yesterday, Quanta found himself paying attention to everything around him with a new kind of awareness. He was thinking about energy, frequency, and vibration. Everything around him was alive with invisible activity, like Wi-Fi signals carrying information through the air or Bluetooth connections linking devices together. The whole neighborhood was alive with frequencies he'd never noticed before. He couldn't see it, but he could sense it.

When he reached Nova's house, he was surprised to see she was already on the front porch with her backpack and that same worn copy of *The Power of Now*. He hadn't expected to run into her this morning, but there she was. She smiled when she saw him, and something about that smile made the morning feel brighter.

"Hey," she said, walking down to meet him. "What are the odds?"

"I know, right? It's like we're headed to the same place or something."

Nova giggled and asked, "So, what's new?"

"Oh, you know, the usual. My dad and I just had an interesting conversation about Tesla and energy and frequency."

Nova's eyes lit up. "Really? What did he say?"

As they walked toward school, Quanta shared the conversation he had with his father. Nova listened with the same focused attention she'd shown yesterday, occasionally asking questions or making connections to things her grandmother, Alma, had written about.

"It's like they're all saying the same thing from different angles," she said as they turned onto the street that led to South Ridge High. "Your dad with the science, my grandmother with the spirituality. But they're both talking about energy and consciousness and how everything is connected."

"Yeah, that's what I was thinking too."

They walked in comfortable silence for a few minutes, with Quanta noticing how their footsteps seemed to sync up naturally, how they automatically adjusted their pace to match each other. Another example of that invisible connection, maybe.

"I've been thinking more about what you shared yesterday," Nova said as the school building came into view. "About hearing the word 'Remember' and realizing it was about remembering you're awareness itself. We said we need to figure out what that means practically, so I need to understand your experience a bit more. Was there anything else about that moment you didn't mention?"

Quanta considered the question. "It was like suddenly seeing myself from the outside. Like realizing I'm not my thoughts or emotions or even my body—I'm the awareness that's observing all of that. But you're right, knowing it and actually living it are totally different things."

Nova nodded thoughtfully. "My grandmother called that the 'witness consciousness.' She said most people live their whole lives identified with their thoughts and emotions, never realizing they're the awareness that's observing or witnessing those thoughts and emotions."

"That makes sense. It's like..." Quanta searched for the right analogy. "It's like being in a movie theater watching the movie of your life play out on the screen—you get so caught up in the story that you forget the real you is the one watching the movie, not the character on the screen. Or thinking you're the apps on your phone instead of realizing you're the phone itself."

"That's perfect," Nova said with genuine enthusiasm. "The apps are all the different thoughts and feelings and roles you play, but you're actually the device that's running all of them."

They'd reached the school parking lot, and students were beginning to gather in their usual groups before the first bell. Quanta saw Andy and a few other guys from the football team near the main entrance, but for the first time in years, he didn't feel the automatic pull to join them.

"There's my homeroom," Nova said, pointing toward the sophomore wing. "But I'll see you at lunch?"

"Actually," Quanta said, "would you want to sit with me and my friends? I mean, if you're comfortable with that. They're good people, they're just not really into... deep conversations."

Nova smiled. "I'd like that. And don't worry—I can talk about normal teenage stuff too. I haven't completely lost touch with reality."

"See you at lunch then."

As Nova headed toward her building, Quanta made his way to his locker. The familiar chaos of a school morning increased as more students arrived. Instead of the background noise that he usually tuned out, he found himself aware of it as a kind of collective energy field.

All these people, all these minds, all broadcasting their own frequencies of thoughts and emotions. Anxiety about tests, excitement about weekend plans, frustration with parents, hopes about relationships. It was like being in a room full of radio transmitters all operating on different channels.

"Morning, Q," Andy said as Quanta approached his locker. "You look... I don't know, more awake today."

"I feel more awake."

"Good. Because yesterday you were acting like someone had unplugged your brain."

Quanta laughed. "Maybe someone plugged it back in."

The first few classes passed in a blur of familiar routine, but Quanta was paying attention in a different way. In English with Mr. Suzinski, while they continued to discuss symbolism in literature, he started thinking about how symbols were just energy patterns that carried meaning from one mind to another. In Spanish with Miss Clark, while they practiced pronunciation, he considered how language itself was a form of frequency transmission— sound waves carrying information through the air.

Everything his father had said that morning was starting to make sense in ways he hadn't expected. Energy, frequency, vibration—it wasn't just abstract physics concepts. It was the foundation of how everything in the world actually worked.

By lunch time, he was eager to continue the conversation with Nova. He found her at the salad bar in the cafeteria, and together they made their way to his usual table where Andy, Tyler, Jessica, and a few others were already deep in discussion about the upcoming winter dance.

"Everyone, this is Nova," Quanta said as they sat down. "She just moved here from... where was it again?"

"Colorado," Nova said with an easy smile. "My mom got a new job, so here we are."

"Cool," Jessica said. "What's Colorado like? I've never been there."

"Beautiful. Lots of mountains and outdoor stuff. Very different from here, but I don't mean that in a bad way."

The conversation flowed naturally from there—talk about classes, teachers, the differences between schools in different states. Nova was good at this, Quanta realized. She could engage with surface-level topics without seeming bored or condescending, but he could see her paying attention to the deeper currents underneath the words.

"So what do you think of South Ridge so far?" Tyler asked.

"It's nice. The people seem friendly. Though I have to say, some of the classes feel a little..." She paused, searching for the right word. "Limited."

"Limited how?" Andy asked.

"Like they're only teaching one way of looking at things. Take history, for example. We learn about dates and events and who won which war, but we don't really talk about why people make the choices they make, or what patterns keep repeating throughout human history."

Quanta felt his attention sharpen. This was exactly the kind of thing he'd been thinking about but hadn't known how to articulate.

"What do you mean by patterns?" Jessica asked.

"Well, think about it. Throughout history, you always have people in power and people without power. And the people in power always do the same things to stay in control—they keep the people without power distracted, divided, and focused on fighting each other instead of questioning the system and who's really in charge of it."

The table had gone quiet. Quanta could see his friends processing this idea, some looking intrigued, others looking slightly uncomfortable.

"That sounds pretty conspiracy theory-ish," Tyler said with a nervous laugh.

"Does it?" Nova asked mildly. "Or does it just sound like how power really works? Think about social media, for example. Have you ever noticed how the algorithm in each app shows you content that makes you angry or upset? That's not an accident. Angry, divided people are easier to control than calm, unified people."

Andy shifted in his seat. "Okay, but that's just how algorithms work. They show you stuff that gets a reaction."

"Right. And who programmed those algorithms? Who benefits when people are constantly angry and distracted?"

Quanta watched his friends' faces as they grappled with these questions. He could see them trying to dismiss what Nova was saying, but also unable to argue with the logic of it.

"I never really thought about it that way," Jessica said slowly.

"Most people don't," Nova said. "That's kind of the point. The system works best when people don't realize it's a system."

The bell rang, signaling the end of lunch period, and everyone began gathering their things. As they walked toward their afternoon classes, Andy fell into step beside Quanta.

"Your new friend is... intense," he said.

"In a good way or a bad way?"

"I'm not sure yet. She makes some good points, but it's kind of heavy, ya know? Like, I just want to get through high school, play football, and maybe go to college or just get a job. I don't really want to think about whether everything is some kind of conspiracy."

Quanta understood what Andy meant, but he also realized that he couldn't go back to not thinking about these things. Once you started seeing the patterns, once you started asking the deeper questions, it was impossible to pretend they didn't exist.

"Yeah," he said finally. "I get it."

But as they parted ways for their afternoon classes, Quanta was thinking about energy and frequency again. Andy's discomfort with Nova's ideas wasn't just intellectual—it was energetic. The vibration of what she was saying didn't match the frequency of the reality he wanted to live in. And that was okay. People could only receive information that resonated with their current level of awareness.

The afternoon classes dragged on with their usual mixture of routine and restlessness. In PE, while running laps again, Quanta was thinking about how physical exercise was really just a way of moving energy through the body. In social studies, while Mrs. Koon lectured about the Industrial Revolution again, he considered how major historical changes always happened when enough people shifted their thinking about what was possible.

Everything was starting to feel connected in ways he'd never noticed before. Not in some mystical, supernatural way, but in practical, observable ways. Like Tesla had said—energy, frequency, vibration. The whole universe operating like some vast, intricate network where everything influenced everything else.

When the final bell rang, Quanta felt a surge of anticipation about going to Nova's house. He met her at her locker, and together they walked through the gradual exodus of students heading home or to after-school activities.

"So," Nova said as they left the building, "what did you think of lunch?"

"Interesting. You definitely gave them some things to think about."

"Too much?"

"Maybe for some of them. But I think that's okay. Not everyone is ready to hear certain things at the same time."

Nova nodded. "My grandmother used to say that truth is like light—you can only handle as much as your eyes are adjusted for. If you try to show someone too much too quickly, they'll just close their eyes."

They walked through the familiar streets of Quanta's neighborhood, but now he was seeing them through a different lens. Each house contained families living their own versions of reality, most of them probably unaware of the invisible forces that shaped their thoughts and choices. It wasn't their fault—the system was designed to keep people focused on surface-level concerns. Work, school, sports, plays, PTA meetings, homework, bills, social drama, and entertainment. All the things that kept them too busy and distracted to ask deeper questions.

"Here we are," Nova said as they reached her house.

The moving boxes were gone from the driveway, and the place was starting to look like someone lived there. Mickey's car wasn't in the driveway, which meant she was still at work.

"Come on," Nova said, leading him up the front porch steps.

Before they could walk in, Sol came barreling over to great Quanta and seemed very interested in meeting his new friend as well.

"Sorry about this, let me run him back home," Quanta said.

"No worries at all. I've seen this little cutie in your yard and have been wanting to meet him. Let me say hello and then I'll show you what I found."

Sol approached Nova with that same intense awareness Quanta had noticed the night before. He looked at Nova with those amber eyes, tilted his head slightly, and then sat down directly in front of her.

"Wow," Nova said, kneeling down to Sol's level. "There's something different about your dog. He's so... aware. Like he's actually listening to what we're saying."

"His name is Sol," Quanta said. "I named him that when we got him three years ago. I'd just learned in Spanish class that Sol means sun, and something about that word always felt special to me. Like it connected to light and energy somehow."

"You named him after the sun?" Nova's asked.

"Yeah. My dad thought it was cool that I made the connection between the sun and energy. My mom just liked that it was simple." Quanta scratched behind Sol's ears. "But it's weird—it's like the name chose itself. Sol's always been different from other dogs. More... intuitive, I guess."

Nova studied Sol with the same focused attention she brought to everything else. "It's like he can sense things that other animals can't. Energy things."

"That's exactly what it's like," Quanta agreed.

Sol seemed to approve of Nova's assessment. He stood up and allowed her to pet him. Then he looked back at Quanta with an expression that seemed to say *She gets it*. With that, Quanta picked him up and rushed him back home. He was eager to see what Nova had to show him.

Quanta returned to her house within minutes. Nova led him into the living room, which was still mostly boxes but had a couch and coffee table set up. Nova threw her backpack on the floor and walked over to the coffee table, which contained several of Alma's journals and what appeared to be a small wooden box.

"After I got home last night, I dug deeper into my grandmother's things," Nova said, sitting on the couch and patting the cushion beside her. "And I found this."

She opened the wooden box, revealing a collection of tuning forks, each pair a different size and marked with a specific frequency. There were also several index cards covered in Alma's neat handwriting.

"What are they?"

"According to my grandmother's notes, these are tuned to different frequencies that correspond to different brainwave states. Like... like physical tools for tuning your mind the same way you'd tune a guitar."

Nova picked up one of the tuning forks and showed him the number etched on it. "This one is 528 Hz—she called it the 'love frequency.' And this one..." She picked up another fork. "This one is 40 Hz, which supposedly enhances focus and awareness."

"Do they actually work?"

"Let me show you," Nova said, selecting two tuning forks marked with the same frequency—256 Hz. She struck one against the wooden box, creating a clear, pure tone that filled the room. Then she held it near the second 256 Hz fork without making contact. Almost immediately, the second fork began vibrating on its own, producing the exact same tone.

"Whoa," Quanta said, watching in amazement.

Nova then tried the same experiment with forks of different frequencies—striking the 256 Hz fork and holding it near a 512 Hz fork. Nothing happened. The second fork remained silent.

"See? Tuning forks only respond to their exact frequency match," Nova explained, setting them down. "Remember when we talked about resonance before? This is the physical demonstration. And if it works with metal forks, why wouldn't it work with consciousness? Sound waves are just vibrations, and our brains send out vibrations too."

Nova set the tuning forks aside and picked up one of the cards. "But she wrote that the real tools are simpler than that—breathing techniques, gratitude practices, visualization exercises. The forks are just... training wheels, I guess."

Quanta thought about his father's explanation of thoughts as electromagnetic signals. "So people work the same way as those tuning forks—we only resonate with others who are on our frequency?"

"Exactly. Or like how a radio can tune into different stations depending on which frequency you dial it to."

Nova picked up one of her grandmother's journals. "But that's not even the most interesting thing I found. Look at this."

She opened the journal to the page where a bookmark rested and began to read:

"'The awakening always begins with the dissolution of time. When the seeker steps outside the stream of past and future, into the eternal now, reality reveals its true nature. This is when the voice speaks, when the call becomes clear. Energy, frequency, vibration—these are not just words but the very language of creation itself.'"

Quanta felt that familiar chill. "The call?"

"Keep listening." Nova turned the page. *"'The one who hears will begin to understand that thoughts are not private events contained within the head, but electromagnetic transmissions that shape the fabric of reality itself. Every thought is a signal, every emotion is a command sent to the quantum field. Most humans are unconscious transmitters, broadcasting random signals that create chaotic, reactive lives. But the awakened ones learn to broadcast deliberately, to tune their frequency to match their highest intentions.'"*

Nova looked up at him. "Quanta, I think what happened to you in that classroom was the universe trying to get your attention."

"But why me? Why now?"

Nova turned to another marked page. "Listen to this: *'The universe does not choose randomly. It calls to those whose names carry the resonance of light, to those born at the intersections of cosmic cycles, to those whose souls have agreed to serve as bridges between the sleeping and the awakened. They will find each other through resonance, like tuning forks vibrating at the same frequency.'*"

They sat in silence for a moment, both processing the implications of what they'd just read.

"So what does this mean?" Quanta asked finally. "What are we supposed to do with this information?"

"I think," Nova said slowly, "we're supposed to learn how to tune our frequency deliberately. How to become conscious transmitters instead of unconscious ones."

"How do we do that?"

Nova smiled and picked up one of the cards from the box. "I think we experiment. My grandmother left detailed instructions for what she called 'frequency work.' Practical techniques for shifting your energy state, for raising your vibration, for broadcasting more coherent signals."

"Like meditation?"

"Meditation is part of it. But it's more practical than that. It's about becoming aware of your thoughts and emotions throughout the day, about consciously choosing what frequency you want to transmit instead of just reacting to whatever happens to you."

Quanta thought about his conversation with his father that morning, about thoughts as electromagnetic signals that could influence the energy fields around you. "My dad said something similar this morning. About thoughts being like radio transmitters."

"Once again, your dad sounds like he understands more than most people. Certainly makes sense given his profession."

"Yeah, I'm starting to realize that."

Nova opened another journal and showed him a page covered with what looked like exercises and techniques. "Want to try something?"

"Like what?"

"Just a simple frequency shift. My grandmother wrote that the easiest way to raise your vibration is through gratitude. It changes your electromagnetic signature almost instantly."

"Okay."

"You've already been noticing how different thoughts create different feelings in your body. Now just use that sensitivity deliberately. Think of three things you're genuinely grateful for. But don't just think about them—feel the appreciation in your body. Like, really feel how it shifts something inside you."

Quanta closed his eyes and considered the question. What was he genuinely grateful for?

Meeting Nova was the first thing that came to mind. The way she understood things he'd never been able to explain to anyone else. The feeling of not being alone with these big questions anymore.

He could feel something shift in his chest as he focused on that appreciation. A warmth that seemed to spread outward from his heart.

Second was his father's willingness to discuss concepts that most adults would dismiss as crazy. The way Justin looked at him with those knowing eyes, like he was waiting for Quanta to catch up to something he'd always understood.

The warmth in his chest grew stronger, and he could sense the feeling extending beyond his body somehow.

Third was Sol's mysterious awareness, the way his dog seemed to know things that should be impossible for an animal to know. The comfort of having a companion who operated on a different level than most of the world.

When he opened his eyes, Nova was watching him with a slight smile. "How do you feel?"

"Different. Lighter, somehow. And more... connected to things."

"That's your frequency shifting. You can genuinely feel it when your vibration changes."

"That's incredible."

"And it affects everything around you too. Sol will definitely pick up on this when you go back home. Animals are much more sensitive to frequency shifts than humans are."

"So, if I can change my frequency through gratitude..."

"Then you can change it through other emotions too," Nova explained. "Fear, anger, and worry lower your vibration. Love, joy, and appreciation raise it. And the frequency you broadcast determines what you attract back into your life."

Quanta thought about the Law of Attraction concepts he'd heard mentioned in passing but never really understood. "Like a magnet."

"Exactly. Or like how YouTube recommends videos based on what you've been watching—your viewing frequency determines what content gets pulled into your feed."

They spent the next hour going through more of Alma's journals and practicing different frequency techniques. Some were simple, like the gratitude exercise. Others involved specific breathing patterns—inhaling for four counts, holding for seven, exhaling for eight—that seemed to naturally shift his state of awareness. There were visualization exercises where he practiced imagining light or energy flowing through different parts of his body, and techniques for consciously shifting his attention between different emotional states.

With each exercise, Quanta could feel something shifting in his awareness. It was like discovering muscles he hadn't known he had, or finding controls for his internal experience that had always been there but hidden.

"This is amazing," he said as they finished a technique that involved imagining light flowing through different parts of his body. "Why don't they teach this stuff in school?"

Nova's expression grew more serious. "Because people who know how to control their own energy are much harder to manipulate. If everyone knew how to change their vibe on purpose instead of just reacting to everything, the whole control system would fall apart."

"The system we talked about at lunch?"

"Exactly. Fear, anger, division, distraction—those are all low-frequency states that make people easy to manipulate. But joy, love, gratitude, awareness—those are high-frequency states that make people powerful and independent."

Quanta looked out the window at the neatly arranged rows of homes, each one hiding its own version of normal. Behind those front doors were people moving through the motions of daily life, never realizing they might have the power to shape their reality instead of just reacting to it.

"So the voice you heard," Nova continued, "it might have been the universe trying to wake you up to your own power. To remind you that you're not just a passive observer of your life—you're an active creator of it."

"Through frequency?"

"Through frequency. Through the electromagnetic signals you broadcast every moment of every day."

"I should probably head home soon," Quanta said, though he was reluctant to leave. "This is a lot to process and it's getting late."

"Of course. But..." Nova hesitated. "Would you want to keep exploring this stuff? I mean, together?"

"Absolutely. This feels important."

"It does. Like we're supposed to understand these things for a reason."

As they gathered up the journals and tuning forks, Quanta was thinking about energy, frequency, and vibration in entirely new ways. It wasn't abstract physics anymore—it was practical knowledge about how to navigate life consciously instead of just reacting to whatever happened around him. And it went beyond just him. He was thinking about his friends and classmates back at school—all the stress and anxiety he saw every day. If these simple techniques could create such noticeable shifts in how he felt, maybe they could help others too. The thought felt important, though he wasn't sure why yet.

"Nova," he said as they reached the front door, "thank you for sharing all this with me. I really thought I was losing it the other day."

"Thank you for being ready to hear it. My grandmother always said that teachers appear when students are ready, but it works both ways. Students appear when teachers are ready too."

"Are we teachers or students?"

"I think we're both."

Quanta grinned and turned to walk back to his house. When he walked in, he was greeted by Sol and his mom.

"How was your visit with Nova?" Anne asked. "Did she show you whatever it was her grandmother left her?"

"Yeah. Some journals and things. Stuff about energy and frequency and how thoughts affect reality."

Anne's expression shifted slightly. "Well, that sounds... interesting."

"Interesting indeed," Quanta said. "Dad was telling me this morning about Tesla and electromagnetic fields, and how our thoughts send out measurable frequencies. Then Nova pulls out these journals, and her grandma was writing about the exact same thing. It seemed to be more than just theory."

"Hmm." Anne didn't look entirely convinced, but she also didn't seem worried. "Well, just remember to keep your feet on the ground, okay? Real life still happens whether we're thinking about frequencies or not."

"I know, Mom."

But as he headed upstairs to his room, Quanta realized that real life was exactly what he was learning about. The energy underneath all the surface-level events. The invisible forces that shaped everything from his own emotional states to the larger patterns of human behavior.

He was beginning to understand that the voice he'd heard in Mr. Rike's classroom wasn't some mysterious supernatural experience. It was the universe speaking through his own deeper awareness, finally getting his attention, trying to remind him of capabilities he'd always had but had forgotten how to use.

Energy, frequency, vibration. The language of creation itself.

And tomorrow, he would continue learning how to speak
it fluently.

Chapter 4: The Observer

Thursday morning brought a different kind of energy to the Jones household. Quanta was downstairs earlier than usual, drawn by the smell of coffee and the sound of his father already moving around the kitchen. He'd been thinking about everything that had happened over the past few days, and he had questions that felt too important to wait.

The house felt quieter at this hour, more peaceful. Sol had followed him downstairs and was now sitting by the kitchen window, watching the early morning light filter through the trees in their backyard. There was something about this time of day that felt full of possibility, as if the world was resetting itself for whatever might unfold.

Justin was at the counter, preparing his usual morning routine, but instead of his typical stack of papers to grade, he had a book open beside his coffee mug—*Becoming Supernatural* by Joe Dispenza. He looked up when Quanta entered, a slight smile crossing his face.

"You're up early," his dad said, closing the book and giving Quanta his full attention. "Everything okay?"

"Yeah, just... thinking about stuff." Quanta poured himself some milk and gestured toward the book. "What's that one about?"

"Dr. Dispenza's research on how meditation and mental focus can heal people's bodies. He's documented cases where people have overcome serious illnesses just by changing how they think and feel."

Quanta felt that usual glimmer of intrigue, the same feeling he'd been getting whenever these concepts came up. "Like how?"

Justin set down his coffee mug and leaned against the counter, clearly ready to engage in the kind of conversation they'd been having more frequently this week. "Well, people learn specific meditation techniques that help them get into deeper states of consciousness. When they do this regularly and focus their intention on healing, their bodies actually start to change—tumors shrink, immune systems get stronger, even genetic expression can shift."

"You mean their thoughts can change their physical health?"

"Exactly. And here's the thing—this connects to the observer effect in quantum physics."

"Right, like how observation changes reality," Quanta said, making the connection. "So Dispenza's work is basically the same thing happening with healing?"

"Yep! Whether you're observing tiny particles and changing their behavior, or focusing your consciousness on healing and changing your biology, it's the same fundamental principle—consciousness actively participates in creating physical reality."

"I've discussed this with Nova as well," Quanta said recalling their first conversation. "About how we participate in creating reality just by being aware of it."

Justin's eyebrows rose with interest. "Wow! So, Nova understands the connections between consciousness and reality? That's impressive for someone so young. The observer effect isn't just limited to quantum particles in laboratories. It seems to operate at every level of existence. When you change your state of consciousness, you literally change what becomes possible in your life."

"I understand the concept, but how does that work exactly?"

"Think about it this way," Justin said, moving to sit across from Quanta at the kitchen table. "If consciousness can affect reality at the quantum level, and quantum particles make up everything in the universe, then maybe consciousness affects reality at every level. Maybe what you pay attention to, how you observe the world around you, influences what shows up in your experience."

Quanta felt that familiar chill of recognition. "Like... like if you're always looking for problems, you'll find them?"

"Or if you're looking for opportunities, those will show up instead. Your state of awareness might be creating your reality rather than just perceiving it. That's what Dispenza's research suggests—that we're not victims of our genetics or circumstances, but active participants in creating our lives through consciousness."

Anne appeared in the doorway, still in her robe, looking slightly bewildered as she took in the scene of father and son deep in conversation over quantum consciousness before seven in the morning.

"What is it with you two this week and these deep conversations before the coffee has even set in?" she said, though her tone carried more amusement than complaint.

Both Justin and Quanta laughed. "He asked," Justin said, closing the book and standing up. "And it's good to see him thinking about these concepts. Most kids his age are only interested in social media and video games."

"Well, save some of the universe-solving for after school," Anne said with a smile, moving toward the coffee maker. "Quanta needs to get going, and I need caffeine before I can handle discussions about consciousness affecting reality."

As Quanta grabbed his backpack and headed for the door, he felt energized by the conversation. His dad's research kept connecting to everything he was experiencing with Nova, creating a web of understanding that was growing stronger each day. It was like having pieces of a puzzle that were finally starting to reveal the bigger picture.

The walk to school had become something he looked forward to. The conversations with Nova were giving him a new lens through which to view everything he was learning, and today felt full of potential. When he reached Nova's house, she was walking toward the street, apparently having just finished helping her mom load some boxes into the car.

"Perfect timing," she said, falling into step beside him as they headed toward school. "How are you feeling today?"

"Good. Different. Like all these pieces are starting to fit together."

"The frequency work from yesterday?"

"That, plus my dad was telling me about research on how consciousness can actually rewire the brain and affect physical reality. This guy Joe Dispenza has documented cases where people have healed serious illnesses just through meditation and changing their brainwave states."

Nova's gaze sharpened with interest. "That makes total sense. If consciousness is the foundation of reality, then changing your consciousness should be able to change anything, including your body."

"It's wild to think about. We've been taught that we're basically powerless over what happens to us, and that the only solution is to seek a fix or cure externally instead of looking within ourselves. But maybe that's completely backwards."

"Right. Maybe we're way more powerful than we think, but nobody's taught us that we even have this power, let alone how to use it."

As they walked, Quanta was looking forward to his upcoming classes in a way he hadn't for months. Instead of just sitting through lectures and absorbing information passively, he was eager to see how these consciousness concepts might show up in different subjects. Today, he was especially curious about science with Mr. Wagner.

"Random question," Nova said, as if reading his thoughts. "Are there any teachers who would know anything about what we're exploring, or does everyone just stick to the state curriculum in fear of losing their job?"

"If anyone in this school would know, it would be Mr. Wagner. He's my favorite teacher and by far the most knowledgeable in my opinion. Definitely the most open-minded. I have him third period today." Quanta paused, then added, "My dad met him at the open house last year and they ended up talking for like an hour about physics. He was impressed that a high school teacher actually understood the deeper implications of the science he was teaching."

"That sounds promising. At least you'll have one teacher who gets it."

They spent the rest of the walk discussing what they hoped to learn, both from Mr. Wagner and from their continued exploration of consciousness together. When they reached South Ridge High, they separated toward their respective wings with plans to meet at lunch and compare notes on their morning classes.

The first two periods passed without much incident, though Quanta was paying attention differently in each class. Instead of just passively absorbing information, he was looking for connections to the consciousness concepts he was learning. Then came third period science with Mr. Wagner.

Walking into the classroom, Quanta immediately noticed the energy felt different from earlier in the week. While it still had the standard institutional setup—white walls, fluorescent lighting, rows of black lab tables—Mr. Wagner had transformed the space with interesting scientific equipment and demonstrations that looked like they got used regularly rather than sitting as decorative props.

There were posters showing not just the standard scientific charts, but also more thought-provoking images: the electromagnetic spectrum, diagrams of wave-particle duality, even a quote from physicist Max Planck about consciousness being fundamental to matter. The whole room felt alive with curiosity and genuine inquiry.

Mr. Wagner himself was a portly, enthusiastic man in his late forties with thinning black hair and eyes that sparkled with genuine passion for his subject. He wore a wrinkled button-down shirt and a tie that had clearly seen better days, but there was something about his presence that commanded attention without demanding it. He moved around the classroom with the easy confidence of someone who genuinely loved what he was teaching.

"Good morning, future scientists," Mr. Wagner said as students settled into their seats, his voice carrying both warmth and excitement. "Today we're going to explore one of the most fascinating and mysterious aspects of reality—how the act of observing affects the observed."

Quanta's attention sharpened immediately. After everything he'd been discussing with Nova and his father, walking into a science class about observation felt like the universe was orchestrating something significant.

"Now," Mr. Wagner continued, moving to the front of the classroom and scanning the faces of his students, "how many of you have heard of the observer effect?"

Quanta raised his hand along with a couple other students, as he had just mentioned this to his friends at lunch earlier in the week. He caught Mr. Wagner's eye and saw a spark of interest there.

"Interesting, more than I thought. For those who haven't heard of it, the observer effect is one of the most mind-bending discoveries in the history of science. It suggests that the very act of observing something changes it. Not just influences it—actually changes the fundamental nature of reality itself. In other words, when we observe something, we're not just watching—we're participating in what becomes real."

Sarah Williams, who always asked thoughtful questions, raised her hand. "But how is that possible? How can just looking at something change it?"

"Ah," Mr. Wagner said, his eyes lighting up with the kind of enthusiasm that made it clear he'd been hoping someone would ask that question. "That's exactly the question that has puzzled scientists for the better part of a century. Let me show you something that might help illustrate the concept."

Mr. Wagner moved to a sophisticated demonstration setup at the front of the room, complete with laser equipment, precision slits, and projection screens. Quanta could see this wasn't the simplified equipment most high school science classes used—this looked like professional grade lab equipment.

"We're going to conduct a version of what's called the double-slit experiment," Mr. Wagner said, his hands moving confidently over the equipment as he made some final adjustments. "It's one of the most important experiments in the history of physics, and it reveals something truly extraordinary about the nature of reality." *(A visual summary of this concept appears in the Concept Glossary.)*

He dimmed the lights and activated the laser. "First, let's talk about what light is. Light is made up of tiny particles called photons. Now, if I shine this light through these two parallel slits onto the screen behind them, what do you think will appear?"

"Two lines of light?" Jessica Martinez suggested.

"That's exactly what you'd expect," Mr. Wagner agreed. "If light is made of particles shooting through the slits, you should get two bright lines on the screen, right? But watch what actually happens."

He activated the full apparatus, and instead of two distinct lines of light, a series of alternating bright and dark lines appeared on the projection screen.

"Instead of just two lines, we get this pattern of light and dark stripes," Mr. Wagner explained, pointing to the screen. "That happens because light is acting like a wave. Where the waves line up, they make brighter stripes. But where they cancel each other out—like when one wave's high point hits another's low point—it creates darker stripes, because there's no light hitting the screen there. So light is acting like a wave, not individual particles."

Mike Reynolds, one of the football players on Quanta's team, looked confused. "But wait, you said light is made of photons, which are particles. How can it be both?"

"Excellent question," Mr. Wagner said with genuine pleasure, clearly delighted that his students were engaging with the concept. "And that's where the observer effect comes in. When we set up detectors to see which slit each individual photon goes through—when we try to observe the path of the light—something remarkable happens."

He made some adjustments to the apparatus, adding sophisticated detection devices near the slits. "Now watch what happens when we observe which path the light takes."

As soon as the detectors were activated, the interference pattern on the screen disappeared, replaced by exactly what Jessica had predicted—two distinct lines of light.

"When no one is observing, photons act like waves—they go through both slits at once. When they are observed, however, they act like particles—they go through just one of the slits. The act of observation changed the behavior of the light itself," Mr. Wagner said, letting that sink in as he looked around the classroom. "When we weren't watching, the photons behaved like waves and created an interference pattern. When we set up detectors to observe them, they behaved like particles and created two separate lines. This phenomenon is called wave-particle duality—a core principle of wave theory. Wave theory shows us that at the quantum level, everything exists as probability waves until consciousness collapses those waves into definite particles. It's not just light—it's the fundamental way reality works."

The classroom was completely silent. Quanta could see his classmates struggling to process what they'd just witnessed, their faces showing varying degrees of confusion, amazement, and disbelief. He seemed to grasp it more than the others, but he still had questions.

"Let me try to clarify a bit further. Think of it like reality is shy," Mr. Wagner explained with a grin. "When no one's watching, particles feel free to be themselves—flowing like waves through both slits at once, creating these beautiful interference patterns. But the moment consciousness peeks at them, they get self-conscious and snap into being well-behaved particles, going through just one slit like they're supposed to."

"But that's impossible," Sarah said finally, voicing what several others were clearly thinking. "How can light know whether it's being observed or not?"

"That," Mr. Wagner said with a look of quiet intensity, "is the question that led to some of the most profound discoveries in modern physics. Because it turns out that this isn't just true for light—it's true for all matter at the quantum level. Electrons, atoms, even larger molecules exhibit this same behavior."

Quanta raised his hand. "So you're saying that everything knows it's being watched?"

Mr. Wagner paused, studying Quanta with the kind of attention that suggested he was evaluating how much depth to go into with his answer. "That's actually being actively researched by physicists around the world. The relationship between consciousness and quantum physics is still being explored. What we can say definitively is that the act of measurement—which requires some form of observation—fundamentally alters the behavior of subatomic particles."

"But what does that mean for everyday life?" Quanta pressed, genuinely curious about the implications.

"Well," Mr. Wagner said carefully, "if observation requires consciousness, and observation affects quantum particles, then consciousness affects physical reality. Just to reiterate, consciousness in this sense means awareness itself—the part of you that can observe your thoughts and experiences. And if that awareness can affect quantum particles, and everything is made of quantum particles, then consciousness affects everything. In other words, your awareness doesn't just watch reality—it helps shape it. Some of the leading research on this is being done downtown at our top universities. I'm sure your father will know more about the latest developments than I do, given his work in quantum physics."

Quanta felt a spark of recognition. Mr. Wagner knew about his father's research.

After demonstrating how the observation changed the light's behavior several more times to make sure everyone understood the concept, Mr. Wagner moved to another sophisticated piece of equipment—what looked like a spectrum analysis device connected to various sensors.

"Now, let's talk about another fascinating aspect of observation," he said, activating a large display that showed the full electromagnetic spectrum. "How much of reality do you think we can actually perceive with our normal senses?"

"All of it?" Mike guessed, still looking slightly dazed from the previous demonstration.

Mr. Wagner shook his head with a smile. "Actually, humans can only see a tiny fraction of the electromagnetic spectrum—less than 1%. Look at this."

He pointed to the narrow band of visible light in the middle of a much larger spectrum that included radio waves, microwaves, infrared, ultraviolet, X-rays, and gamma rays. The visible portion was barely a sliver compared to the vast ranges of electromagnetic energy surrounding it.

"Do you guys remember learning ROYGBIV in science class when you were younger? All the colors of the rainbow – red, orange, yellow, green, blue, indigo, violet. This is the small sliver being shown here. This is all the human eye can see. That means over 99% of the remaining electromagnetic energy around us right now—in this very classroom—is completely invisible to our normal senses. Just because we can't see something doesn't mean it's not there."

He activated some of the sensors connected to his equipment, and numbers began appearing on a digital display. "Right now, this room is filled with radio waves from dozens of stations, cell phone signals, Wi-Fi networks, infrared radiation from our body heat, ultraviolet light filtering through the windows, and cosmic radiation from outer space. We're swimming in an ocean of electromagnetic energy that we can't see."

"So what else might be there that we can't perceive?" Sarah asked, leaning forward with interest.

"Well, that's where science gets really interesting," Mr. Wagner said, his eyes taking on the kind of excitement that suggested this was his favorite part of the lesson. "There are theories suggesting that consciousness itself might be everywhere around us, like an invisible field of energy and information that connects everything. Most scientists refer to this field as the 'quantum field,' although they have yet to land on an agreed upon name for this phenomenon."

"You mean consciousness could be like Wi-Fi?" Tyler asked suddenly. "Invisible but everywhere?"

"That's correct," Mr. Wagner said with approval. "An invisible field that carries energy and information and can influence physical systems when properly tuned into."

As the class period wound down, Mr. Wagner returned to the main point. "The key takeaway is this: observation isn't passive. When we observe something, we're not just watching—we're helping to decide what actually happens. At the tiniest level, everything exists as multiple possibilities at once, until someone observes it and it becomes one specific thing."

The bell rang, but Mr. Wagner raised his hand to indicate he had one final thought.

"Before you go, I want you to think about this: if consciousness affects reality at the quantum level, and if we can only perceive less than 1% of what's around us, what might be possible if we learned to expand our awareness? What if observation isn't just about seeing what's there, but actually participating in creating what becomes real?"

As students gathered their books and headed for the door, Quanta caught Mr. Wagner's eye.

"Mr. Jones, I'd be curious to hear what your father thinks about today's demonstration. I have a feeling he might have some interesting insights to add."

"I'll definitely ask him," Quanta said, feeling excited about the conversation they'd have later.

At lunch, Quanta found Nova at their usual spot in the cafeteria and immediately launched into an enthusiastic recap of Mr. Wagner's class.

"He really demonstrated the observer effect?" Nova asked, her eyes wide with interest. "With real equipment?"

"With real equipment. We could see how the light changed behavior when it was being observed versus when it wasn't. It was incredible—the pattern completely changed the moment we started observing which path the photons took."

"That's crazy. What did everyone think?"

"Most looked pretty confused, but you could see they were really trying to understand it. And Mr. Wagner mentioned my father's work. I think he knows my dad's ahead of the curve on this stuff."

They were joined by Andy, Tyler, and Jessica, who slid into seats around them with their lunch trays.

"Hey, Q," Andy said with a smirk, setting down his tray. "Isn't this that observer thing you were asking us about the other day at lunch? How did you know about it before we learned it in class?"

Tyler nodded, looking impressed. "Yeah, you were talking about consciousness affecting reality or something. That's exactly what Mr. Wagner demonstrated today."

"Wait, you knew about this already?" Jessica asked, looking between Quanta and Nova with curiosity.

Quanta felt a moment of recognition at how everything was connecting. "My dad's mentioned it before. He's always researching this kind of stuff. This proves consciousness isn't just along for the ride. We're participating in creating what we experience."

"That makes sense," Jessica said. "No wonder you knew about it. Your dad must talk about some pretty advanced topics at home."

"Sometimes," Quanta said. "Though I'm just starting to really understand what it all means."

"It's pretty crazy when you think about it," Tyler said. "Like, reality isn't actually solid the way we think it is. Even this table we're sitting at."

"Yeah," Quanta said, thinking more about Mr. Wagner's demonstration and recalling some facts from conversations with his dad. "Everything is just energy vibrating at different frequencies, which behave like waves until observed. So, this table is really just energy patterns that our brains interpret as solid matter. In other words, the waves turn to particles and form the physical table, but only after we look at it."

He looked around the cafeteria, thinking through what this meant on a larger scale. "So that would also mean... this whole building, the houses outside, the skyscrapers downtown, cars, trees—none of them exist until we observe them. Like a video game that only renders the scene when the player gets there, not wasting resources on areas nobody's looking at." He shook his head slightly, the realization almost too big to wrap his mind around.

"That's exactly what some interpretations of quantum mechanics suggest," Nova said, joining the conversation. "Most people think the world is just this fixed, solid thing sitting there waiting for us to observe it. But some physicists believe reality isn't fully formed until observation. It's being generated in real-time through our awareness, which is helping to create what we experience with our five senses."

After his friends moved on to other topics, Nova leaned closer to Quanta, lowering her voice.

"You see what's happening, right? You're starting to understand these concepts before they're even taught in class. Your awareness is expanding."

"It does feel like that." Quanta replied. "Like I'm tuning into information that was always there, but I just couldn't perceive it before."

Nova smiled. "That's exactly how it works. As your consciousness expands, you naturally become aware of deeper layers of reality."

She paused, the continued, "The whole idea of observation collapsing possibilities reminds me of this concept called superposition."

"Wait," Quanta said, his eyes lighting up with recognition. "This sounds like something my dad mentioned Tuesday—Schrödinger's cat. Is that the same thing? I think Mr. Wagner was about to present this as well, but the bell rang."

"You got it." Nova said with a smile. "Superposition just means that something can exist in more than one state at the same time—until it's observed. Think of it like this—imagine you have a coin that you flip, but instead of landing heads or tails, it's spinning in the air. While it's spinning, it's both heads and tails at the same time. That's superposition. But the moment someone catches it and looks at it, it collapses into being either heads or tails."

Quanta processed this. "So reality exists in multiple possibilities until consciousness observes it?"

Nova continued eagerly. "Yes! And what Schrödinger was showing is how weird this gets when you apply it to bigger things. In his experiment, a cat in a box could be both alive and dead at the same time until someone opens the box to check."

"That..." Quanta struggled for words as the implications hit him. "That changes everything about how reality works."

"It really does," Nova said. "And most people have no clue that this is how the universe works at the deepest level. They think reality is fixed and solid, but it's actually flexible and responds to consciousness."

Quanta connected the pieces. "So when Mr. Wagner said consciousness participates in creating reality..."

"He meant it literally," Nova confirmed. "Every moment, through our observation and attention, we're collapsing infinite possibilities into the specific reality we experience.

Scientists call this collapse decoherence—it's when all those multiple possibilities suddenly become one definite reality through observation."

During his afternoon classes, Quanta started thinking about superposition, decoherence, and the observer effect in entirely new ways. The idea that reality existed in multiple possibilities until consciousness observed it felt revolutionary, like learning that everything he'd been taught about the nature of existence was incomplete.

After school, Quanta walked home with Nova, both of them still buzzing with excitement from the day's revelations. Everything was connecting—the conversations with his father, Mr. Wagner's demonstration, even the way his classmates were starting to engage with these ideas.

"You know what's really wild to think about?" Quanta said. "If individual consciousness can affect quantum particles, what happens when you have millions of people all thinking about the same thing?"

Nova's gaze sharpened, suddenly focused. "You mean collective consciousness?"

"Exactly. Like, what if consciousness doesn't just work individually, but collectively too?"

"That's a fascinating idea," Nova said. "What made you think of that?"

"Well, everyone always talks about how the TV show *The Simpsons* predicts the future, right? Like, they'll show something crazy on the show, and then years later it actually happens and then they blast it all over social media. Most people think it's just coincidence or that the writers are psychic or something."

"But you're thinking there might be another explanation?"

"What if it's not that the show that is predicting the future, but that so many people watch it and think about the events presented on the show, that their collective consciousness somehow makes those future events more likely to happen in real life? Like, millions of minds all focused on the same possibilities, collapsing them into actual reality."

Nova stopped walking for a moment, processing the implications. "That would mean consciousness affects reality not just at the quantum level, but at the social and historical level too."

"Right. And it would explain why certain ideas seem to emerge in multiple places at the same time, or why some cultural predictions seem to come true while others don't."

"The more people who see it and think about it, the more likely it is to occur," Nova said, her voice growing more excited. "It's like... like consciousness creates probability fields, and the more attention something gets, the stronger the field becomes."

They continued walking, both lost in thought about the implications of consciousness operating on collective scales.

They slowed to a stop before parting ways.

"This is getting really deep," Nova said with a smile. "I love how everything keeps connecting."

"Me too. See you tomorrow?"

"Definitely. I have a feeling there's a lot more to explore."

They said goodbye and headed to their respective houses, both still processing the day's revelations.

When Quanta walked into his house, Sol greeted him with that familiar knowing look, and he could feel the subtle but unmistakable shift in energy that he'd come to associate with their house—that sense of being in a space where consciousness and reality interacted more freely.

"Dad?" he called out, setting his backpack down by the front door.

"In the study," came Justin's voice from down the hall.

Quanta found his father surrounded by books and papers, clearly deep in research mode. The study was Justin's sanctuary, filled with quantum physics texts, consciousness research, and theoretical works that most people would find incomprehensible. But now, having experienced what he had over the past few days, Quanta looked at those books with new appreciation.

"How was school today?" Justin asked, looking up from a paper he'd been reading and giving Quanta his full attention. "Learn anything interesting?"

"Actually, yeah. Mr. Wagner's class was incredible. He demonstrated the double-slit experiment with real equipment. We could see how the light changed from wave behavior to particle behavior once we started observing it."

"What went through your mind when you saw that?"

"It was mind-blowing. Like, you know intellectually that consciousness affects reality, but seeing it happen right in front of you..." Quanta paused, searching for the right words. "It made everything we've been talking about feel real in a completely different way. It's like everything connects. Tesla's ideas about energy and frequency, the techniques Nova showed me for shifting my internal state, and now scientific proof that consciousness affects physical reality. It's all the same thing, just looked at from different angles."

Justin smiled with obvious pleasure. "Mr. Wagner's one of the good ones. He understands that science is about asking the big questions, not just memorizing formulas and getting the right answers on tests. He's showing the scientific foundation that explains why those techniques work."

"He mentioned that some of the leading research on consciousness is being done downtown at local universities. He seemed to know about your work."

"I remember meeting him at the open house last year. We had a great conversation about physics. He's got a good understanding of where the field is heading, even if he has to be careful about how much he can discuss in a high school classroom."

"Dad, do you have any books about consciousness research? After what Mr. Wagner demonstrated today, I'm really curious to learn more about how consciousness affects reality."

Justin stood and moved to one of his bookshelves, scanning the titles before pulling several books. "Here's Dean Radin's *The Conscious Universe*—it's a comprehensive overview of the scientific research on psychic phenomena and consciousness. Very rigorous, very well-documented."

He handed Quanta the book, then reached for another. "And here's Michael Talbot's *The Holographic Universe*, which explores the idea that reality might be structured like a hologram—where every part contains information about the whole. It connects quantum physics to mystical experiences in ways that are both scientifically grounded and personally transformative."

The third book he pulled was *The Untethered Soul* by Michael Singer. "And this one is perfect for understanding the difference between thoughts and the awareness observing them. Singer has some remarkable insights about how to live from the observer perspective rather than being controlled by the voice in your head."

Quanta looked at the books with growing excitement. "These were just sitting here on your shelf?"

"I've been waiting for you to be ready for them," Justin said with a knowing smile. "The universe has a way of providing exactly what we need when we need it. A few months ago, these books would have seemed too abstract or complicated. But after everything you've been experiencing..."

"They feel exactly right," Quanta finished.

"And now you have both the direct experience and the scientific framework to really understand what these authors are talking about."

"Thanks, Dad. This is what I was hoping for."

"Just remember," Justin said, settling back into his chair, "these aren't textbooks to memorize for a test. They're invitations to expand your understanding of what's possible. Read them with curiosity, ask questions, and trust your own experience above everything else."

"I will."

"And Quanta? If you have questions or want to discuss what you're reading, I'm always here for you. Not many people are interested in these deeper aspects of reality, so I welcome the opportunity for meaningful conversation."

As Quanta headed to his room with the books, he felt profound gratitude for how everything was unfolding. Just a few days ago, he'd been feeling isolated and disconnected, questioning his sanity after the experience in Mr. Rike's classroom. Now he had Nova to explore these concepts with, a father who understood and supported his journey, and a teacher who could provide scientific context in the classroom.

The universe really did seem to be providing exactly what he needed exactly when he needed it.

In his room, Sol settled into his favorite spot on the bed while Quanta arranged the three books on his desk. Looking at them—*The Conscious Universe*, *The Holographic Universe*, *The Untethered Soul*—he felt like he was looking at doorways into deeper understanding.

Tomorrow, he would continue this exploration with Nova. This weekend, he would dive into these books. And somehow, he knew this was still just the beginning of understanding what was truly possible when you recognized that consciousness was fundamental to reality.

He was no longer just remembering who he was. He was discovering the laws that governed reality itself—laws that most people remained completely unaware of. And with that awareness came a growing sense of responsibility and

excitement about what he might be capable of creating in
his life.

Chapter 5: The Frequency of Thought

Friday morning found Quanta lying in bed before his alarm, watching patterns of light shift across his ceiling as the sunrise filtered through his bedroom window. He'd been awake for nearly an hour, not from restlessness but from a growing sense of anticipation about the day ahead. Yesterday's revelations—Mr. Wagner's demonstration, the walk home with Nova, and receiving those books from his father—had left him feeling like he was standing at the edge of something infinite and unexplored.

Sol was curled up at the foot of the bed, but even in sleep, his ears twitched occasionally as if he were monitoring frequencies beyond normal hearing. Quanta had noticed this more since Monday's awakening—how Sol seemed to be perpetually tuned into subtle energies that most people couldn't perceive.

As he lay there, Quanta was becoming aware of his own thoughts in a way he'd never experienced before. Instead of being caught up in the constant stream of mental chatter, he could step back and observe it—using the awareness he'd awakened to in Mr. Rike's classroom. He could watch thoughts arise and fade away like clouds passing through an empty sky.

The frequency techniques Nova had taught him were becoming more natural and precise. He could now easily distinguish between the heavy, constricted feeling of worried thoughts and the lighter, more expansive quality of grateful ones. It was like developing a new sense for measuring the energy quality of different mental states.

This wasn't just a philosophical understanding anymore—it was a direct, felt experience. He could literally sense the difference between high-frequency and low-frequency mental states in his body. It was like discovering he had an internal instrument that could measure different frequencies of consciousness.

He decided to experiment more deliberately with what Nova had taught him about frequency work. Closing his eyes, he focused on three things he was genuinely grateful for: the consciousness research books waiting on his desk, the growing friendship with Nova, and his father's willingness to discuss these concepts openly.

As he held each thought in his awareness, he could feel a subtle but distinct shift in his energy. It was like tuning a car radio to a clearer station—the static of morning anxiety gave way to something more harmonious and alive. The change wasn't just mental; he could feel it in his body, a lightness that seemed to expand outward from his chest and actually affect the space around him.

"Interesting," he murmured, sitting up and looking at Sol, who had opened his eyes and was watching him intently. "You felt that too, didn't you, buddy?"

Sol's small tail gave a wag, as if to say *Now you're getting it.*

Downstairs, Quanta's parents were already in their morning groove, but today felt different from the usual weekday rush. His father was at the kitchen table with his coffee and another book—this one titled *The Field* by Lynne McTaggart—while his mother moved around the kitchen with an unusual lightness to her step.

"Good morning," Anne said, glancing up from packing lunches. "You're looking particularly alert for a Friday morning."

"I feel alert," Quanta said, and realized it was true. Instead of the usual Friday fatigue that came from four days of institutional routine, he felt energized and curious about what the day might bring.

"Sleep well?" Justin asked, looking up from his book with interest.

"Really well. I keep thinking about those books you gave me last night. I'm really curious about what I'll learn from them."

"Well," Justin said, clearly pleased with that response, "those books explore some fascinating research. Scientists have discovered that focused thoughts can affect physical things in small but measurable ways."

Quanta sat down across from his father. "Like how?"

"Imagine a computer program that's supposed to pick random numbers, like randomly choosing 1 or 2. Scientists have people try to influence it just by thinking 'pick more 1s' or 'pick more 2s.' Sounds impossible, right? But when researchers test this with thousands of people over thousands of trials, they find that focused intention does change the results slightly."

"You mean thoughts can affect computers?"

"In tiny ways, yes. The effects are small, but they're real and consistent. It's like your consciousness has this subtle influence on the world around you."

Anne paused in her lunch preparation and looked between them. "Are you two saying that thoughts can actually change things in the real world?"

"That's what the research shows," Justin replied simply. "The question isn't whether it happens—it's how much and under what conditions."

"But that would mean..." Anne trailed off, clearly processing the implications.

"It gets even more interesting," Justin continued. "You've been developing sensitivity to your own frequency changes, so have you ever noticed how some people just make you feel calmer or more energized just by being around them? When your thoughts and emotions are in harmony with your heart rhythm, you broadcast a different kind of energy that other people can sense. It's like the difference between playing a single instrument versus conducting a symphony where everything is perfectly synchronized."

"You mean like sending out good vibes or bad vibes?" Quanta asked.

"Yes, but it's measurable. When someone is really centered and peaceful, their heart rhythm and brain waves sync up in a coherent pattern. Other people nearby—even pets—often start matching that rhythm without realizing it."

"That's incredible," Quanta said. "So, learning to control your own energy isn't just personal—you're actually affecting everyone around you."

"Right," Justin said with a meaningful look. "Which means that working on yourself is really a service to all those around you. When you maintain higher frequencies, you're helping to lift up everyone in your environment. You're literally creating 'good vibes' as you mentioned."

As Quanta headed out for school, he decided to put his morning discoveries into practice. Instead of just letting his mind wander randomly, he began experimenting with consciously choosing what to focus on. When he noticed himself thinking about an upcoming test with anxiety, he gently shifted his attention to curiosity about what he might learn instead. The change in how he felt was immediate and noticeable.

It was like discovering he had controls for his own experience that he'd never known existed.

When he reached Nova's house, she was waiting on the front steps with her backpack and a small notebook that was bound in worn leather and had the appearance of something well-used and important.

"Hey," she said, standing up and walking beside him. "What's new?"

"I think I'm starting to understand how this stuff actually works."

"What do you mean?"

"I was just experimenting with consciously shifting my thoughts, and I could feel the energy change in my body. It's like thoughts have frequencies that you can tune just like a radio."

Nova's eyebrows raised with interest. "That's amazing. Most people take forever to develop that kind of sensitivity. You're picking this up super-fast."

"It helps having good teachers," Quanta said. "Both you and my dad are showing me different pieces of the same puzzle."

"Speaking of which," Nova said, holding up the leather notebook, "I brought something I think you're ready for. More advanced frequency techniques from my grandmother's notes."

"Like what?"

"Ways to use thought frequency for creating changes in your life, not just feeling better in the moment. But we should probably wait until after school to go through it properly."

They spent the rest of the walk discussing Quanta's experiments with gratitude and frequency shifting. Nova shared some additional techniques for maintaining higher frequencies throughout the day, especially in challenging situations like difficult classes or peer pressure.

"The key," she explained, "is remembering that you're not your thoughts—you're the awareness watching your thoughts. Once you get that, you can start choosing whatever frequency you want instead of just reacting to whatever happens."

The first few periods of school provided perfect opportunities to practice what Nova had described. Instead of getting caught up in frustration with repetitive lessons or other students' lack of engagement, Quanta experimented with consciously shifting his focus to find deeper meaning in whatever was being taught.

In one class, instead of zoning out during a lecture about historical events, he found himself genuinely curious about why people made the choices they did. In another, when half the class was on their phones instead of paying attention, he focused on appreciating what the teacher was trying to share rather than getting annoyed at their disrespect. Each time he consciously shifted his attention, the experience became more engaging—not because the content had changed, but because his relationship to it had changed.

By the time he reached science class, Quanta was eager to see what Mr. Wagner had in store for them.

"Good morning, scientists," Mr. Wagner said as students settled in, using the greeting he started every class with. "Today we're going to explore something that builds directly on yesterday's discussion about consciousness and observation. We're going to continue with the electromagnetic spectrum but expand to how everything—including thoughts—generates measurable frequencies."

Quanta felt a thrill of anticipation. This was exactly what he'd been experimenting with that morning.

Mr. Wagner moved to a sophisticated device that looked like a combination of computer and scientific instrument. "This is an EEG machine—short for electroencephalogram—it measures the electrical activity happening in your brain. Don't worry, I won't ask you to spell it on the next test. Just think of it like a heart monitor, but instead of tracking your heartbeat, it tracks the electrical signals your brain cells create when they communicate with each other."

He attached sensors to his own head and activated the display screen. Immediately, wave patterns began scrolling across the monitor—complex, constantly shifting patterns of electrical activity.

"These are my brain waves right now," Mr. Wagner explained. "When I focus my attention, the patterns change. When I relax, they change again. Watch what happens when I shift into different mental states."

As he spoke, the patterns on the screen shifted noticeably. When he focused intently on explaining a complex theory, the waves became more rapid and organized. When he closed his eyes and took a deep breath, they slowed and became more rhythmic.

"The fascinating thing," Mr. Wagner continued, "is that these frequencies don't stay contained within your head. They're energy fields that extend into the space around you. In a very real sense, your thoughts are broadcasting signals just like when music is streamed from your phone to your wireless headphones."

He moved to another part of his demonstration setup. "But here's what makes it even more interesting. Watch what happens when I really focus my intention on shifting into what's called a 'coherent' state."

Mr. Wagner closed his eyes and took several more deep, rhythmic breaths, each inhale and exhale perfectly timed to the second. As he did, the chaotic wave patterns on the screen began to organize themselves into smoother, more regular rhythms. The patterns repeated at precise intervals and were in sync with each breath.

"Scientists refer to this as being in 'coherence' – when your mind and body are perfectly synchronized," he explained, opening his eyes while maintaining the breathing pattern. "When your heart rhythm, brain waves, and nervous system all sync up, you generate what's essentially a more powerful and organized energy field. Think of it like a dual-engine plane. When both engines are perfectly synchronized, you fly smoothly and powerfully toward your destination. But when they're out of sync—like when your mind is worried about tomorrow while your heart wants to enjoy today—you're basically flying with engines fighting each other. You might still get where you're going, but it takes more fuel and creates a lot of turbulence."

"And that affects other people?" Sarah asked, clearly fascinated.

"Studies show that people in coherent states can influence the heart rhythms and brain waves of others nearby, even without direct contact. It's as if coherent consciousness creates a field that naturally draws other people into more organized states."

Tyler raised his hand. "So if someone's really anxious or angry, they could make other people feel that way too?"

"Unfortunately, yes. Chaotic emotional states tend to create disorganized energy patterns that can negatively influence others. But the good news is that coherent, positive states have an even stronger effect. One person in genuine coherence can often shift the energy of an entire room."

Sarah asked a follow up question. "So other people can pick up our thoughts?"

"Not exactly like reading minds," Mr. Wagner replied, "but people do unconsciously respond to the energy fields you're generating. Have you ever noticed how some people make you feel calm just by being around them, while others make you feel anxious or agitated, even when they're not saying anything?"

Several students nodded, clearly recognizing the experience.

"That's partly because you're picking up on their frequency. Calm, centered people generate coherent energy patterns that tend to influence others toward coherence. Anxious, scattered people generate chaotic patterns that can create similar states in those around them."

Mike Reynolds looked skeptical. "But that sounds like you're saying thoughts are contagious."

"In a way, they are," Mr. Wagner said. "Research shows that people in groups unconsciously synchronize their brain waves, heart rhythms, and even breathing patterns. We're much more connected than most people realize."

Quanta raised his hand as this sounded awfully familiar to the collective consciousness discussion he and Nova had yesterday. "So if thoughts generate frequencies, and frequencies can influence other people, does that mean we can learn to control what frequency we're broadcasting to those around us?"

"That's precisely the right question," Mr. Wagner said with enthusiasm. "And the answer is yes. Meditation practices, breathing techniques, even conscious shifts in attention can dramatically alter the energy you broadcast. Some researchers believe this is one reason why certain people seem to have unusual abilities to influence their external reality—they've learned to broadcast more coherent frequencies."

"Are we talking about manifestation here?" Tyler asked.

Mr. Wagner paused, choosing his words carefully. "The research shows manifestation is real, though scientists are still figuring out exactly how it works. What they do know is that it works better when you're both focused and in a positive, calm state."

After class, Quanta felt like his understanding had expanded exponentially. The consciousness concepts he'd been learning weren't just philosophical ideas—they were proven, measurable phenomena with practical applications.

At lunch, he enthusiastically updated Nova on what he had just learned in Mr. Wagner's class.

“He showed us brain waves changing in real time based on different mental states,” Quanta said. “And he confirmed that thought frequencies extend beyond the brain and can influence other people.”

“That’s incredible,” Nova said. “It’s like having scientific validation for everything my grandmother wrote about.”

“And it explains so much about why some people just feel good to be around while others suck the life right out of you. Now I understand what energy vampires are,” Quanta joked.

Andy, Tyler, and Jessica arrived at their table, setting down their lunch trays and joining the conversation.”

“Hey, you guys talking about Mr. Wagner’s class again?” Andy asked with a grin. “That brain wave stuff was pretty wild.”

“It makes you think about how much we don’t know about our own minds,” Jessica said. “If thoughts are generating energy fields, what else might be happening that we’re not aware of?”

“It’s kind of scary when you think about it,” Tyler added. “If people can unconsciously influence each other through thought frequencies, how do you know which thoughts are actually yours?”

Nova edged forward, clearly intrigued. “That’s such a good point. Learning to tell the difference between your own energy and what you're picking up from others is essentially the first thing you need to learn."

"How do you do that?" Jessica asked.

"Practice noticing what your natural energy feels like when you're calm and centered. Then when you're around other people, you can feel when your energy changes and ask yourself if that change is coming from you or from them."

"That's like... mental self-defense," Andy said, looking thoughtful.

"Indeed. Once you understand that consciousness and energy are connected, you realize you need to be more careful about what energies you're around and what energy you're putting out."

After lunch, Quanta continued to piece all this new information together. How much of what he experienced was his own consciousness, and how much was influenced by the collective frequency of everyone around him? The idea that individual awareness might be much more interconnected than people realized was both fascinating and slightly overwhelming.

In PE, while warming up, he experimented with consciously maintaining his own frequency instead of getting caught up in the competitive energy that usually dominated the gym. The experience was remarkable—he felt more centered and focused than usual, and he noticed that his presence seemed to have a calming effect on some of his classmates.

By the time the final bell rang, Quanta was eager to explore the advanced techniques Nova had mentioned that morning. They walked home together through the autumn afternoon, the conversation flowing naturally between theoretical understanding and practical application.

"So, what's in the special notebook?" Quanta asked as they approached Nova's house.

"Techniques for using thought frequency to create specific changes in your life. My grandmother called it 'conscious creation'—learning to match the frequency of what you want instead of just reacting to what's happening now."

"That sounds like manifestation. Tyler actually asked about this in Mr. Wagner's class today."

"It is, but it's much more precise than most people think. It's not just about positive thinking or visualizing what you want. It's about matching your inner frequency with the frequency of what you want to create. This is one of several 'Laws of the Universe' called the Law of Correspondence that essentially says 'as within, so without'—meaning your inner world creates your outer world. Thoughts are part of it, but emotions and feelings are what really drive the frequency—they're like the power source behind your intentions."

When they reached Nova's house, she led him to the back porch, where they could sit comfortably without the possibility of her mother overhearing their conversation when she got home from work. The autumn air was crisp but not cold, and the afternoon sun created a warm, peaceful atmosphere.

"Before we dive into the advanced techniques," Nova said, settling into one of the porch chairs, "given your dad's understanding of the science behind all of this, has he shared any materials with you, or does he mostly just talk about the high-level concepts?"

"Actually, yeah. Just last night he gave me three books about consciousness research. He said he'd been waiting for me to be ready for them."

"Really? What kind of books?" Nova asked.

"One is called *The Conscious Universe* by Dean Radin, another is *The Holographic Universe* by Michael Talbot, and the third is *The Untethered Soul* by Michael Singer," Quanta replied.

Nova recognized one immediately. "Oh, Michael Singer. He was one of my grandmother's favorites. She said his understanding of witness consciousness was incredibly clear and practical. She used to quote him all the time— especially his insights about ego and not being controlled by the voice in your head."

"What's witness consciousness again?" Quanta asked.

Nova answered, "It's what we've been talking about—just the state of awareness where you observe your thoughts, emotions, and experiences without getting caught up in them or trying to change them."

"Oh, that's right. So just being the witness or the observer instead of the observed—realizing that we're not our thoughts, but the awareness observing them."

"Yep, he explains the observer-observed relationship in such a simple way. Like how you can watch your thoughts and emotions without reacting to them. My grandmother said he was one of the few authors who made the distinction between awareness and thoughts crystal clear for everyday people. That's the foundation of everything. Once you really get that you're the one watching your thoughts, not the thoughts themselves, you can start taking control instead of just being pushed around by whatever pops into your head."

Nova opened the leather notebook and showed Quanta pages covered with diagrams, frequency charts, and detailed instructions written in Alma's neat handwriting.

"The basic principle," she began, "is that everything in the universe has its own frequency signature. This is another Law of the Universe – the Law of Vibration, which states that everything in the universe is constantly moving and vibrating at its own unique frequency."

Health has a frequency, abundance has a frequency, love has a frequency, fear has a frequency. When you learn to match your internal frequency to the frequency of what you want to create, you start attracting those experiences into your life."

"But how do you know what frequency something has?"

"That's where sensitivity training comes in. Remember how you could feel the difference between grateful thoughts and worried thoughts this morning?"

"Right, grateful thoughts felt warm and uplifting."

"Exactly. Each emotion, each state of consciousness, each type of experience has its own feeling signature. With practice, you can learn to recognize the frequency of almost anything by how it feels in your body."

Nova turned to a page filled with a detailed frequency map—different emotions and experiences organized according to their vibrational characteristics.

"This is what my grandmother called the 'frequency scale,'" she explained. "At the bottom are the lowest frequencies—fear, jealousy, hatred, revenge, greed, superstition, anger, shame, despair. These feel heavy, constrictive, and disconnected. At the top are the highest frequencies—desire, faith, love, enthusiasm, hope, joy, peace, gratitude. These feel light, expansive, and unified."

Quanta studied the chart with fascination. "So, consciousness development is basically learning to maintain higher frequencies?"

"That's part of it. But the really powerful application is learning to match your frequency to specific outcomes you want to create. If you want better health, you practice feeling the frequency of vibrant wellness. If you want better relationships, you practice feeling the frequency of deep connection and love."

"And this actually works?"

"According to my grandmother's notes, it works because of the Law of Attraction—like frequencies attract each other. Remember those tuning forks I showed you? When you strike one tuning fork, any other fork tuned to the same frequency will start vibrating automatically, even from across the room. If a fork is tuned to a different frequency, then it obviously won't vibrate. Consciousness works the same way—when you consistently broadcast the frequency of what you want, you naturally attract similar frequencies into your experience. The Law of Vibration essentially serves the Law of Attraction."

Nova turned to another page showing specific techniques for frequency alignment. "Want to try one?"

"Definitely."

"Let's start with something simple. Think of an area of your life where you'd like to see improvement—maybe school, sports, relationships, creativity, whatever feels important to you."

Quanta considered the question. "I guess I'd like to feel more confident and natural in social situations. Sometimes I feel like I'm watching from the outside instead of really connecting with people."

"Perfect. Now, instead of focusing on the current situation where you feel disconnected, I want you to imagine what it would feel like to be completely comfortable and confident in social gatherings. Don't worry about the specific details—just focus on the feeling."

Quanta closed his eyes and tried to imagine feeling completely at ease with people. At first, it was difficult because his mind kept jumping to memories of awkward social moments. But gradually, he began to sense what it might feel like to be genuinely relaxed and confident around others.

"Can you feel a difference in your body when you focus on that?" Nova asked.

"Yeah, it's like... lighter and more open. Less of that tight feeling in my chest."

"That's the frequency of social confidence. The more you practice accessing that feeling, the more you'll naturally attract situations and opportunities that match it."

They spent the next hour going through different techniques for frequency alignment, emotional clearing, and what Nova's grandmother had called "frequency anchoring"—creating specific physical or mental triggers that could instantly shift your vibration to a desired state. It was like programming a shortcut into your nervous system, so that a simple gesture, word, or mental image could immediately bring back the feeling of gratitude, love, or whatever high-frequency state you wanted to access.

"The secret to making this practical," Nova explained as they worked through a technique for maintaining coherence during stress, "is understanding that you're not trying to control your external circumstances. You're learning to choose your internal frequency regardless of what's happening around you."

"So instead of trying to change what's happening outside of me, I focus on changing what's happening inside of me? Like, I can't control if someone's being difficult, but I can control how I respond to it?"

"You nailed it. When you can maintain your inner peace no matter what's going on externally, you actually become a stabilizing influence that helps shift the energy of the entire situation. Let's dive a bit deeper. Think of a time when you felt completely confident and at peace. Really immerse yourself in that memory—see what you saw, hear what you heard, feel what you felt. Use as many of your senses as possible."

Quanta recalled a moment from last summer when he'd been sitting by the lake at their cabin, watching the sunset reflect on the water, feeling completely relaxed and at peace, connected to everything around him.

"Now, while you're in that state, press your thumb and forefinger together," Nova instructed. "Hold that physical gesture while you stay completely immersed in the feeling."

He followed her instructions, anchoring the sensation of deep peace and relaxation to the simple physical gesture.

"Great. Now clear your mind, think about something completely different for a moment... okay, now press your thumb and forefinger together again."

The instant he made the gesture, the peaceful, relaxed feeling flooded back through his system.

"That's incredible," he said, releasing the pressure and feeling the state fade, then pressing again and having it return immediately. "It's like a switch for consciousness."

"That's exactly what it is. My grandmother called these 'coherence anchors.' Once you build several of them, you can access any state you want almost instantly, regardless of your external circumstances. It's like saving someone's phone number as a favorite—when you need that connection, it's just one tap away instead of scrolling through your entire contact list."

"Love it," Quanta said as they finished practicing this technique. "It's like having actual tools for creating your experience instead of just hoping things work out."

"Right. Most people think they're victims of circumstance, but really they're creators and are just simply unaware of it. They're broadcasting frequencies all day long without realizing it, and then wondering why they keep attracting the same kinds of experiences."

As the afternoon sun began to set, Quanta felt profoundly grateful for the journey he'd been on this week. From Monday's awakening to today's advanced frequency training, each day had built upon the last in ways that felt both surprising and strangely orchestrated.

"Nova," he said, "thanks again for sharing all this with me. I feel like I'm finally understanding what's possible."

"We're just getting started," she replied with a smile. "There's so much more to uncover."

When Quanta arrived home that evening, he found his father in the living room reading another book while dinner preparations created comfortable sounds and smells from the kitchen.

"How was school today?" Justin asked, looking up with genuine interest.

"Incredible. Mr. Wagner demonstrated how different mental states create different brain wave patterns, and showed us that thought frequencies extend beyond the brain and can influence other people."

"Ah, electromagnetic field effects. That's cutting-edge research. I'm glad he's covering these kinds of topics in his class. What did you think about the implications?"

Quanta felt the same ease of communication they'd been developing all week. "It makes sense of so many things I've been experiencing. Like how you can feel different people's energy, or how your own mental state seems to affect what happens around you."

"Sounds like you're getting it. The boundaries between self and environment are much more fluid than most people realize. Consciousness doesn't just observe reality—it helps shape it by interacting with the energy field around us. The same field that mostly everyone is completely unaware of."

"Dad, can I ask you something about how to apply this knowledge?"

"Of course."

"If consciousness affects reality through frequency, and we can learn to control our frequency, does that mean we can actually influence what shows up in our lives?"

Justin paused, clearly considering how to respond to such a direct question about manifestation and conscious creation.

"The research suggests that clear and focused intention combined with elevated and heartfelt emotions can change your frequency and influence external reality," he said carefully. "The effects are usually subtle, but they're statistically significant across large numbers of trials. Whether that scales up to major life changes..." He paused. "Well, that's where the science gets more speculative, but the theoretical framework certainly supports it."

"What do you mean by elevated and heartfelt emotions?"

"When your thoughts, feelings, emotions, and intentions are all aligned and working together rather than in conflict. When your brain and heart are in coherence. Most people have scattered attention and contradictory desires, which creates what you might call 'frequency static.' But when someone achieves internal coherence—when all aspects of their consciousness are broadcasting the same signal— that's when the most significant effects seem to occur."

That evening, Quanta was drawn to his desk where his new books sat waiting. He picked up *The Conscious Universe* and began reading the introduction, while Sol settled nearby, occasionally lifting his head as if sensing the shift in Quanta's energy as he absorbed the new information.

As Quanta processed everything he'd learned that week, he felt a profound shift in his understanding of what it meant to be human. Consciousness wasn't just a byproduct of brain activity—it was an active, creative force that was constantly shaping reality through frequency and intention. And more importantly, it was something he could learn to use consciously rather than just being driven by unconscious patterns and reactions.

He flipped to a passage in Dean Radin's book further digesting what he'd learned about frequency and coherence and began to wonder about something that felt both exciting and slightly impossible. If his internal state could affect the brain waves of people around him, and if consciousness could influence quantum particles in laboratory experiments, what might be possible when someone learned to maintain coherent frequencies consistently?

Looking up from the book, Quanta realized that this was exactly what he was learning to do. Not through wishful thinking or magical beliefs, but through understanding the science of consciousness and developing practical skills for frequency management.

He was learning to become a conscious creator rather than just going through life on autopilot and playing the victim card.

And tomorrow, he would continue developing these abilities, exploring what was possible when someone truly understood the frequency of thought and learned to broadcast it intentionally.

For the first time in his life, Quanta felt like he was discovering his real power—not power over others, but power to consciously participate in creating his own experience. And that, he realized, was just the beginning of what was possible when you understood the true nature of consciousness and reality.

The frequency of thought was the frequency of creation itself. And he was finally learning how to tune in.

Chapter 6: The Controllers

Three weeks had passed since Quanta's introduction to frequency anchoring and the Laws of the Universe, and the transformation in his daily experience had been remarkable. What once felt like random events happening to him now seemed more like a carefully orchestrated dance between his internal frequency and external reality. His growing awareness—the same consciousness he'd awakened to in Mr. Rike's classroom—had become like a sixth sense, allowing him to perceive the energetic quality of situations and people in ways he'd never imagined possible. He'd been practicing the coherence techniques Nova had taught him, working through Dean Radin's research on consciousness affecting physical systems, and experimenting with the frequency anchoring methods that allowed him to shift his emotional state almost instantly.

The weather had turned crisp and clear, with December bringing that quality of light that made everything feel more vibrant and alive. Sol had become even more attuned to Quanta's energy shifts, often positioning himself nearby whenever Quanta practiced his frequency work, as if the dog were somehow participating in or amplifying the process.

During these past few weeks, Quanta had noticed changes beyond just his ability to manage his own frequency. His grades had improved without additional studying—not because the material was easier, but because his mind felt clearer and more focused. His relationships with friends and classmates had shifted subtly; people seemed more drawn to spend time around him, and conflicts that used to drain his energy now felt manageable. Even his parents had commented on the change in his overall demeanor.

Most significantly, he'd begun to notice patterns in the world around him that he'd never seen before. The way certain news broadcasts made him feel scared or agitated even when he wasn't paying close attention. How some music seemed to lift his spirits while other songs left him feeling depressed. The difference between teachers who genuinely cared about their students' development versus those who only seemed focused on grades and control.

It was as if developing his consciousness had given him a new sense for detecting the quality of energy and intention in his environment.

On this particular Saturday morning, Quanta woke up naturally around sunrise, his internal clock having adjusted to a more natural rhythm since he'd begun his consciousness practices. Instead of a loud alarm that used to wake him from a dead sleep, he'd been experiencing what he could only describe as an authentic awakening to reality, as if his consciousness was finally emerging from the fog of unconscious sleep, no longer keeping his head buried in the sand like the rest of the world—this wasn't the shallow 'woke' mentality he saw online, but genuine awareness of how things actually worked.

He lay in bed for a few minutes, practicing the morning gratitude techniques Nova had shown him, feeling his internal frequency shift from the grogginess of sleep to a more coherent, energized state. As he did, he reflected on how much had changed since his initial awakening. The voice that had commanded him to "Remember" felt like a distant memory, yet its message had become the foundation of everything he was discovering about himself and reality.

Downstairs, Justin was in the kitchen earlier than usual for a weekend, sitting at the table with his coffee and a printed research paper rather than one of his usual books. There was something in his father's posture that suggested the content of his reading was anything but peaceful.

"Morning, Dad. You're up early for a Saturday."

Justin looked up, and Quanta immediately noticed something different in his father's expression—a mixture of concern and determination that he hadn't seen before. There was also a quality of protective alertness, like someone who had discovered an important truth that others needed to know.

"Good morning. Actually, I wanted to talk to you about something. I've been reading some research that connects to what you've been learning about consciousness and frequency, but from a different angle. A more concerning angle, unfortunately."

Quanta sat down with his father, immediately sensing the shift in energy around the conversation. After weeks of practicing frequency sensitivity, he could feel that whatever his father wanted to discuss carried significant weight.

"What kind of research?"

Justin held up the paper, and Quanta could see it was titled "Subliminal Frequency Modulation in Mass Media: A Technical Analysis." The document looked official, with university letterhead and what appeared to be classified markings.

"This is from a colleague at another university who studies the intersection of technology, media, and consciousness. He's been documenting how certain frequencies can suppress awareness rather than enhance it—the opposite of what you and Nova have been exploring. And he's uncovered evidence that this suppression is not accidental—it's systematic and intentional."

"What do you mean by systematic?"

"Well, you know how you've learned that different frequencies can affect consciousness—how coherent states feel different from chaotic ones, how love has a different frequency than fear?"

"Right."

"It turns out that the same principles can be used in reverse. Instead of helping people achieve higher frequency states, certain technologies and media can be strategically designed to keep people in lower frequency states—fear, anxiety, anger, confusion. States that make them more susceptible to outside influence and less likely to think clearly or question authority."

Quanta felt a chill run through him as the implications began to sink in. "You mean like... on purpose? Someone is deliberately doing this?"

"That's exactly what I mean. And the people orchestrating this—referred to as 'the elites' in this research—understand consciousness and frequency manipulation far better than most scientists, having had access to this knowledge for decades—possibly even centuries—giving them a staggering head start over the rest of humanity."

Justin turned the research paper around so Quanta could see the detailed analysis. "Look at this data. They've analyzed the frequency content of major television networks, movie studios, radio stations, along with the top steaming and social media platforms. There are specific frequencies embedded in the content that disrupt coherent brain wave patterns and promote lower consciousness states."

Quanta studied the charts, recognizing some of the brain wave patterns from Mr. Wagner's EEG demonstrations. But these patterns were the opposite of the coherent, organized states they had observed in class. These looked chaotic, scattered, purposefully designed to create mental confusion.

"But why on earth would anyone want to do this?"

"Control," Justin said simply. "Think about it from a strategic perspective. If you understand how consciousness works, you have two fundamental choices: you can either help people become more aware, independent, and empowered, or you can use that knowledge to keep them unconscious, suppressed, and dependent on a system that you own. The elites chose the latter because conscious, empowered people are much harder to control, manipulate, and profit from."

Before Quanta could respond fully, his phone buzzed with a text from Nova: *"Need to talk to you today ASAP. Found something in my grandmother's journals that you need to see. It's about the other side of consciousness research— the dark side. This is bigger than we thought."*

"But here's what they didn't count on," Justin continued with growing conviction. "Consciousness is like water— you can try to dam it up, redirect it, even pollute it, but eventually it always finds a way to flow freely. Every person who develops these abilities becomes a crack in their control system. And once consciousness starts flowing through those cracks, the whole dam starts to crumble."

Quanta showed the text to his father, who read it with a knowing expression that suggested this is exactly what he's talking about.

"Sounds like Nova's grandmother understood this aspect as well," Justin said. "Why don't you go see what she's discovered? We can continue this conversation when you get back. But Quanta..." He paused, making sure he had his son's full attention. "Once you start seeing how this system works, you can't unsee it. It changes how you view almost everything—media, education, healthcare, politics, entertainment, even social interactions. Are you ready for that level of awareness?"

Quanta thought about the journey he'd been on for the past several weeks, how each revelation had opened doors he couldn't close again. Yet rather than feeling overwhelmed by these discoveries, he also thought about the growing sense of power and freedom he'd experienced as his consciousness expanded.

"I think I'm ready. I mean, if this knowledge exists, and if people are using it to manipulate others, shouldn't I know about it? Shouldn't everyone know about it? Isn't awareness always better than ignorance?"

"Yes," Justin said with conviction. "Awareness is always better than ignorance, even when the truth is uncomfortable or challenging. But remember what you've learned about frequency management. Don't let this information drop you into fear or anger—that would just trap you in the same low-frequency states the elites want people in. Stay centered, stay curious, and remember that consciousness itself is more powerful than any system designed to suppress it."

An hour later, Quanta was back at Nova's house, but this time the atmosphere felt charged with a heavier kind of urgency—as if what they were about to uncover carried even more weight than before. Nova had several of Alma's journals spread out on the table, along with newspaper clippings, printed articles, photocopied documents, and handwritten notes organized into distinct piles.

The leather-bound journals were open to pages he'd never seen before, filled with diagrams that looked more like military intelligence reports than spiritual teachings. There were charts analyzing media content, frequency measurements of various technologies, and detailed psychological profiles of different manipulation techniques.

"I've been going through more of my grandmother's stuff," Nova said immediately, her usual calm demeanor replaced by focused intensity. "And I found a whole section I'd never seen before—it was hidden under a false bottom in one of her journal boxes. She didn't just study how to expand consciousness. She also spent years studying how to suppress it. And what she found is pretty disturbing."

Nova opened one of the journals to a page named "The Frequency War: A Hidden History." The page was filled with notes written in the same careful handwriting Quanta had seen before, but the content was darker, more urgent, with an undertone of warning that made the hairs on his arms stand up.

"According to my grandmother's research, there are people—she called them 'the elites'—who have known about consciousness and frequency manipulation for hundreds of years. But instead of using this knowledge to help people grow and reach their potential, they've been using it to keep people asleep, easy to control, and dependent upon them."

"That's the same term used in the research my dad just showed me before I came over—'the elites.' Interesting how they both used the same name. Any specifics on when all this began?"

Nova riffled through several pages showing historical timelines. "My grandmother traced it back to at least the early 1800s, but she suspected it went much further. She found evidence that certain secret societies and power groups have had access to consciousness research long before it became public knowledge. They've been testing and refining these techniques for generations."

She jumped to another page showing a frequency analysis of different types of media content, with detailed measurements and observations. "They're doing this through everything. TV shows, news, movies, social media, even the frequencies hidden in music and popular ads. They've basically taken the same stuff we've been learning and turned it into tools for keeping entire populations asleep and easy to control. It's like using consciousness science in reverse—instead of waking people up, they're lowering their frequency and restricting their awareness."

Quanta felt his stomach tighten. "This is hard to believe, but it does make sense when you think about how screwed up the world is today. They are using this information to harm people instead of help them."

Nova pointed to a chart showing brain wave patterns from various research sources. "My grandmother documented how news broadcasts designed to create fear and anxiety literally put people into what she called 'susceptible states'— where they're more likely to believe whatever they're told without questioning it."

The patterns were unmistakable and deeply disturbing. Certain types of content created the chaotic, low-frequency brain states that were the exact opposite of the coherent states Quanta had been learning to cultivate. It was like seeing a blueprint for mental hijacking.

"When my dad first told me about this earlier this morning," Quanta said slowly, "I asked him *why*. Why would anyone want to suppress consciousness instead of expand it? He said the main reason was control—and now, looking at all this, it's really sinking in. I'm still trying to wrap my head around how people could coordinate something this massive though... across so many systems, affecting millions of lives."

"Control for sure, but also money. These journals show the elites have built this huge, connected system that must've taken forever to set up. They don't just suppress consciousness randomly; they've figured out exactly how to keep different groups of people in different types of unconscious states. The elites definitely don't want the masses awake, empowered, and armed with vital information to think for themselves and make their own decisions. Those kinds of people don't buy things they don't need, don't support wars they don't believe in, don't accept authority without question, and don't stay trapped in jobs and lifestyles that don't serve them. That's not good for business."

Nova pulled out another part of Alma's research, this one focused on "The Education-to-Corporate Pipeline." The pages showed a flowchart that looked like a factory assembly line: Elementary School → Middle School → High School → College → Corporate Job → Retirement → Death.

"But there's another layer to this system that's even more alarming," Nova continued, showing Quanta the evidence. "The entire educational system isn't designed to help people discover their purpose or develop their consciousness. It's designed to create compliant workers who will spend fifty years of their lives in jobs that drain their energy and creativity."

"And this isn't even a new observation," she added. "Over a hundred years ago, John D. Rockefeller's education board poured massive donations into shaping the educational system we still have today. One of his top advisers, Frederick Gates, even admitted their dream was for students to 'yield with perfect docility' to the system's molding hands—not to raise philosophers or poets, but obedient citizens. That's a fancy way of saying the system was designed from the beginning to produce compliant workers, not awakened thinkers."

Quanta felt a chill of recognition as he thought about his own academic anxiety and the pressure to get good grades so he could get into a good college. "You mean the whole 'study hard, get good grades, go to college, get a good job' path was designed to keep us compliant?"

"Unfortunately, yes. They sell you the 'American Dream'— work hard for decades, sacrifice your present happiness for future security, climb the corporate ladder, and maybe you'll be happy when you retire at sixty-five, perhaps even later. But here's the trap: by then, most people are too exhausted, too programmed, and too financially dependent to ever question whether there might be better ways to live."

Nova showed him more of Alma's data. "Student debt creates financial dependence that keeps people trapped in jobs they hate because they can't afford to leave. Why do you think college has become so expensive lately? The system creates artificial scarcity around education and healthcare, forcing people to work for corporations that provide benefits they should naturally have access to."

"Taking this a step further," Nova pressed on, "student loans are just the opening move. We're conditioned to borrow until we're hundreds of thousands in debt in our early twenties, and then we're sold the dream of homeownership with a thirty-year mortgage that ties people to paychecks for decades. Those two debts stack with healthcare costs and benefits that are locked to employers, so a 'good' job stops being a choice and becomes survival. Lose the job and you risk the roof over your head; keep the job and you trade years of your life for monthly payments. And now, with corporations rapidly adopting AI to replace human labor, even the illusion of job security is fading. For the first time since World War II, today's younger generation has less wealth than their parents did at the same age—all while carrying more debt and working longer hours just to keep up with rising costs. That's how most people end up running the rat race—not because they want to, but because the system brainwashed them into believing it's the only life worth wanting."

"And most corporate jobs don't actually contribute anything meaningful to society," Quanta realized, connecting the dots. "People spend their lives on conference calls, attending countless meetings, moving numbers around on spreadsheets, or creating marketing campaigns to make people buy stuff they don't need."

"Right. The system is designed to absorb human energy and creativity into activities that serve corporate profits rather than human wellbeing or consciousness development," Nova explained. "Think about it—if you're working forty to sixty hours a week at a job that sucks the life out of you, commuting in traffic, worrying about bills, and exhausted when you get home, when do you have time to question reality or develop your consciousness?"

"So the academic pressure we all feel isn't really about education—it's about programming us to accept a life of compliance and external validation," Quanta said, understanding the deeper implications.

"Precisely. Real education would teach you to think critically, develop your consciousness, discover your unique purpose, and create value through your natural talents. Instead, the system teaches you to memorize information, follow instructions without questioning, compete against classmates instead of collaborating, and measure your worth through grades and test scores."

She shifted to another entry; this one filled with analysis of advertising and consumer psychology. "Unconscious people are perfect consumers and compliant citizens. They live in fear. They buy products to fill emotional voids, they believe whatever they're told by authority figures or news media outlets, they stay distracted by entertainment and social media, and they remain too scattered and reactive to organize effective resistance to systems that exploit them."

Nova pulled out a folder filled with classified government documents. "My grandmother somehow got access to intelligence research on 'mind control programs.' These are documented programs designed to influence public opinion and behavior through frequency manipulation, subliminal messaging, and psychological conditioning."

Quanta examined the documents with growing alarm. The technical language was difficult to follow, but the intent was clear: these were systematic methods for influencing large populations without their knowledge or consent.

"This is like science fiction," he said, but even as he spoke, he realized it wasn't fiction at all. It was documented scientific research being applied in the real world.

"It unfortunately gets worse," Nova said, opening another journal to a section titled "The Consciousness Prison." "The elites use sophisticated psychological techniques to keep people trapped in what my grandmother called 'the frequency prison'—a state of chronic low-level stress, fear, confusion, and reactivity that makes higher consciousness development nearly impossible. It's basically a matrix. Not like the movie where we're physically plugged into a computer-generated simulation, but a manufactured reality designed to keep people unconscious while the real controllers operate from behind the scenes. Most people think they're living in the real world, but they're experiencing a carefully constructed illusion, both mentally and emotionally. Through media, education, culture—all of it designed to keep consciousness asleep and compliant."

She began reading from Alma's notes: *"'The frequency prison operates on multiple levels simultaneously. First, they create artificial problems that generate fear and stress—economic uncertainty, political division, health scares, environmental threats. Then they position themselves as the solution to these problems, creating dependency. They flood everyone with contradictory messages that create confusion and doubt about basic reality. All while keeping us divided and arguing with each other about surface-level issues while they maintain control from the shadows. They promote entertainment and social media that glorifies lower consciousness behaviors like violence, materialism, instant gratification, and narcissism. And they structure educational and work environments to reward compliance and conformity while discouraging critical thinking and consciousness development.'"*

Quanta felt slightly overwhelmed by the scope and sophistication of what Nova was describing. "So when people are watching the news and feeling anxious or angry..."

"They're being deliberately programmed into low-frequency states that make them easier to control," Nova finished. "And the worst part is, most people have no idea it's happening. They think their thoughts and emotions are their own, but they're being influenced by carefully crafted frequency manipulation that they're not even consciously aware of."

Nova reached for another journal and flipped to a part named "The Technology of Control." This section contained detailed information that looked like something from an advanced physics laboratory.

"My grandmother found out that the elites have access to technologies most people don't even know exist. Frequency machines that can influence your mood and behavior from far away. Hidden audio and visual stuff embedded in media. Even electromagnetic frequencies sent through cell phone towers and Wi-Fi that can mess with your brain."

She showed him a chart measuring energy emissions from various sources. "She found that certain frequencies commonly used in modern technology can disrupt natural brain wave patterns and make it difficult for people to achieve the coherent states we've been practicing."

"You mean our own technology is working against us?"

"Some of it, yeah. And not by accident—on purpose. The elites know that technology can either help expand consciousness or suppress it, and they've chosen to develop the suppressive stuff while keeping the good technologies hidden."

"But perhaps the most destructive part of their system," Nova said, skimming through pages marked with red ink, "is how they poison us and then profit from keeping us sick."

She showed him pages filled with research on food additives, pharmaceutical interventions, and what Alma had labeled "The Sickness Industrial Complex."

"Look at this," Nova continued, reading from Alma's notes. *"'They deliberately put chemicals in our food supply that disrupt brain function, lower consciousness, and create chronic health problems. High fructose corn syrup, artificial preservatives, pesticides, fluoride in the water—all of it designed to keep people's brains foggy and their bodies sick. And it started when we were kids. We were taught to follow the government's food pyramid—loaded with refined grains and processed carbs—believing it was healthy. But that misinformation helped spark today's epidemics of obesity, diabetes, and chronic illness.'"*

Quanta studied the documentation with growing alarm. "And then they charge people huge amounts of money to treat the symptoms?"

"You got it. The medical system isn't designed to heal people—it's designed to create permanent customers. Even studies from leading medical institutions have suggested that medical error—including misdiagnosis—

ranks among the top causes of death in America, just behind heart disease and cancer. They treat symptoms with drugs that often create new symptoms, requiring even more drugs. Meanwhile, the actual cures—nutrition, exercise, consciousness work, natural healing—get dismissed as unscientific or dangerous."

Nova pointed to a chart showing the relationship between processed food consumption and mental health disorders. "My grandmother found that the same chemicals that suppress consciousness also create anxiety, depression, and attention problems. Then they diagnose these as mental illnesses and prescribe drugs that further suppress consciousness."

"So people get trapped in a cycle where the food makes them sick, the medicine keeps them sick, and they never have the mental clarity to question the system," Quanta realized.

"Right. And if you're constantly dealing with health problems and medical bills, you're too distracted and financially stressed to develop your consciousness or question authority. It's the perfect control mechanism— keep people physically compromised, mentally foggy, and financially desperate."

Nova showed him more evidence. "The same corporations that profit from processed food also invest in pharmaceutical companies. They literally profit from both making people sick and keeping them sick. And they suppress research on natural healing and consciousness-based health approaches because healthy, conscious people don't need their products."

"That's why they don't want people knowing about the mind-body connection we've been learning about," Quanta said, connecting it to their consciousness work. "If people understood that their thoughts and emotions affect their physical health, and that coherent states promote healing, the entire medical-industrial complex would collapse."

They spent the next hour going through page after page of Alma's journals, documenting everything from subliminal messaging techniques used in advertising to the consciousness-suppressing effects of certain food additives, from the psychological manipulation methods used in nightly news programming to how modern technology can affect people's minds and moods.

"It's like there's a whole invisible war going on," Quanta finally said, feeling the weight of the information settling over him like a heavy blanket, "and most people don't even know they're in it."

"That's exactly what it is," Nova agreed. "A frequency war. On one side, you have the elites using science to maintain control and keep people unconscious. On the other side, you have people like my grandmother, your father, and Mr. Wagner trying to help people wake up and develop their consciousness. The rest of humanity is caught in the middle, completely unaware that this battle is even happening."

"And we're choosing where we fit in."

"We already chose," Nova corrected. "The moment we started developing our consciousness, we became part of the resistance. Every time you practice frequency anchoring, every time you choose love and gratitude over fear, every time you stay centered instead of getting caught up in media manipulation, you're fighting back."

Nova pulled out the oldest and most worn journal of all. The leather cover was cracked and faded, and the pages inside had the yellow tint of age. "This contains my grandmother's most important work. She called it 'The Liberation Protocols'—specific techniques and strategies for breaking free from elite consciousness programming and helping others do the same."

She opened to a page that seemed to radiate hope despite the serious nature of the content. The handwriting here was different—more urgent, more passionate, as if these words had been written with particular care and intention.

"The main takeaway is this," Nova began reading: *"'The elites' power depends entirely on keeping people unconscious. Their manipulation techniques only work on those who remain unaware of their own consciousness and how it functions. Once someone develops sufficient self-awareness and frequency mastery, they essentially become immune to most forms of external manipulation. More importantly, they begin to naturally help others break free from the programming, just by being around them and maintaining their own coherent state.'"*

"Like what Mr. Wagner demonstrated with coherence affecting other people's brain waves?"

"Yes, but on a much larger scale. My grandmother discovered that conscious people naturally help others become more conscious, just by maintaining their own high frequency states. Back to the tuning fork that helps other tuning forks of the same frequency come into resonance. That's why the elites work so hard to prevent consciousness development—they understand what researchers call the '1% rule': that just 1% of a population operating at higher consciousness can significantly influence the behavior and awareness of the entire group. They know that even this small number of truly conscious people can begin to unravel their entire control system."

Nova flipped to another section filled with specific techniques and practices. "She called conscious people 'frequency lighthouses'—beacons of coherent energy that help guide others out of the darkness of the frequency prison. But she also warned that this comes with responsibility. Once you understand how the system works, you become responsible for using that knowledge ethically and to help others break free from the chains of mental manipulation."

"This actually makes everything we've been learning even more important," Quanta said, feeling a surge of determination rather than fear. "The frequency techniques, the coherence work, learning to maintain our own center—it's not just personal development. It's actual immunity to manipulation. Every time we choose love over fear, or stay present instead of getting caught up in media drama, we're becoming unmanageable."

As the day wore on, they explored more of the Liberation Protocols. There were techniques for detecting frequency manipulation in real time, methods for maintaining coherent states even in challenging environments, and strategies for sharing consciousness information with others without overwhelming them or triggering their psychological defenses.

"One of the most important principles," Nova explained, "is not letting this knowledge make you fearful, angry, or paranoid. Those emotional states would just trap you in the same low frequencies the elites want everyone in. The goal is to remain in a state of compassionate awareness— seeing clearly what's happening while maintaining your connection to higher frequency states. Think of consciousness development like antivirus software for your mind. Once you understand how manipulation works and you've developed your own awareness, these techniques just bounce off you. You can see them coming—the fear-based messaging, the attempts to trigger reactive emotions, the programming designed to keep people scattered and powerless. But instead of falling for it, you stay centered and make conscious choices."

"My dad said the same about not being fearful, but I have to be honest, my initial response was anger. I mean, this is essentially mass psychological warfare against innocent people, but I now understand that's how they'd want me to react."

Nova smiled for the first time that day, and Quanta could feel the shift in energy as she accessed one of her coherence anchors. "By remembering that consciousness always wins in the end. The elites can only control people who remain unconscious. Every person who wakes up reduces their power. And the fact that we're having this conversation, that people like your father and Mr. Wagner are teaching these concepts, that consciousness research is becoming more mainstream—all of this means the awakening is already happening."

She then turned to a section titled "The Great Awakening." "My grandmother predicted that we'd reach a tipping point where consciousness development would accelerate exponentially. She believed we're living in that time right now—a period when more people are waking up to their true nature than ever before in human history."

"What happens when we reach that tipping point?"

"The frequency prison collapses," Nova said with conviction. "When enough people understand their own consciousness and develop immunity to manipulation, the elites' control systems simply stop working. You can't fool conscious people with unconscious tricks. And conscious people naturally organize themselves in ways that serve the highest good of humanity rather than the narrow self-interest of a select few."

When Quanta returned home that evening, he found his father waiting for him in the study, surrounded not just by research papers, but also by several additional books and what appeared to be communication equipment he'd never seen before.

"How did it go with Nova?" Justin asked, looking up from a paper titled "Electromagnetic Frequency Weapons: A Threat Assessment."

"Intense and overwhelming. Her grandmother documented everything—how the elites use frequency manipulation, media programming, even technological interference to keep people unconscious. It feels like discovering there's a whole hidden level of reality I never knew existed. Just a lot more detail supporting what you showed me this morning."

"And how are you processing it emotionally?"

Quanta considered the question carefully, checking in with his internal state. "At first, I was angry and scared, but I now understand that those reactions would just trap me in the same low-frequency states the elites want people in. Now I feel... determined. Ticked off even, but not in a negative way. Like I now have even more incentive to practice consciousness development. It's not just for personal growth—it's actual resistance to a system of control."

Justin nodded with approval. "That's exactly the right response. This knowledge isn't meant to make you paranoid or angry—it's meant to make you free and empowered. Once you understand how consciousness manipulation works, you become immune to it."

"Dad, how long have you known about this aspect of consciousness research?"

"I've suspected it for years," Justin admitted. "Any serious consciousness researcher eventually discovers this darker application of the science. But I wanted you to develop a solid foundation in consciousness development first, so you'd be prepared to handle this information without getting overwhelmed or dropping into fear-based thinking."

"And now?"

"Now you're ready to use this knowledge responsibly. You understand your own consciousness well enough to not be manipulated by external forces. You know how to maintain coherent states regardless of what's happening around you. And most importantly, you can help others develop these same capabilities."

Justin pulled out another research paper, this one with multiple university logos and international collaboration markings. "There's something else you should know. The consciousness research community isn't just discovering these manipulation techniques—we're also developing countermeasures and liberation technologies."

"Like what?"

"Biofeedback systems that help people achieve coherent states more easily and detect when they're being subjected to frequency manipulation. Educational programs that teach media literacy and critical thinking specifically designed to counter elite programming techniques. Even helpful technologies that can protect people from the consciousness-suppressing effects of modern devices and wireless signals."

Justin showed him images of various devices and technologies. "There are researchers developing what they call 'consciousness enhancement technologies'—devices that can help accelerate natural consciousness development and provide protection against external manipulation."

"So there's actually hope for changing this system?"

"More than hope," Justin said with growing excitement. "There's a growing global movement of scientists, educators, technologists, and conscious individuals who are working to make consciousness development mainstream and accessible to everyone. They are out there promoting the positive applications of consciousness research."

He pulled out a membership directory for an organization Quanta had never heard of. "There are networks of consciousness researchers sharing information and developing strategies for mass awakening. The elites may have had a head start and superior resources, but consciousness itself is beginning to wake up on a global scale."

"What does that mean for us? For people like Nova and me?"

"It means you're part of the first generation that will grow up with full access to consciousness development techniques and protection against manipulation. You're like digital natives, but for consciousness. While older generations have to unlearn several decades of programming, you're developing these capabilities from the beginning."

Justin's expression became more serious. "The more conscious you become, the more you become capable of helping others break free and become awake and aware. But the elites will not give up their control systems without a fight."

"Are we in danger?"

"Not in the way you might think," Justin replied thoughtfully. "The elites' power depends on secrecy, fear, and unconsciousness. The more people who know about these systems and develop immunity to them, the less power they have. Their main weapons are deception and manipulation, which don't work on conscious people. Physical force would only wake more people up and expose their methods."

"So our protection is consciousness itself?"

"Exactly. Consciousness is both the target they're trying to suppress and the ultimate defense against suppression. The more conscious you become, the safer you are from their manipulation, and the more you contribute to everyone else's safety by helping to accelerate the collective awakening."

That night, Quanta lay in bed with his mind racing despite his efforts to maintain coherent frequency states. The world felt fundamentally different now—not darker, exactly, but far more complex and high-stakes than he'd ever imagined. He could sense the frequency manipulation attempts in the background of modern life like a subtle static he'd never noticed before, but he could also feel his own consciousness as a source of clarity and power that no external force could truly touch.

Sol was curled up at the foot of the bed. Looking at his companion, Quanta realized that animals were naturally immune to most forms of elite manipulation because they lived from intuition and present-moment awareness rather than from the mental programming that made humans so susceptible to external control.

He picked up one of the books from his nightstand and found a passage that felt particularly relevant to everything he'd learned that day: *"The implications of consciousness research extend far beyond academic curiosity or personal development. If consciousness can affect physical reality in measurable ways, and if this capability can be enhanced through training, then we're looking at nothing less than the next stage of human evolution. The question isn't whether these abilities exist—the evidence is overwhelming. The question is whether we'll develop them consciously and responsibly, for the benefit of all humanity, or whether they'll be suppressed and manipulated by those who would use them for control rather than liberation."*

Setting the book aside, Quanta understood that his journey was no longer just about personal development or even helping his immediate friends and family. He was part of a larger awakening, a frequency war between those who would suppress human consciousness for control and profit, and those who would help it flourish for the benefit of all life.

The elites might have sophisticated tools for consciousness manipulation and vast resources at their disposal, but they had made one crucial mistake: they had underestimated the power of consciousness itself. Once awakened, awareness could not be put back to sleep. Every person who understood their true nature as consciousness became immune to external manipulation and naturally helped others remember their own power.

Tomorrow, he would continue practicing his frequency techniques with even greater purpose. He wasn't just developing personal abilities—he was building immunity to control systems and preparing to help others do the same. The frequency war was real, but consciousness itself was about to prove who the real victor would be.

Chapter 7: Inner Creates Outer

Two weeks had passed since Quanta's jarring introduction to the reality of elite consciousness manipulation, and the knowledge had settled into his awareness like a new lens through which he viewed the world. Rather than falling into the fear and anger that such information might have triggered in the past, he was becoming more determined, more focused, and paradoxically more peaceful about his role in what Alma had called "the frequency war."

The December weather had turned cold, with the kind of clear winter air that seemed to amplify everything—sounds carried farther, colors appeared more lucid, and the bare trees formed intricate networks of branches against the gray sky. Snow had begun to dust the landscape intermittently, creating a sense of pristine possibility that matched Quanta's evolving understanding of reality itself.

During these two weeks, Quanta had been using this time to deepen his consciousness practices, working through Michael Talbot's research on the holographic nature of reality and experimenting with increasingly sophisticated frequency techniques. He'd also begun to notice something remarkable: the more he understood about external manipulation systems, the more immune he became to their effects. It was as if awareness itself created a natural shield against unconscious influence.

What fascinated him most was how understanding the elite manipulation systems had enhanced his own consciousness development rather than diminishing it. It was like discovering that someone had been secretly drugging the water supply—once you knew about it, you could choose to drink from pure sources instead. The knowledge hadn't made him paranoid; it had made him more selective and deliberate about what frequencies he allowed into his consciousness.

He'd also been experimenting with what he privately called "reality testing"—consciously choosing his internal frequency and then observing how external circumstances seemed to shift to match. The results were subtle but consistent enough that he could no longer dismiss them as coincidence. When he maintained states of gratitude and curiosity, helpful information and supportive people seemed to appear naturally. When he briefly slipped into frustration or doubt, obstacles and complications would manifest almost immediately.

As another weekend began, Quanta woke up with an unusual sense of anticipation, as if something significant was about to shift in his understanding. Sol was already alert, his ears perked and his eyes fixed on Quanta with that knowing expression that had become so familiar over these weeks of consciousness development.

"What is it, buddy?" Quanta asked softly, sitting up and immediately tuning into his internal frequency. There was something different in the energy of the day—a quality of potential that felt almost electric, like the air before a thunderstorm but without any sense of threat or disturbance.

As he lay back down for a moment, practicing the morning coherence techniques that had become as natural as breathing, Quanta once again reflected on how dramatically his life had changed. The confused, anxious teenager felt like a different person entirely. In his place was someone who understood the fundamental nature of consciousness, could deliberately manage his own frequency states, and was beginning to grasp the profound implications of what it meant to be an aware and creative person in a responsive universe.

Downstairs, his dad was in the kitchen reading a handwritten letter rather than his usual research papers and books. Justin was still in his pajamas and Quanta could sense that whatever he was reading contained significant news.

"Good morning," Justin said, holding up the letter with obvious enthusiasm. "I just received this from Dr. Vasquez whose made some remarkable progress in her research on consciousness that I think you'll find fascinating. She's one of my colleagues that I'm always running into at conferences."

Quanta sat down across from his father, immediately sensing the shift in energy around whatever this communication contained. "What kind of progress?"

"Breakthrough research on what they're calling 'reality formation'—the scientific study proving that consciousness doesn't just observe what happens, but actually creates it. They can now measure how thoughts directly affect physical reality. This obviously goes well beyond the observer effect you previously learned about."

Quanta felt that familiar spark of recognition, the electric sensation that accompanied truly significant information. "That sounds like what Nova and I have been exploring with frequency work and the manifestation techniques from her grandmother's notes."

"Right, but now they have the rigorous scientific framework to explain how it works at the quantum level. Dr. Vasquez writes that consciousness appears to function like a creative force that literally shapes the quantum field into physical manifestation. And the more coherent and focused the consciousness, the more powerful and precise the reality-shaping effect becomes. In other words, your thoughts can literally create physical reality, and the clearer your intention, the stronger the results."

Justin set down the letter and looked at his son with renewed interest and a mixture of pride and anticipation. "She's specifically interested in working with the younger generation who have been developing these capabilities from the beginning of their conscious awareness journeys, rather than trying to teach older minds to overcome decades of limiting beliefs and subconscious programming."

"You mean people like me and Nova?"

"Exactly. She believes that your generation might be the first to grow up with full conscious access to these reality-creation abilities as a natural part of human development. But there's something else in her letter that I think you'll find particularly relevant to what you've been learning."

Justin turned the letter around so Quanta could see the elegant handwriting filled with technical terms and detailed observations. He initially wondered why she didn't just email his dad, but now understood and had a better appreciation for this preferred method of communication given the sensitive material at hand. "She mentions something called the Law of Correspondence—the principle that inner reality creates outer reality. According to her research team's findings, this isn't just a spiritual concept or philosophical idea, but a measurable scientific phenomenon that operates according to precise quantum mechanical principles."

Quanta was about to say that Nova had already introduced him to this universal law several weeks ago when his phone buzzed with a text from her: *"Ready for the next level? Found some additional info on the Law of Correspondence buried in my grandmother's notes. This explains not just how consciousness works, but how to use it deliberately to create specific outcomes. Can you come over this morning? I think today might be another breakthrough."*

Quanta showed the text to his father, grinning. "This is the second time she's texted me about the same exact stuff we're discussing, right as we're talking about it."

Justin read it and then smiled with a look of deep satisfaction. "Synchronicity never ceases to amaze me. When consciousness is aligned with its true purpose and highest development, the universe tends to provide exactly what's needed exactly when it's needed. Go see what Nova has discovered. I have a feeling today is going to be significant for both of your developmental journeys."

"What makes you think that?"

"Because you're both at the point where you can direct your consciousness intentionally instead of just reacting to whatever comes up. That's the transition from being a victim of circumstances to being the creator of your circumstances. It's the difference between being a passenger and taking the wheel."

Quanta made his way over to Nova's again, but the vibe was noticeably different this time—less frantic than before, more like they were stepping into the calm before a storm. The winter sun was bright despite the cold, and everything seemed to sparkle with an almost magical quality of aliveness.

Nova had a single journal open on the table, along with several more drawings and diagrams. There were also multiple sheets of paper covered with mathematical equations and frequency calculations.

"So, you know how you can feel your energy shift with different thoughts given the frequency work and coherence techniques you've been practicing?" Nova began, her usual calm demeanor now infused with barely contained excitement. "Well, I've been working with the Law of Correspondence stuff from my grandmother's notes, and I think I've figured out how to use what you've already been developing to create specific changes in your life. No wonder the elites don't want people waking up."

She opened the journal to a page named "The Architecture of Reality Creation." The page showed the relationship between internal consciousness states and external manifestation, with detailed notes explaining the precise mechanics of how thoughts and emotions became physical reality.

"It's not just that conscious people can't be manipulated," Nova continued, her eyes bright with discovery. "It's that conscious people can change reality itself by understanding how the Law of Correspondence works. Every thought, every emotion, every feeling you have is literally sending out a signal to the universe, and reality changes to match that signal."

Quanta studied the diagrams with growing fascination and recognition. They showed energy patterns flowing from internal states to external manifestations, with specific frequencies corresponding to specific types of reality experiences. It was like seeing a framework for how consciousness and physical reality interfaced with each other.

"So when I practice love and gratitude and feel that warm, expansive energy..."

"You're sending out the positive signals of abundance and joy," Nova finished, pointing to a specific diagram that illustrated this exact process. "And the universe responds by bringing you experiences, people, and situations that match that signal. But here's what makes it even more powerful—the more aware you become of this process, the better you can fine-tune your results to match exactly what you want."

She turned to another page showing a step-by-step process for conscious reality creation, complete with detailed instructions and troubleshooting guides for common obstacles.

"My grandmother called this 'Intentional Manifestation'—using what you know about the Law of Correspondence to create specific things you want rather than just wishing for the best or hoping stuff works out."

"How is that different from what we've been doing with frequency work and anchoring techniques?"

"Frequency work was about managing how you feel inside and letting reality naturally change to match, which definitely works. Intentional Manifestation is about deciding what you want to create and then getting your thoughts, feelings, and emotions all lined up to send that specific signal out to the universe so you can attract what you want. Remember discussing the Law of Attraction? These universal laws are all interconnected. While the Law of Correspondence explains that your internal state creates your external reality, the Law of Attraction is what actually pulls those matching experiences into your life."

Nova then pulled out a comprehensive workbook filled with exercises, techniques, and detailed case studies. "She figured out a complete system for this and tested it for decades. It works through five main steps that build on one another."

"What are the steps?"

"These steps will feel familiar because they build on everything you've already been practicing," Nova explained, pointing to the detailed framework in Alma's notes. "The gratitude work from our first session, the coherence techniques you learned from Mr. Wagner's demonstration, the frequency anchoring we've been developing—it all connects into this complete system. The first step is Clarity with Elevated Emotion—setting a clear intention and pairing it with the elevated emotions you'd feel if it were already real. Second, Belief and Mental Rehearsal—training your subconscious to accept your desired outcome as natural by emotionally rehearsing it as if it's already happening. Third, Alignment through Inspired Action—taking action that reflects the identity of the version of you who already lives that reality, not just chasing an outcome. The fourth step is Detachment—trusting the quantum field to handle the "how" and "when," and releasing control over the path it takes. And finally, Gratitude and Embodiment—living in appreciation while fully embodying your future self through your thoughts, habits, and environment. When these five things are working together, manifestation becomes natural."

"That sounds incredibly powerful, but also like it requires a lot of discipline and consistency."

"It does, but that's why my grandmother developed all these supporting techniques. Look at this."

Nova showed him a page describing something called "Reality Anchoring"—a more advanced version of the frequency anchoring they'd already learned, but specifically designed for maintaining manifestation frequencies even in challenging circumstances.

"The main thing to understand," Nova explained as they began working through the theoretical framework, "is that you're not trying to force reality to change through willpower or anything like that. You're not just trying to wish things into existence or chasing after them. Instead, you're getting your inner world so lined up with what you want that reality naturally shifts to match it and presents it in your outer world. Think of it like your mind is a movie projector and your life is the screen. Most people try to change the movie by messing with the screen—getting upset at what's playing, trying to cover up the parts they don't like. But that never works. If you want to change the movie, you change the film in the projector, not the screen. Your inner thoughts and feelings are the film; your outer life is just what gets projected onto the screen."

"Do all possible realities already exist somewhere?"

"According to quantum physics, absolutely. Every possible outcome already exists as potential in what scientists call the quantum field of infinite possibilities. What consciousness does is collapse those potentials into actual experience by observing and choosing which reality to tune into through consistent internal alignment. Just like we talked about with superposition. Basically, whatever you focus on consistently is what becomes real in your life."

Nova flipped to a page titled "The Quantum Buffet," and Quanta could see why his father had mentioned synchronicity earlier—this was exactly the kind of information he was ready to understand and apply.

"My grandmother used this analogy all the time: reality is like an infinite buffet where every possible meal already exists. Most people walk through the buffet unconsciously, just grabbing whatever they see first or whatever other people tell them to get. But conscious creators know exactly what they want, go straight to that choice, and make it their reality through clear intention and elevated emotion."

"And I'm gonna take a wild guess the elites don't want people to know about the buffet, or that they even have a choice in what they select?"

"Exactly right. If people understood that they could consciously choose their reality instead of just accepting whatever circumstances they find themselves in, the entire control system would collapse overnight. You simply cannot control people who know they're the creators of their own experience."

As they continued working through the material, Quanta began to understand why the consciousness manipulation systems were so sophisticated, pervasive, and desperately maintained. The elites weren't just trying to control people's behavior, exploit their energy, or suppress their consciousness by keeping them locked in the 'frequency prison'—they were trying to prevent them from discovering their fundamental creative power as conscious beings.

"This explains everything," he said suddenly, feeling pieces of a vast puzzle clicking into place. "The media programming designed to keep people in fear, the education system and corporate structures designed to produce workers instead of thinkers, the profit-based healthcare system, the poison contained in our food supply—it's all designed to prevent people from awakening to their power as true creators of their own reality."

"That about sums it up," Nova agreed with enthusiasm. "As long as people believe they're victims instead of creators, they remain controllable and exploitable. But once someone understands that their inner reality creates their outer reality, they become essentially ungovernable by any type of authority or government."

Nova turned to the most advanced section of Alma's notes, with pages that seemed to glow with possibility and profound wisdom.

"She called this level 'Reality Mastery'—being able to create any experience you want while making sure it's good for everyone else involved."

"How do you make sure it's good for everyone? That seems like it could be subjective or easily manipulated by ego."

"That's the crucial part, and my grandmother spent years figuring this out. She developed an approach she named 'Clear Intention'—wanting things not from ego, fear, or trying to get something from other people, but from genuine love, wanting to help others, and working with consciousness's natural tendency to expand and evolve. When what you want is good for everyone, the entire universe supports your manifestations completely, making it far more likely that what you desire will become reality. On the flip side, if your desires are self-serving and based in fear or doubt, they will obviously not become reality."

"How can you tell the difference?"

"She figured out several ways to test this. The best one is a practice she termed the 'Expansion Test'—clear intentions make you feel more open, connected, and alive when you think about them. Ego-based desires make you feel tight, separate, or anxious, even if they seem cool on the surface."

They spent more time exploring specific techniques for developing clear intention and practicing the preliminary steps of intentional manifestation. Quanta was naturally gravitating toward creating experiences related to consciousness expansion, helping others awaken to their own creative power, and contributing to the transformation of educational systems.

"That's perfect," Nova said when he shared his natural focus areas. "This is re-emphasized in the journal... manifestations work best when you're trying to help people wake up and become more aware. When you're creating things to help others instead of just getting stuff for yourself, the universe supports you more. Let's take a look at some real examples of how this works," Nova continued as she flipped through the pages.

"Here's one where my grandmother manifested a complete healing from a serious illness that doctors said was incurable. She started by making it clear that what she really wanted wasn't just physical health, but the experience of vitality and aliveness that would allow her to serve others more effectively."

Quanta studied the detailed notes, which read like a combination of scientific journal and spiritual practice guide.

"Then she used reality anchoring to embody the frequency of perfect health so completely that it became her inner reality even while her physical body was still showing illness symptoms. The key was keeping that inner alignment consistent, no matter what the external symptoms looked like."

"How long did it take?"

"According to her notes, about three months of consistent practice before the physical symptoms began changing, and six months before doctors confirmed complete healing. But she wrote that the real transformation happened inside within the first few weeks—once she got consistent inner alignment with health and vitality, the external manifestation became inevitable."

Nova turned to another case study that was even more remarkable.

"This one was about completely switching careers to teach this awareness stuff full-time while still being able to support her family. She got clear about wanting to help people wake up, then practiced feeling like someone who loves what they do and has money flowing in easily."

"What happened?"

"Within four months, she received an unexpected inheritance that covered her family's expenses for two years, three different organizations offered her teaching positions, and she began attracting private students who could afford to pay top dollar for awareness training. All of this emerged naturally without her having to push or struggle for any of it."

"That seems almost too good to be true."

"That's precisely what she wrote about—how most people have been so programmed to expect struggle and not having enough that they can't believe reality creation could be that natural and easy. They think this is all "woo-woo" stuff. But she documented dozens of similar examples, all following the same basic steps."

As the afternoon progressed, they worked through increasingly sophisticated techniques and explored more advanced applications of the Law of Correspondence. Nova shared methods for creating group manifestations, techniques for manifesting on behalf of others, and approaches for addressing seemingly impossible situations through conscious reality creation.

"What's really important," Nova explained as they practiced something called "Future Memory Creation," "is that you're not trying to force anything to happen. You're just getting yourself so lined up with what you want that it naturally shows up in your life. Remember, you need to detach and trust the process."

"Future Memory Creation?"

"It's a technique where you create such a vivid and emotionally real inner experience of what you want that your mind literally remembers it as something that already happened, even though it hasn't occurred yet. This sends an incredibly powerful and consistent signal to the quantum field."

They continued working with this technique, with Quanta practicing creating future memories of various scenarios— from simple things like acing his next math test without stress, to bigger goals like feeling completely confident talking to anyone at school, to eventually teaching other students everything he'd learned about consciousness.

"The main thing to remember," Nova guided him, "is making the inner experience so real and emotionally authentic that your subconscious mind accepts it as actual memory rather than imagination. When that happens, your entire inner system aligns with that reality as if it's already done."

As the day progressed, Nova opened to the final section on the Law of Correspondence.

"This is what she defined as 'The Great Work,'" Nova said, her voice taking on a serious quality that suggested they were approaching the most profound material yet. "It's about mastering these abilities so completely that you can become a teacher and guide for others who are ready to wake up. Not trying to force anyone or convince people who aren't interested, but being able to recognize those who are naturally drawn to consciousness development and helping them discover their own creative power."

She turned to pages filled with teaching methodologies, techniques for recognizing readiness in others, and approaches for sharing consciousness concepts without overwhelming people or triggering their resistance.

"The neat part is," Nova continued, "that once you've developed these abilities for yourself, you naturally become a bridge that helps others cross from unconsciousness to awareness. But it requires real mastery—you have to embody these principles so completely that you're living proof of what's possible."

"So, it's not about trying to wake up people who don't want to be awakened?"

"Exactly. It's about becoming so clear, so centered, and so genuinely happy that the people who are ready to grow will naturally be drawn to you. They'll start asking questions about how you stay so calm or why you seem to have such good luck or what you do to manage stress. And that's when you can begin sharing what you've learned."

Nova showed him techniques for recognizing spiritual readiness in others, methods for introducing consciousness concepts gradually, and ways to avoid common pitfalls like coming across as preachy, religious, or superior.

"My grandmother figured out that the best way to teach this stuff isn't by hammering people with a bunch of facts. Instead, you help them experience it for themselves so they can feel how much difference it makes in their own lives."

"Like how Mr. Wagner demonstrated the observer effect instead of just talking about it?"

"Perfect example. When someone experiences their own thoughts affecting physical reality, they don't need to be convinced—they know it's real. That's much more powerful than any explanation."

They spent time practicing techniques for becoming more effective at helping others, including methods for maintaining their own center while teaching, ways to recognize when someone is ready for deeper information, and approaches for handling skepticism or resistance without taking it personally.

"Here's the deal," Nova explained, "you can only give people what you've mastered yourself. You can't teach manifestation if you're still struggling with it—people will sense you're being fake. But when you're really living these principles and they're working for you, people want to know how you're doing it."

As they wrapped up, Quanta started thinking about his friends and classmates at school. All the stress and anxiety he witnessed daily, the way people seemed trapped in reactive patterns, believing they were powerless over their circumstances. "Nova," he said thoughtfully, "do you think other people our age could learn these techniques? I mean, if it works this naturally for us..."

"That's exactly what my grandmother hoped for," Nova replied with a knowing smile. "She believed the most powerful way to spread consciousness development was through young people teaching other young people. When someone your own age shows you that these abilities are real and achievable, it's much more believable than adults preaching about it."

When Quanta returned home that evening, he found his father waiting for him in the study grading some papers, with Dr. Vasquez's letter nearby.

"How did it go with Nova?" Justin asked with obvious curiosity and anticipation.

"Absolutely remarkable," Quanta replied, sitting down and feeling the weight of profound new understanding. "She showed me her grandmother's complete system for using the Law of Correspondence to consciously create reality. But more than that, she showed me how to eventually help others discover these same abilities. It's not just about personal manifestation—it's about becoming skilled enough to help and guide others who are ready to wake up."

"And how are you processing that level of creative power and responsibility?"

Quanta considered the question carefully, checking in with his internal state and the profound shifts he could feel occurring in his understanding of himself and reality.

"At first, it felt overwhelming to realize that I could eventually become someone who helps others discover their creative power. But then I realized that I've actually been creating my reality unconsciously my whole life—everyone has. The difference is now I can do it deliberately and skillfully, and help others learn to do the same."

Justin nodded with obvious approval and deep satisfaction about his son's developmental progress.

"That's the key distinction between ego-based teaching, which often creates dependence and confusion, and authentic guidance, which empowers others to discover their own capabilities. When you're sharing from a place of genuine mastery and service rather than neediness or superiority, people naturally benefit from being around you."

"Dad, do you really think I could eventually become good enough at this to help others?"

"I think it's not only possible, but inevitable," Justin replied with profound conviction. "You're developing these abilities during your formative years, which means they'll become as natural as breathing. And young people often learn best from other young people who've mastered something they want to understand."

Justin then glanced over to the letter. "Dr. Vasquez isn't the only one interested in this work. The same network of scientists, educators, and researchers I previously mentioned are documenting these phenomena and developing ways to teach these capabilities more widely."

"You mean this could actually become mainstream rather than remaining hidden or pushed aside?"

"Eventually, yes. Though it will probably take time and will definitely face heavy resistance from those institutions and power structures that benefit from keeping people unconscious of their creative power. That's why what you and Nova are learning is so critically important—your generation will help establish these capabilities as normal human function rather than rare or mystical abilities."

Justin continued, "There are already pilot programs being developed to teach these principles in professional settings, research projects documenting the measurable effects of individual consciousness on physical systems, and even some forward-thinking businesses experimenting with consciousness-based approaches to innovation and problem-solving."

"What does that mean exactly?"

"People using clear intention and manifestation techniques to solve complex problems, create breakthrough innovations, and even influence larger social and environmental challenges. The results are still being studied, but the preliminary data is remarkably promising."

"So, there's a whole movement of people working with this?"

"Hopefully it's more of an evolution than movement. Consciousness itself appears to be evolving toward greater self-awareness and creative capability, and humans are the vehicles through which this evolution is expressing itself. You and Nova are now part of that evolutionary wave."

That night, Quanta lay in bed with a sense of profound possibility expanding through his awareness like ripples in a cosmic pond. The journey that started several weeks ago had led him to an understanding of reality that was far more magnificent, empowering, and responsibility-laden than he'd ever imagined possible.

He was not just a passive observer of experience, as he'd been taught in school and in life up to this point. He was not even just a conscious participant in reality, as he'd learned through his initial awakening. He was an active creator of reality itself, with the power to shape his experience and help others discover their own creative capabilities.

Every thought he had, every emotion he felt, every frequency he maintained was literally broadcasting a frequency into the quantum field of infinite possibilities, and physical reality was constantly reorganizing itself to match those frequencies. The Law of Correspondence was absolute and inescapable—as within, so without. As his internal consciousness expanded and evolved, his external reality would inevitably reflect that expansion and evolution.

The elites might have had a head start, but as more people awakened to their true nature as creators and began practicing intentional manifestation with clear intention and elevated emotion, the entire world would inevitably transform to reflect higher levels of awareness, compassion, wisdom, and service to the greater good of all humanity.

Instead of reaching for a book, Quanta simply lay there processing everything he'd learned about manifestation and his potential role as a guide for others. The five-step system Nova had shared felt solid and practical— something he could implement rather than just understand theoretically.

But what excited him most was the realization that he was naturally drawn to helping others discover their own creative abilities. It wasn't about proving how much he knew or trying to impress anyone. It was about recognizing when someone was genuinely ready to grow and being skilled enough to offer real guidance.

Tomorrow would mark the beginning of a new phase in his development. He would start practicing the manifestation techniques Nova had taught him, beginning with simple, clear intentions and gradually building toward more sophisticated creations. More importantly, he would begin observing his classmates and friends with new eyes, learning to recognize the subtle signs that indicated someone was ready to question conventional reality and explore their own consciousness.

The thought of eventually being able to help other students discover what he'd learned filled him with quiet anticipation. Not through preaching or trying to convince anyone, but by embodying these principles so completely that curious people would naturally be drawn to ask questions.

As sleep began to overtake him, Quanta felt a deep sense of purpose settling into his awareness. He was no longer just learning for himself—he was preparing to become a bridge that could help others cross from unconsciousness to awareness, whenever they were ready to make that journey.

Chapter 8: The Bridge

Thursday morning Quanta was in the hallway between second and third period, standing at his locker and practicing what Nova had taught him about future memory creation. Instead of just grabbing his books and rushing to class like everyone else, he took thirty seconds to create a vivid mental experience of crushing his upcoming Spanish test—not through cramming or stress, but by accessing a calm, clear state where the answers flowed naturally.

The five-step manifestation system was starting to feel more natural, though he still had to think about each step. Instead of just hoping things would work out, Quanta was starting to create his experiences more intentionally— using focus and emotion to guide him. The results were steady enough that he didn't doubt the process, just how well he could keep it going.

What fascinated him most was how the process seemed to connect him to something larger—like invisible forces that had always been there but that he'd never known how to consciously engage. It wasn't about forcing anything or trying to control external circumstances. It was more like tuning into a frequency that was already broadcasting and allowing himself to receive what was being offered.

"Q!" Andy's voice cut through his concentration as his friend approached with a mix of confusion and slight envy.

"Man, what's your secret lately? Everything just seems to be working out for you these days."

Quanta closed his locker and studied his friend's face, using the awareness techniques Nova had taught him to really observe what was happening beneath the surface. Andy had been his closest friend since elementary school, but over the past few weeks, Quanta had started to notice things about their interactions that he'd never seen before. The way Andy used humor to deflect anything serious, constantly making jokes whenever conversations got too deep. How he seemed uncomfortable with genuine emotions and always redirected to safer topics like sports or video games. The restless energy he projected whenever someone tried to have a meaningful conversation, as if depth made him anxious.

But underneath all of that, Quanta could sense something else—a genuine curiosity about the changes he was observing in Quanta, mixed with a kind of longing that Andy probably wasn't even aware of himself.

"You think so?" Quanta asked, genuinely curious about Andy's perspective and hoping to understand what his friend was picking up on.

"I don't know, man. You're like... calmer or something. And you have this weird luck lately." Andy shifted his backpack to his other shoulder and leaned against the lockers. "Like in PE yesterday when Mr. Cunningham was picking teams and you got picked first even though Tyler's obviously better at volleyball. Or how you never seem stressed about tests anymore even though we're all freaking out about midterms. And how did you win that 50/50 raffle at the basketball game the other night?"

This was exactly the kind of moment Nova had described—when someone starts noticing your energy shift and asking questions about what's different. Andy wasn't ready for the full explanation about consciousness and manifestation, but maybe there was something smaller and more practical that Quanta could share.

"I've just been practicing some stress management stuff," Quanta said casually as they walked toward their next class. "Just focusing on what I want to happen instead of worrying about what might go wrong. And paying attention to how different thoughts make me feel."

Andy chuckled and shook his head. "Dude, that's not how the real-world works. Bad stuff happens whether you think positive thoughts or not. My dad lost his job last month, and he's like the most optimistic person I know. Always talking about how everything happens for a reason and all that garbage. Didn't stop him from getting laid off."

Quanta felt a flash of the old urge to argue or try to convince Andy that consciousness could affect reality, but Alma's notes had been clear about this: you can't teach someone who isn't ready to learn, and trying to force understanding usually just creates resistance. All you can do is embody the principles so clearly that curious people start asking better questions.

"Yeah, that really sucks about your dad," Quanta said sincerely. "I hope he finds something even better soon. That kind of transition has got to be stressful for your whole family."

"See, that's what I mean," Andy continued, apparently not ready to drop the subject. "You used to worry about everything, even my stuff. You did enough worrying for both of us. Now you're all zen about everything. It's like you've joined some kind of meditation cult or something."

"Not a cult," Quanta laughed. "Just experimenting with different ways of thinking about things. Like, instead of assuming the worst possible outcome, what if I assumed the best possible outcome? Think of it like being the remote control for your own experience. Your awareness is like the remote. Worried thoughts are just one channel among many that your mind can tune into. Once you realize you're holding the remote, you can choose to watch something else, something more positive or uplifting. The anxious channel will always be available, but you don't have to stay tuned to it."

Andy was quiet for a moment, processing this. "But what if you're just setting yourself up for failure? What if you expect good things and then reality crushes you?"

"Then I deal with that when it happens," Quanta replied. "But in the meantime, I get to feel better and think more clearly and probably handle challenges more effectively. Plus, I've noticed that when I'm in a better state, I notice more opportunities and solutions that I would have missed if I was focused on everything that could go wrong."

The bell rang before Andy could respond, and they hurried to their respective classes. But Quanta could sense that the conversation had planted a seed. Andy wasn't ready to change his entire worldview, but he was beginning to question whether his habitual pessimism was actually serving him.

In Spanish class, Quanta was sitting next to Sarah, who had always been an above average student. While Miss Clark was getting ready to teach how to conjugate verbs, Quanta noticed Sarah staring at her textbook with an expression of deep frustration, her shoulders tense and her breathing shallow.

"Everything okay?" he asked quietly, genuinely concerned about her obvious distress.

Sarah glanced at him, then back at her book, clearly debating whether to share what was going on. "I'm failing this class," she finally admitted in a whisper. "I understand the concepts when I read them, and I can explain them perfectly when I'm talking to my parents. But the moment I sit down for a test, my mind goes completely blank. It's like there's this wall between what I know and what I can demonstrate under pressure."

Quanta recognized this immediately—it was exactly the kind of limiting belief pattern that Alma's techniques could address. Sarah wasn't lacking intelligence or study skills; she was trapped in a fear-based pattern that was blocking her natural abilities. Her test anxiety was creating a feedback loop where fear of failure was causing the failure she was afraid of.

"That sounds incredibly frustrating," he said, choosing his words carefully. "Have you ever noticed if there are specific thoughts going through your head right before your mind goes blank?"

Sarah looked at him with surprise. Most people offered study tips or tutoring suggestions when she mentioned her academic struggles. No one had ever asked about her internal experience during the moments when everything fell apart.

"Actually, yeah," she said slowly, as if she'd never articulated this before. "It's like this voice that says *You're going to mess this up like always* or *Everyone else is smarter than you* or *The teacher and your classmates are going to think you're an idiot.* I know it's not rational, but I can't seem to stop it from happening."

"What if you tried something different next time you hear that inner voice?" Quanta suggested, drawing on the techniques he'd been learning about frequency management and conscious thought direction. "Instead of fighting it or getting upset about it, what if you just acknowledged it like *Oh, there's that worried voice again* and then chose to focus on something else? Like remembering a time when you understood the material perfectly, or imagining yourself calmly working through the test questions step by step."

"You think that would actually work?" Sarah asked, hope creeping into her voice.

"It's definitely worth as shot. The worst that could happen is you get the same results you're already getting. But there's a good chance it could help you access what you already know instead of getting blocked by anxiety."

Sarah stared at him for a moment, as if seeing him differently than she had before. "That's... really insightful. Where did you learn that approach?"

Before Quanta could answer, Miss Clark called for their attention and began her lesson. But throughout the class, Quanta could feel Sarah's curiosity like a subtle energy shift. She was ready for this kind of information, even if she didn't realize the broader implications yet.

After Spanish, Quanta had a few minutes before his next class and decided to walk past the guidance counselor's office. Through the open door, he could hear Mr. Brytus talking with a student who looked overwhelmed and exhausted.

"I just can't keep up anymore," the student was saying. "I'm studying constantly, but my grades keep getting worse. My parents keep adding pressure, my teachers keep assigning more work, and I feel like I'm drowning."

Quanta recognized the frequency of powerlessness and overwhelm that was radiating from the conversation. Here was another student trapped in reactive patterns, believing that the external environment controlled their experience and that the only solution was to work harder and stress more.

He continued walking, but the encounter reinforced his growing sense that there were many students who could benefit from the consciousness tools he was learning. The traditional approaches to academic stress—more studying, better time management, multi-tasking, increased pressure—weren't addressing the root cause of how students related to challenges and pressure.

At lunch, Quanta was sitting with his usual group, but instead of just passively participating in conversations, he was observing the energy dynamics around the table with his developing awareness. Nova stopped by briefly to say hello but had to go to the library to work on a research project. Jessica was cycling through the same complaints about her parents' divorce proceedings that she'd been expressing for weeks, caught in a loop of resentment and helplessness. Tyler was obsessing over his grade in English, convinced that Mr. Suzinski had it out for him personally and that there was nothing he could do to improve the situation. Mike was stressed about football tryouts for next year, certain he wasn't good enough to make varsity and that the coaches would never give him a fair chance.

Everyone was trapped in their own version of victim consciousness—believing that external circumstances controlled their experience and that they had no power to change anything meaningful. A month ago, Quanta would have joined in with his own complaints and contributed to the collective negative energy of limitation and powerlessness. Now, listening to the frequency of their conversations, he felt a mix of compassion for their struggles and determination to offer different possibilities.

"You know what's interesting?" he said during a brief pause in Tyler's rant about English class. "I read somewhere that successful people tend to focus on solutions rather than problems. So, instead of spending energy thinking about why something won't work, they spend that same energy figuring out how it could work."

"That's easy to say when you don't have real problems," Tyler shot back defensively. "Some of us have to deal with unfair teachers and impossible standards. Not everyone gets to coast through life with good luck and supportive parents."

"I'm not saying the problems aren't real," Quanta replied calmly, maintaining his center despite Tyler's hostility. "I'm just wondering if there might be different ways to approach them that could actually help instead of just making us feel worse about situations we can't control."

Jessica looked up from her phone, apparently intrigued by this direction in the conversation. "What do you mean exactly?"

This was another opening—Jessica was naturally curious, and unlike Tyler, she wasn't immediately defensive about examining her approach to challenges.

"Well, take your parents' situation," Quanta said carefully, aware that he was entering sensitive territory. "You can't control what they're doing or how they're handling their divorce. But you can control how you respond to it and where you focus your attention. What if instead of focusing on how unfair and stressful it all is, you focused on how you want to feel regardless of what they're going through? Or what kind of person you want to be during this difficult time?"

"That sounds like you're telling me to pretend everything's fine when it's not," Jessica said, but her tone was curious rather than defensive.

"Not pretending everything's fine. More like... choosing where to put your energy and attention. If you spend all your mental and emotional energy thinking about how bad the situation is, you feel terrible and nothing changes. But if you focus on what you can control—like how you treat yourself during a difficult time, or what kind of support you need, or how you want to handle your own emotions—at least you're building your own strength and resilience."

Jessica was quiet for a moment, processing this perspective. "I never thought about it that way. I guess I have been spending a lot of energy being upset about things I can't change. But it feels wrong somehow, like I should be upset about my family falling apart."

"You can be upset about it," Quanta clarified. "I'm not suggesting you suppress your feelings or pretend you're happy about difficult situations. I'm just wondering if there might be ways to process those feelings that actually help you rather than keeping you stuck in cycles of stress and helplessness."

"Like what kind of ways?" Mike asked, apparently interested despite his earlier skepticism.

Quanta felt a moment of excitement. This was another example of what Nova had described—multiple people becoming curious at the same time, ready for deeper conversations about consciousness and personal power. But he also knew he needed to be careful not to overwhelm them with concepts they weren't ready for.

"Mostly just paying attention to how different thoughts make you feel," he said, keeping his language practical and accessible. "For example, worried thoughts make me feel tight, anxious, and scattered. Grateful thoughts make me feel more relaxed, open, and clear-headed. And I'm starting to notice that when I feel better, I make better decisions and handle challenges more effectively."

"But what if there's nothing to be grateful for?" Jessica asked. "What if everything really is falling apart?"

"Even then, there are usually small things," Quanta replied. "Like having friends who listen to you, or teachers who care about helping you learn, or just the fact that you're healthy enough to be in school. I'm not talking about pretending big problems don't exist. I'm talking about noticing good things that are also true at the same time. You just need to focus on the positive side of things instead of dwelling on the negative. Even the toughest situations have a positive side—you just have to be willing to look for it."

"That's probably just coincidence though," Tyler said, but without his earlier hostility. "You feeling better and things going better. Doesn't mean your thoughts actually changed anything."

"Maybe," Quanta agreed. "But if it is just coincidence, what's the harm in feeling better while dealing with the same problems? And if it's not coincidence... well, that could be really interesting to explore."

"You really think our thoughts can affect what happens to us?" Mike asked, genuine curiosity in his voice.

This was the edge of what Quanta could share without moving into territory that would sound too over the top or unbelievable. "I think our thoughts definitely affect how we feel, and how we feel affects how we act, and how we act affects what happens to us. So, at minimum, there's an indirect connection. Whether there are more direct connections..." He shrugged. "I'm still figuring that out."

The conversation gradually moved on to other topics, but Quanta could sense the shift in energy around the table. Instead of the heavy, negative frequency that usually dominated their lunch discussions, there was a lighter, more curious quality. People were listening to each other instead of just waiting for their turn to vent about their problems.

After lunch, Quanta had study hall, which he usually spent in the library doing his homework. He'd been experimenting with studying in a state of calm focus rather than stress and anxiety, and his comprehension and retention had improved dramatically. Instead of cramming information through force and repetition, he was learning to access a relaxed state of curiosity where understanding flowed naturally.

He was settling into his favorite corner table when he noticed Nova at one of the computer stations, apparently researching something that required intense concentration. They'd barely spoken at school since their Saturday conversation—not from any distance or awkwardness, but because they were both focused on integrating what they'd learned rather than constantly processing new information.

"Hey," he said quietly as he approached her station. "Find anything interesting?"

Nova looked up with a smile that immediately shifted to curiosity when she saw his expression. "You look like someone who's been experimenting. How's the manifestation practice going?"

"Really well, actually. Small stuff mostly, but it's been consistent. And I think I'm starting to understand what your grandmother meant about being a bridge for others."

"Tell me more," she said, closing her browser window and giving him her full attention.

Quanta described his conversations with Andy, Sarah, and the lunch table group, paying attention to Nova's reactions as he spoke. She listened with the kind of genuine attentiveness that made him feel heard and understood—something he was beginning to realize was rare among people their age.

"That's exactly right," she said when he finished. "You're not trying to convince anyone or prove anything. You're just offering different perspectives when people are ready to hear them. And you're doing it from a place of genuine care rather than ego or superiority."

"It feels natural," Quanta said. "Like I'm finally using abilities I've always had but never knew how to access consciously."

"That's because you are. We all have these abilities. Most people just never learn how to use them intentionally." Nova paused, then added with obvious excitement, "I've been doing some research on something that might interest you. Have you ever thought deeply about how the interconnected nature of consciousness works through the quantum field?"

"Not really, but I've occasionally heard Mr. Wagner say that everyone is more connected than people realize. Last time he said that was when he initially told us about the quantum field the day he conducted the double slit experiment."

"Well, my grandmother said this was another one of the universal laws—the Law of Divine Oneness which states that everything and everyone in the universe is connected. She used this analogy of a spider's web—if you touch one strand, a vibration is sent through the entire web and affects everything connected. Similarly, our actions and thoughts affect the entire universe because everything is connected through the quantum field—the same invisible field of energy and information all around us that links everything together."

Quanta felt that familiar spark of recognition. "So, when we develop these abilities, we're not just helping ourselves—we're affecting everyone else through this connection?"

"Exactly. My grandmother's notes suggest that when people develop consciousness abilities like we're doing, it doesn't just help them individually. Because we're all connected through this invisible web of energy, our individual development actually makes it easier for others to develop the same abilities."

Nova pulled up a new browser window and showed him some additional studies. "Look at these documented cases where groups of people practicing meditation had measurable effects on entire communities, even on people who weren't meditating themselves. It's basically like when one person learns something new, it creates this invisible path that makes it easier for others to learn the same thing."

"That's incredible. So there really is this interconnected consciousness that we're all part of through the quantum field?"

"That's what the evidence suggests. And it explains why consciousness development can potentially accelerate globally. As more people wake up to these abilities, it becomes easier for others to wake up too because we're all connected through the same field. We're creating this ripple effect where more people start to get it."

They spent the remainder of the period exploring research about collective consciousness and its connection to the quantum field. Nova found some more information on the 1% effect that they initially saw in Alma's journals. There was a lot of detailed research on group meditation affecting entire communities, and experiments demonstrating how consciousness connections work through the field. What emerged was a picture of reality that was far more interconnected and responsive than conventional science acknowledged.

"This makes everything feel so much more meaningful," Quanta said as they prepared to leave for their next classes. "Every person we help, every conversation that opens someone's mind, every moment of embodying higher consciousness—it's all contributing to something much bigger than our individual lives."

"Right on. And it's why your instinct to become a bridge for others is so important. You're not just helping random people—you're participating in the evolution of human consciousness itself."

As they walked to their classes, Nova mentioned something that made Quanta stop in his tracks. "Speaking of which, I recently uncovered a pretty intriguing aspect to all of this. That's what prompted my additional research here. My grandmother wrote about the importance of introducing these consciousness principles to the younger generation through any means possible, even within educational settings. She wrote about how to introduce this info in learning centers or schools without triggering resistance from parents or administrators."

"Really? She wrote about that specifically?"

"She did. She believed that awakening young people wasn't just about helping them deal with anxiety or getting better grades. It was all about true consciousness education during their formative years as this was one of the most powerful forms of resistance against the control systems we talked about."

"So education itself could be a form of resistance?" Quanta asked.

"Think about it. Who do you think controls the national curriculum and decides what schools are allowed to teach—and what they're not? We know the elites' power depends on keeping people unconscious from childhood through adulthood. But if students start developing these capabilities early, before they're fully programmed into victim consciousness, they become immune to this control. A generation of conscious teenagers would eventually become conscious adults who couldn't be manipulated by fear, division, or scarcity programming."

"So teaching these techniques to other students isn't just about helping them grow or manage stress—it's actually about helping humanity break free from the frequency prison?"

"Exactly. Every student who learns to manage their own consciousness disconnects from the matrix of those control systems. And our generation might be the one that brings the whole thing down, just by remembering who we really are and teaching others to remember too."

"So where do we even begin? What did your grandmother's notes suggest?" Quanta asked.

"Things like study groups initially focused on awareness, peak performance, and anxiety management to get people to open up their minds. Essentially the same consciousness principles, but presented as practical life skills. She thought students teaching other students would be the most effective way."

"That's what I've been trying to do. The good part is nobody would really question students helping other students with stress and studying."

"Right. Let's look through those notes next time we meet. I think there might be some strategies that could work in our school."

When Quanta finally arrived home around 4:30 PM—he'd stayed after school to help Sarah with some Spanish work using the anxiety management techniques they'd discussed—he found his mother in the kitchen preparing dinner while his father graded papers at the kitchen table. The scene was familiar, but Anne's energy felt different than usual—more curious, more present, as if she was paying attention to things she normally missed.

"How was school?" she asked, but her tone suggested she was genuinely interested rather than just going through parental motions.

"It was great. I had some interesting conversations with friends about different ways to handle stress and problems. And I helped a classmate with some test anxiety issues that were affecting her grades."

Anne paused in her vegetable chopping and looked at him with surprise. "That's not typical teenage conversation. And helping with test anxiety? That's pretty sophisticated for someone your age."

"I know. But I think people are more interested in this stuff than we usually assume. They just need someone to bring it up in a way that doesn't sound preachy or weird. Everyone deals with stress and pressure, especially around midterms. Most people are desperate for better ways to handle it."

Justin stopped what he was doing, his interest piqued. "What kind of responses are you getting when you suggest different approaches?"

"Mixed, but more positive than I expected. Some people are immediately defensive, like they think I'm judging their problems or suggesting everything is their fault. But others get curious and start asking questions about specific techniques they could try. It's like Nova said—you can sense when someone is ready for deeper conversations about consciousness and personal power."

"And how does it feel to be having these kinds of exchanges with your peers?" Anne asked, settling into a chair across from him with genuine curiosity.

This was the first time his mother had shown real interest in his consciousness development rather than just tolerance or vague concern about him getting too involved in "weird stuff." Quanta could feel her openness and decided to share more than he usually would.

"It feels like I'm finally being useful in a way that matters," he said honestly. "I can help people feel less stuck and powerless without having to pretend I have all the answers. It's more about asking better questions or offering different perspectives that they might not have considered."

"That's a very mature approach," Anne said thoughtfully. "And it sounds like you're developing some real leadership abilities. The best leaders aren't the ones who tell people what to do—they're the ones who help people discover their own capabilities."

"I hadn't thought of it as leadership, but I guess that's what it is. Except it doesn't feel like trying to control people or get them to follow me. It's more like helping them discover what they already know but maybe haven't been able to access."

Justin smiled with obvious pride. "That's the best kind of leadership—helping others find their own power rather than trying to accumulate power over them. It sounds like you're developing wisdom beyond your years."

"Speaking of which," Anne said, clearly building up to something she'd been thinking about, "I had an interesting conversation with Mr. Brytus today. I just happened to bump into him while running a quick errand after work. Anyway, he mentioned that several students have been asking about stress management resources and study techniques. Apparently, there's been a significant increase in students seeking help with anxiety and academic pressure."

Quanta felt a moment of excitement mixed with responsibility. What Nova's grandmother had written about—bringing consciousness education into schools right under the radar of the very systems meant to suppress it—stuck with him. If other students were already looking for tools to manage their minds and emotions, maybe this was the opening she'd envisioned. Maybe there were opportunities to share what he was learning in more formal ways to quietly reshape the system from within.

"Did he say what kind of help they're specifically looking for?"

"Mostly practical techniques for managing anxiety and improving focus. Things that could help them perform better academically rather than just cope with stress. He mentioned that a lot of students are overwhelmed by the pressure to excel, and the traditional 'study harder and put in more hours' approach isn't working for many of them."

"That's totally the kind of stuff I've been learning about," Quanta said, ideas beginning to form rapidly. "I wonder if there would be interest in some kind of student-led study group or workshop series? Something focused on peak performance where students can be shown how to get into the zone and enjoy learning instead of just stressing about it. They can learn how to tap into natural abilities they don't even know they have. We wouldn't just be helping individual students cope with stress. We'd be teaching them that they have real power over their own experience. Imagine if an entire group of teenagers understood that they're not victims of circumstances—that they can actually influence what shows up in their lives through clear intention and elevated emotion."

"That's a fascinating idea," Justin said. "A generation of young people who understood their own creative power would change everything. You could frame it in terms of performance psychology and optimal learning states rather than consciousness development. Same principles, but in language that wouldn't trigger resistance from parents or administrators who might be suspicious of anything that sounds too alternative."

"But if it actually helps students improve their grades and reduce their stress levels, the school administration should be very supportive," Anne added. "They're always looking for programs that address student mental health while also improving academic outcomes."

As they continued discussing possibilities over dinner, Quanta felt a new dimension of purpose opening up. Instead of just helping individual friends in casual conversations, there might be opportunities to reach larger groups of students with practical applications of consciousness principles.

"Not to go down a rabbit hole," Quanta said directly to Justin, "but Nova also mentioned that her grandmother believed consciousness education for adolescents was a form of resistance against the control systems we discussed. The research paper you showed me on the elites' frequency manipulation through television, movies, social media. And then Dr. Vasquez's letter about targeting younger people at the beginning of their consciousness journeys. I feel like it's all pointing to something much bigger than helping students develop capabilities tied to academic performance or emotional well-being—it's about helping our generation become immune to the control systems that keep people unconscious."

Justin nodded with a meaningful look. "Nova's grandma understood something very important. What's her name, by the way?"

"Alma," Quanta replied.

Justin continued, "Every young person who develops these abilities becomes a threat to those control systems. What you're doing has implications far beyond South Ridge High. Maybe not initially, but eventually. Just keep our conversation in mind regarding the elites and their unwillingness to give up control. They don't want a young generation of conscious, empowered people."

Anne chimed in, "You guys are going a bit over my head, but I suggest starting small in whatever you do next. Maybe with a pilot group of students who are already interested, to test out what works and refine the approach before expanding."

"And having some measurable outcomes," Justin added. "If you could demonstrate that participants improved their grades or reduced their anxiety levels, that would provide evidence for expanding the program. Perhaps even beyond school. I agree with your mom, though. Start small with your peers and small groups and then you can tackle dismantling the control systems for the benefit of all humanity," Justin said with a grin. "Rome wasn't built in a day."

"You're right. I know several students who would probably be interested in the small group approach," Quanta said, thinking of Sarah and some of the others he'd been talking with. "People who are already struggling with stress and looking for better solutions."

"What about Nova?" Anne asked. "She seems to understand these concepts as well as you do. Would she be interested in co-leading something like this?"

"Definitely. She might actually be better at it than I am. She has this way of explaining complex ideas that makes them understandable without dumbing them down."

"Two leaders would be better than one anyway," Justin observed. "Different people respond to different teaching styles, and you'd be able to support each other through the challenges of working with groups."

After dinner, Quanta went upstairs to his room to think more deeply about what this might look like practically. Sol followed him and settled into his favorite spot on the bed, and Quanta found himself appreciating his companion's steady presence as he processed the day's developments and the exciting possibilities that were emerging.

The conversation with his parents had shifted something fundamental in his understanding of his role and potential impact. He'd been thinking about being a bridge for other individuals, but what if there were ways to create bridges for entire groups of students? What if the consciousness principles he was learning could be integrated into peer tutoring, study groups, leadership opportunities, or even formal programs?

The more he thought about it, the more excited he became. There were probably dozens of students in his school who were struggling with stress, anxiety, and academic pressure. Most of them had never been exposed to the idea that their internal state could dramatically affect their performance, or that there were practical techniques for accessing calm, focused, creative states of mind. This would definitely offer a new, innovative way of thinking.

He pulled out his phone and texted Nova: *"Just talked to my parents about the possibility of starting the student group. They're fully on board. Think there might be a way to share consciousness principles in a format that would be supported by the school? Interested in partnering up?"*

Her response came quickly: *"YES! There are ways to teach manifestation and frequency work through practical applications that don't sound overly spiritual or controversial. Want to brainstorm tomorrow after school?"*

"Absolutely. This feels like it could be really significant."

She wrote back. *"It is. You're starting to think like a conscious leader rather than just an individual practitioner. This is exactly what the world needs—people who can bridge consciousness development with practical applications that help others improve their lives."*

"I'm nervous about whether I'm ready for something this big."

Nova reassured him. *"You're ready. Trust the process. The fact that the opportunity is presenting itself means you're prepared to handle it. Plus, we'll be doing this together."*

As Quanta set his phone aside and began preparing for bed, he reflected on how much had changed in just a few days. The five-step manifestation system wasn't just working for his individual goals—it was changing how he related to other people and how he thought about his role in the larger world.

Every conversation, every small manifestation, every moment of choosing a higher frequency instead of reacting from old patterns was contributing to something much larger than his personal development. He was becoming part of a network of conscious individuals who were quietly transforming the world by embodying different possibilities and helping others access their own creative power.

The most remarkable thing was how natural and inevitable it all felt. Instead of trying to force change or convince skeptical people, he was simply offering alternatives when people were ready to receive them. And people were responding with more openness and curiosity than he'd ever expected.

Tomorrow, he would begin exploring how to scale this individual work into group applications. The idea of helping entire groups of students discover their creative power and break free from limiting patterns filled him with excitement and a sense of meaningful purpose.

But for now, he was content to practice the gratitude techniques Nova had taught him, appreciating the perfect unfolding of opportunities and connections that were allowing him to step into his role as a conscious bridge between worlds. As sleep approached, Quanta felt deeply grateful for the journey that had begun with a voice commanding him to "Remember."

That moment had initiated a transformation that was not only changing his own life, but giving him tools and opportunities to help others transform theirs. The bridge between unconsciousness and awareness was being built one conversation, one relationship, one moment of authentic connection at a time.

And Quanta Jones was discovering that he had a natural gift for this kind of architecture.

Chapter 9: Consciousness Rising

The following Monday, as Quanta walked through the familiar hallways of South Ridge High, he was seeing the building not just as a place of mandatory education, but as a potential laboratory for consciousness development. The conversations from the previous week—with his friends, his parents, and Nova—had planted seeds that were now beginning to sprout into concrete possibilities.

Earlier that morning, he'd woken up on his own—no blaring alarm needed. Lately, his body seemed to know when it was time to rise—like something deeper inside him had started keeping time. During his morning gratitude routine, he'd set a clear intention for the day: to remain open to opportunities to serve others while staying grounded in his own coherent frequency. The practice had become so natural that it felt like putting on clothes—an essential part of preparing for the day.

Sol had seemed particularly alert that morning, following Quanta to the front door and sitting attentively as if he understood something significant was about to unfold. When Quanta had knelt down to say goodbye, the dog had looked directly into his eyes with that knowing expression that suggested he was offering his support for whatever lay ahead.

During his history class with Mrs. Koon, instead of passively absorbing information about the Industrial Revolution, Quanta was applying the consciousness principles he'd been learning in ways that felt increasingly natural. He practiced maintaining a coherent frequency while listening, used gratitude anchoring when the material felt dry, and experimented with what Nova had called "expanded awareness"—staying present and focused while simultaneously observing his own thought processes.

The results were remarkable. Not only did he retain the information more easily, but he began to see patterns that weren't being taught in class. He could see how technology had changed the way people thought and lived. How economic changes reflected deeper shifts in how people viewed work and their own power. He started noticing connections between historical events that seemed unrelated but were actually part of bigger changes happening in society.

It was like developing a new sense for perceiving the deeper currents beneath surface-level reality. He could see how the Industrial Revolution hadn't just changed how things were made—it had changed how people thought about themselves. People went from working with natural rhythms to following clock schedules, from working together in communities to working alone in factories, from doing creative work to doing the same repetitive tasks over and over.

When Mrs. Koon asked the class to discuss the social impacts of industrialization, Quanta raised his hand.

"I think the biggest change wasn't just economic," he said, aware that he was about to share a perspective that went deeper than the typical class discussion. "It seems like industrialization changed how people thought about themselves and their relationship to their work and communities."

"How so?" Mrs. Koon asked, clearly interested in this direction.

"Before industrialization, most people's work was directly connected to their survival and their community's well-being. They could see the direct results of their efforts, and their work had meaning beyond just earning money. But factory work separated people from the end results of their labor, which might have made them feel less connected to their purpose and more like cogs in a machine."

Several students looked up from their phones, apparently intrigued by this perspective. Tyler raised his hand.

"That's kind of depressing when you think about it. Most jobs today still feel like that—just doing repetitive tasks for money without any real connection to something meaningful."

"Right," Quanta continued, "and maybe that's why so many people today feel stressed and unfulfilled even when they have good jobs and make a lot of money. If work doesn't feel meaningful, if you can't see how your efforts contribute to something larger than yourself, then even success can feel empty."

Jessica joined the conversation. "So, you're saying the Industrial Revolution didn't just change the economy—it changed how people felt about their lives?"

"It changed consciousness itself," Quanta said, surprised by his own clarity on this topic. "And maybe a lot of the problems we face today—anxiety, depression, feeling disconnected—are partly because we've inherited a way of thinking about work and life that was designed for machines rather than conscious human beings. Perhaps that's why so many adults abuse alcohol and drugs. Even food. It's like their coping mechanism for an unhappy life."

Mrs. Koon was nodding approvingly. "That's a very sophisticated analysis, Quanta. You're connecting historical changes to psychological and social patterns in ways that many historians and sociologists are just beginning to explore."

When the bell rang, several students approached Quanta as they gathered their books.

"Dude, that was actually really interesting," Tyler said. "I never thought about history affecting how people think about their lives."

"It made me realize why I hate the idea of working in a cubicle for forty years," Jessica added. "What's the point if you're just doing meaningless tasks to make money to buy stuff you don't really need to impress people you don't even care about? My dad has a corporate office job and is completely miserable."

"Maybe that's why some people are starting to look for different ways to live and work," Quanta suggested. "What if instead of just accepting that work has to be meaningless, we figured out how to do work that actually feels connected to our purpose?"

"How would you even figure out what your purpose is?" Tyler asked.

This was another example of the kind of opening that Alma had written about—when people start asking questions about meaning and purpose, they're ready for deeper conversations about consciousness and personal power.

"I think everyone has natural talents and interests that point toward what they're meant to contribute," Quanta said carefully. "And perhaps the key is learning to pay attention to what excites you versus what drains you, what feels meaningful versus what feels empty."

As they walked toward their next classes, Quanta could feel that he'd planted more seeds. These weren't students who would normally think about consciousness development or personal growth, but they were starting to ask the kinds of questions that naturally led to those explorations.

In Spanish class, he sat next to Sarah again, who immediately turned to him with an expression of excitement mixed with amazement.

"Quanta, I have to tell you something," she said quietly as Miss Clark organized her materials at the front of the room. "I tried what you suggested about acknowledging the worried voice and then focusing on something else."

"How did it go?"

"It actually worked. I had a math quiz on Friday, and when I felt that familiar panic starting, I did exactly what you said. I acknowledged the voice—*Oh, there's that worried voice again*—and then I focused on remembering how well I understood the material when I studied it. The panic didn't completely go away, but it didn't take over either. I was able to think clearly enough to show what I knew."

"That's incredible," Quanta said, feeling genuinely happy for her breakthrough. "How did you do on the quiz?"

"B-plus. Which might not sound like much, but it's the best I've done on a math quiz all semester. And more importantly, I felt like myself during the test instead of this panicked, confused person who couldn't think clearly."

Quanta felt a quiet sense of clarity—when you help someone access their own capabilities rather than trying to fix their problems for them, they develop real confidence and independence.

“Have you tried it in other situations?”

“Actually, yeah. I used the same technique when my parents started arguing about their divorce stuff on Saturday. I actually meant to tell Jessica since her parents are going through the same thing. Instead of getting caught up in their drama and feeling helpless, I acknowledged that I was feeling scared and upset, and then I chose to focus on taking care of myself—I went to my room, put on headphones, and did homework. It sounds simple, but it was the first time I felt like I had some control over my own experience instead of just being a victim of whatever was happening around me.”

“That’s not simple at all,” Quanta said. “That’s really advanced emotional intelligence. Most adults haven’t figured out how to do that.”

“But here’s what’s really weird,” Sarah continued, lowering her voice even more. “After I did that—after I stopped getting caught up in their argument and focused on staying calm—they actually stopped fighting. Within ten minutes, they were talking normally again. It was like my energy shift somehow affected the whole situation.”

Quanta felt a chill of recognition. “That makes a lot of sense. Think of it like being a tuning fork,” Quanta explained, remembering Alma’s wisdom. “When you strike a tuning fork, any other forks tuned to similar frequencies start vibrating automatically. When you maintained your calm, centered frequency instead of getting caught up in their chaos, your parents naturally started resonating with that same coherence. You became like a lighthouse sending out steady, peaceful energy that helped guide them out of their own storm."

"You really think my staying calm helped them calm down?"

"I think consciousness is way more interconnected than most people realize. When you shifted from reactive panic to centered awareness, you created a field of calm that naturally influenced everyone around you."

Sarah stared at him for a moment, processing this idea. "So, learning to manage my own inner state goes beyond just feeling better—it's actually about affecting my whole environment?"

"That's exactly right. Every person who develops these capabilities becomes like a tuning fork, helping other people find more coherent frequencies just by being around them."

During the break between Spanish and his next class, Quanta decided to walk past Mr. Wagner's classroom to see if his favorite teacher was available for a quick chat. He found Mr. Wagner setting up equipment for what looked like another consciousness-related demonstration.

"Quanta!" Mr. Wagner said, looking up with obvious pleasure. "Perfect timing. I was just thinking about you and wondering how you've been applying some of the concepts we've explored in class."

"Actually, that's exactly what I wanted to talk to you about. I've been experimenting with the coherence techniques you demonstrated, and I'm starting to see some really interesting results."

"What kind of results?"

Quanta described his experience with Sarah, how teaching her to observe her anxiety patterns rather than being controlled by them had led to improved test performance and even seemed to affect her family dynamics.

"That's fascinating," Mr. Wagner said, setting down the equipment and giving Quanta his full attention. "And it makes perfect sense from everything we're learning about field effects and consciousness contagion. When one person in a system shifts to a more coherent state, it tends to influence the coherence of the entire system."

"Consciousness contagion?"

"The phenomenon where emotional and mental states spread from person to person through unconscious synchronization of brain wave patterns, heart rhythms, and energy fields. It's why you can walk into a room and immediately sense whether the people there are calm or anxious, happy or depressed."

"So if someone learns to maintain coherent states consistently..."

"They become what researchers are calling a 'positive contagion source'—someone who naturally helps elevate the consciousness of everyone around them just by being present and centered."

Mr. Wagner pulled out a research paper from his desk. "There are studies showing that even one person in a group maintaining heart coherence can influence the heart rhythms of up to fifteen other people in the same space, without any direct interaction or communication."

"Right," Quanta replied, thinking back to the 1% rule. "So you agree consciousness development isn't just personal— it's inherently social and collective?"

"Yes, which is why what you're doing—learning these principles yourself and then sharing them with others— could have exponential effects. Every person you help develop these capabilities becomes a source of positive influence for dozens of other people."

"Mr. Wagner, can I ask you something? Do you think schools would be interested in teaching these kinds of skills more formally? Like, if there was a way to help students develop emotional coherence and stress management abilities that improved their academic performance?"

Mr. Wagner's eyes lit up with interest. "I think the progressive educators would be very interested," Mr. Wagner said carefully. "Especially here at South Ridge. We're fortunate to have a district that's more open to innovative approaches than you'd find at the state or national level. Plus, your father's reputation in the academic community provides some protection for exploring cutting-edge research applications."

He paused, his expression growing more serious. "But you should know that as word spreads beyond our local district, you might encounter resistance from higher up the administrative chain. There are powerful interests that prefer traditional approaches to education—approaches that don't necessarily encourage independent thinking or personal empowerment. Unfortunately, these traditional approaches—more counseling, medication for anxiety and depression, treatment for attention deficit disorders, punitive discipline systems—aren't addressing the root causes of student stress and behavioral problems."

"What do you think the root causes are?"

"Mostly that we're trying to educate people using methods designed for training machines. We focus on information transfer, memorization, and task completion rather than developing the actual capabilities that allow people to think clearly and freely, create effectively, and navigate challenges with resilience. Our obsession with grades and standardized metrics has replaced genuine learning and understanding. Students become skilled at regurgitating information and following prescribed procedures, but struggle when faced with any kind of real problem."

The words hit close to home. Quanta had spent years perfecting the art of playing the academic game—memorizing, testing, performing—without anyone ever teaching him how to actually think or create. What he'd learned from Nova, Mr. Wagner, and his father—consciousness development, coherence techniques, understanding reality—these were the first skills that felt genuinely useful for real life.

At lunch, Quanta was eager to share his morning experiences with Nova, but when he reached their usual meeting spot in the cafeteria, he saw her in an animated conversation with someone he hadn't expected to see—Emma Richards, a sophomore who was known for being both academically gifted and deeply thoughtful about social issues.

"Hey," Nova said as Quanta approached, "I was just telling Emma about some of the stress management techniques we've been exploring. She's been dealing with some intense academic pressure."

Emma looked at Quanta with the kind of focused attention that suggested she was genuinely interested rather than just being polite. "Nova was telling me about frequency anchoring? It sounds like it could really help with the anxiety I've been having about college applications."

"It definitely could," Quanta said, settling into a seat across from them. "Have you noticed specific thoughts or feelings that tend to trigger the anxiety?"

"Oh, constantly. It's like this voice in my head that's always calculating—if I don't get into the right college, my whole future is ruined. If I don't maintain my GPA, I won't have any options. If I don't excel at everything, I'm going to disappoint everyone who believes in me." Emma paused, then added with a self-deprecating smile, "When I say it out loud, it sounds completely crazy, but in my head it feels totally rational and urgent."

"That doesn't sound crazy at all," Nova said reassuringly. "That's exactly the kind of mental pattern that frequency techniques can help with. What if instead of fighting those thoughts or getting frustrated with yourself for having them, you learned to recognize them as just mental habits that you can choose to engage with or not?"

"Like switching playlists?" Emma asked.

"Exactly. Your awareness is like having control of your mental Spotify. The anxious thoughts are just one playlist among many that your mind can stream. Once you realize you're the one choosing what to play, you can skip to a different playlist anytime—something more upbeat and calming instead of the anxiety soundtrack."

Quanta felt a moment of appreciation for how naturally Nova explained these concepts in ways that felt accessible rather than overwhelming. "Emma, have you ever noticed that the anxiety thoughts tend to pull you into thinking about future scenarios that might never happen?"

"All the time. I spend so much energy worrying about things that are completely out of my control, like what college admissions officers will think of my essay, or whether I'll be able to handle the workload at a competitive school, or what I'll do if I don't get into any of my top choices."

"I thought that might be the case. So, one of the most powerful things you can do is practice bringing your attention back to the present moment, where you have some influence over your experience. Being present may sound straightforward, but it requires practice. You need to stop 'time traveling' in your mind. In other words, you can't dwell on the past or worry about the future. Focusing on the past causes depression and focusing on the future causes anxiety. When you notice yourself focusing too much on your future, you can anchor yourself back into the present moment by focusing on your breathing, or looking around and noticing five things you can see, or even just feeling your feet on the ground. You must always try to keep your energy and attention in the present moment."

"That actually makes a lot of sense," Emma said thoughtfully. "It's like the anxiety is trying to solve future problems by thinking about them obsessively, but since they're future problems, thinking about them now doesn't actually help—it just makes me feel awful in the present."

"Yes! And here's what's really interesting," Nova added. "When you're in a present-moment, coherent state, you make better decisions and notice more opportunities. So, anchoring yourself in the now doesn't just feel better—it makes you more effective at creating the kind of future you want."

They spent the rest of lunch walking Emma through some basic frequency anchoring techniques, showing her how to create positive anchors for confidence and calm, and teaching her the gratitude practices that could shift her emotional state almost instantly.

By the time the bell rang, Emma was practicing the breathing techniques they'd shown her, and Quanta could literally see the change in her energy—less tense, more grounded, with a sparkle in her eyes that suggested she was excited about what she'd learned.

"This is incredible," she said as they gathered their things. "I feel like I just discovered I have superpowers I never knew existed."

"You do," Nova said with a smile. "We all do. Most people just never learn how to access them."

"Would you guys be interested in teaching this to other people? I know so many students who are struggling with the same stuff I am."

Quanta and Nova exchanged a meaningful look. This was exactly the kind of organic interest they were hoping for—

when you help people experience their own capabilities, they naturally want to share it with others.

"Actually," Nova said, "we've been talking a lot about that recently. What if there was a way to share these techniques with students who are interested, in a format that would be practical and helpful rather than boring or overwhelming?"

"I would be so interested in that," Emma said immediately. "And I know other people who would be too. When you're drowning in stress and anxiety, you're willing to try anything that might actually help."

After school, Quanta and Nova walked to her house, both buzzing with anticipation about diving deeper into Alma's educational materials and beginning to design their approach to sharing consciousness principles with other students.

"Before we look at the specific strategies," Nova said as they settled onto her couch with several of Alma's journals spread on the coffee table, "I want to show you something my grandmother wrote about the bigger picture of what we're doing."

She opened to a section titled "The Consciousness Revolution in Education" and began reading: *"'Every awakened individual who learns to embody higher consciousness principles becomes a seed for collective transformation. When these seeds find themselves in educational environments, they have the opportunity to help other young people discover their own innate capabilities before those capabilities become buried under layers of social conditioning and limiting beliefs.'"*

"That's definitely what happened with Sarah and Emma today," Quanta said. "They weren't looking for some big spiritual awakening—they just wanted practical help with stress and anxiety. But in learning to manage their internal states, they're developing the foundation for much deeper consciousness and spirituality work."

"Yep. And here's what's really beautiful about the approach my grandmother developed," Nova continued, turning to another page. "She figured out how to teach the most advanced principles through practical applications that anyone can benefit from, regardless of their level of spiritual interest or development."

She showed him a detailed curriculum that looked like it had been developed by someone with extensive teaching experience. The materials were organized into progressive modules, each one building on the previous while remaining standalone enough that someone could benefit from just one session.

"Module One is basic stress management and emotional regulation," Nova explained. "It covers the connection between thoughts, feelings, and physical states, with practical techniques for shifting out of anxiety and into calm focus. Module Two introduces the connection between thoughts, feelings, and outcomes—this is where people start learning that their internal state affects what happens in their external world. Module Three covers goal-setting with elevated emotion and visualization techniques. Module Four explores the science of peak performance states and optimal experience. And Module Five integrates everything into a comprehensive system for conscious creation."

"That's brilliant," Quanta said, studying the materials with growing excitement. "Someone could go through all the modules and basically learn everything we've learned about manifestation and consciousness development, but it would feel like practical life skills rather than abstract spiritual teachings."

Nova pulled out another journal that contained detailed instructions for facilitating large group learning sessions and interactive exercises. "She also figured out how to create an environment where people feel safe exploring these concepts without it coming across like some weird belief system—or some kind of cult or new religion."

"How do we create this environment?"

"Mainly through asking questions instead of giving answers, encouraging people to experiment and see what works for them personally, and focusing on results rather than ideology. She named it 'empirical spirituality'— testing these principles like scientific hypotheses and keeping what works while discarding what doesn't."

"So our role would be more like experienced friends than teachers?"

"Precisely. The facilitator's job is to create space where people can discover their own capabilities, not to make them believe something. The moment you start trying to convince people, you've shifted from empowerment to manipulation."

Nova then opened to the section on introducing consciousness work in educational settings previously discussed.

"This contains tactical instructions for implementation," Nova said, flipping through the pages. "Specific language frameworks, administrative approaches, even sample proposals that emphasize academic and mental health benefits while avoiding terminology that might trigger concerns about spiritual content."

"What kind of language?" Quanta asked.

"Things like 'evidence-based stress reduction techniques,' 'cognitive behavioral strategies for academic performance,' 'mindfulness-based interventions for student wellness,' and 'peer support for optimal learning states,'" Nova replied, reading from Alma's notes. "All completely accurate descriptions, but framed in language that educators and parents would recognize and support."

"So we become like translators?" Quanta said.

"Exactly. We speak the language of measurable outcomes when talking to administrators, while teaching the deeper principles to students who are ready. But here's the sophisticated part—she created a complete implementation timeline."

Nova showed him charts and phases. "She mapped out how to start small with stress management, gradually introduce consciousness concepts as trust builds, and scale systematically while staying under the radar of larger resistance forces."

"She really thought of everything," Quanta said, studying the detailed plans.

"She had to. She knew this work would eventually attract attention from those who benefit from keeping people unconscious. The key is building strong foundations and protective relationships before becoming too visible."

"Right, Mr. Wagner essentially said the same thing. My dad too. What kind of pushback do you think we'd get?"

"Pressure to stick to traditional approaches, resistance to anything that helps students think independently, attempts to discredit these techniques as unscientific or inappropriate for schools, and even attempts to discredit us or whoever else is teaching. Hopefully it's nothing more than that. Appears all the smart adults we've heard from all agree that as more young people develop these capabilities, the elite's will see it as a threat to their control and who knows how they'll respond."

Quanta understood. "So we need to be strategic about how we present this."

"Indeed, we do. But she also wrote that the awakening is inevitable. Once consciousness development reaches a critical mass among young people, it becomes unstoppable. We just need to plant the seeds carefully and let the natural hunger for these tools do the rest."

"The timing might be perfect," Quanta said. "My mom just had a conversation with Mr. Brytus about the increasing number of students seeking help with stress and academic pressure.

"Speaking of Mr. Brytus," Nova said, thinking about their next logical step, "we should meet with him. If we're going to do these group sessions at school, we'll need his approval. As the head guidance counselor, he oversees all student wellness programs."

"Good idea. If we get his approval, we can use school facilities and it'll look legitimate instead of like some underground club. When should we meet with him?"

"Monday morning? I'll email him tonight. I'll use the language from my grandmother's journal to tee up the discussion."

Quanta nodded, feeling a flutter of nervousness. Pitching this to a school official would be their first real test of whether Alma's strategic frameworks actually worked.

When Quanta arrived home that evening, he headed to his father's study where Justin was preparing for an upcoming lecture.

"How did it go with Nova?" Justin asked.

"Incredible. Her grandmother developed a complete curriculum for teaching consciousness principles in educational settings. It's like a bridge between practical life skills and advanced awareness development."

Quanta explained Alma's system—how it was broken into modules, focused on trying things out rather than just accepting ideas, and had ways to work with people who were skeptical. As he spoke, he could see his father getting more excited.

"This is exactly what the field needs," Justin said when Quanta finished. "Most consciousness education is either too academic and theoretical, or too spiritual and inaccessible. What you're describing sounds like it could appeal to anyone who wants practical tools for improving their life experience."

"Do you think there's a chance the school would actually support this? I mean, this isn't necessarily aligned with the standard state curriculum. I know we discussed how students would react to this, but getting buy-in from the school?"

"I think there's a good chance. At least at the local level. Just stick to what we discussed—start small and go from there. Educational institutions are becoming increasingly aware that traditional approaches to student stress and mental health aren't adequate for the challenges students are facing. If you can demonstrate measurable benefits—improved grades, reduced anxiety, better social interactions—schools will be very interested."

"But remember," Justin added with a more serious tone, "presentation matters. What we talked about before still applies—frame this as performance optimization and stress management techniques. Peak performance, mental clarity, anxiety reduction. Don't lead with consciousness awakening or reality creation. Those concepts can emerge naturally once people experience the benefits, but starting with that language will create unnecessary resistance."

Justin pulled a book from his desk. "I've been reading about similar programs already underway—just not aimed at younger students or introduced through the school system. Mindfulness training, emotional intelligence curricula, stress reduction programs. What you and Nova are developing could be positioned as the next evolution of these existing initiatives."

"So this is already happening at other places?"

"Yes, but the current programs are adult-led and don't touch the deeper material Dr. Vasquez is exploring. A peer-to-peer model like the one you're considering could be far more impactful—teens are often more open to learning from each other than from adults."

"Plus," Justin added with a meaningful look, "young people who have experienced these consciousness shifts themselves can teach from genuine understanding rather than academic knowledge. There's a credibility that comes from having lived the principles you're sharing. And the people you're teaching will respect that."

That night, lying in bed, Quanta sensed a deeper clarity settling in. The day's revelations weren't just personal milestones—they were pointing toward something greater. It was becoming clear that his journey wasn't only about awakening himself, but about paving the way for others to awaken too.

He thought about the warnings of potential resistance to their work. The idea that there might be forces actively working to prevent consciousness education felt both daunting and motivating. If these capabilities were truly as powerful as they seemed, if they really could help people become immune to manipulation and control, then of course there would be opposition from those who benefited from keeping people unconscious.

But that only made the work more important, not less. Every student they helped develop these abilities would be one less person vulnerable to fear-based programming and external manipulation. Every teenager who learned to manage their own consciousness would grow into an adult who couldn't be controlled through traditional means.

The consciousness revolution that Nova's grandmother
had written about wasn't some distant possibility—it was
happening right now, and they were playing an active role
in its unfolding. Tomorrow would mark the beginning of
sharing these capabilities with groups of students rather
than just individuals. But as his excitement grew, so did his
awareness that success would bring challenges. The more
effective their program became, the more attention it
would draw—first from supportive local educators, but
eventually from the larger systems that had invested
decades in keeping young people unconscious of their own
power.

The frequency war was real, and Quanta and Nova were
on the front lines. But consciousness itself was on their
side, and that was an unstoppable force.

Chapter 10: The Field

The Monday morning meeting with Mr. Brytus had gone better than Quanta had dared to hope. He and Nova had spent the weekend preparing their presentation, carefully crafting language that emphasized practical benefits while avoiding terminology that might trigger concerns about spiritual content.

"We'd like to propose a peer-support study group focused on evidence-based stress reduction techniques," Nova had begun, reading from the strategic talking points they'd developed from Alma's notes. "Academic pressure and anxiety are affecting increasing numbers of students, and traditional counseling approaches aren't addressing the root causes."

Mr. Brytus had leaned forward with immediate interest. "What kind of techniques are you thinking about? And what makes you think peer-to-peer support would be more effective than adult-led interventions?"

"Research shows that mindfulness-based interventions, cognitive behavioral strategies for academic performance, and peer support for optimal learning states can significantly improve both mental health and academic outcomes," Quanta had replied, drawing on the scientific language his father had helped him refine. "Students are often more willing to try new approaches when they're introduced by other students rather than authority figures."

"Plus," Nova had added, "we've both been experimenting with these techniques personally and have seen remarkable results in managing stress and improving focus. We'd like to share what we've learned with other students who might benefit."

Mr. Brytus had asked practical questions about meeting format, supervision, and measurable outcomes. They'd explained their plan for weekly hour-long sessions in the library conference room right after school ended, with documentation of participant feedback and any improvements in academic performance or stress levels.

"This actually addresses several concerns I've been hearing from both students and teachers," Mr. Brytus had said thoughtfully. "We've had increasing requests for stress management resources, and I've been looking for innovative approaches that might actually help students develop internal resilience rather than just cope with external pressures."

The approval had come with reasonable conditions: sessions would be voluntary and open to any interested students, they would maintain basic documentation of activities and outcomes, and they would check in with Mr. Brytus monthly to report on progress and discuss any concerns.

"We'll call it the 'Peak Performance Study Group,'" Nova had suggested, using terminology that emphasized academic benefits while remaining completely accurate about their intentions.

Now, three days later, Wednesday afternoon found them in the library conference room, preparing for their first official session. Quanta arranged chairs in a circle while Nova set up materials on the central table: notebooks, pens, and carefully selected items from Alma's collection.

"How are you feeling?" Nova asked quietly as she placed the last of the materials.

"Like I'm about to find out whether everything we've learned actually works with groups, or if we're just two kids who've been fooling ourselves," Quanta replied honestly. His stomach carried that familiar flutter of nervous excitement, but underneath it was something else—a steady confidence that surprised him with its strength.

"Remember what my grandmother wrote about group consciousness," Nova said, opening one of her journals to a marked page. "When individual awareness comes together with shared intention, the collective field becomes more than the sum of its parts. It's like individual drops of water joining together to create a powerful river that can carve through mountains—something no single drop could ever accomplish alone."

The first to arrive was Sarah Williams, carrying herself with new confidence since mastering the anxiety techniques. Emma Richards and Tyler Chen followed, both curious about advanced consciousness concepts. Jessica Martinez arrived last, slightly breathless but determined to explore alternatives to traditional stress management.

"So what exactly are we doing here?" Tyler asked, settling into his chair. "I know it's supposed to be about stress management, but it sounds like you guys have discovered something more interesting."

"We're going to explore techniques for managing your internal state so effectively that you influence your external experience," Nova replied. "But instead of just talking about it, we're going to experiment and see what happens when we work together."

Quanta felt appreciation for how naturally the group had formed—students ready for alternatives to conventional approaches to academic pressure.

"Before we start," Quanta said, settling into his own chair and feeling the circle complete itself, "I want to be clear about something. We're not here to convince anyone of anything or make you believe in concepts that seem too weird or unrealistic. We're here to experiment with techniques that have worked for us, and see if they work for you too. Everything we do is optional, and you should only try what feels right to you personally."

"Practical spirituality," Nova added with a smile. "Testing these principles like scientific hypotheses and keeping what works while discarding what doesn't."

"Okay, that actually sounds reasonable," Tyler said, his skepticism visibly relaxing. "So, what's the first experiment?"

"Group coherence," Nova replied, opening her grandmother's journal to a section they'd studied intensively over the past few days. "We're going to explore what happens when multiple people synchronize their heart rhythms and brain waves simultaneously. According to the research, when people achieve coherence together, they create what's called a 'collective field' that's much more powerful than individual coherence."

Emma asked with interest. "Like how a group of singers can create harmonies that are more beautiful than any single voice?"

"That's a perfect analogy," Quanta said, feeling a surge of excitement as the group's energy began to align around genuine curiosity. Emma just provided an analogy similar to Nova's so he felt they were getting off on the right foot.

"So how do we create this group coherence?" Sarah asked, already pulling out a notebook to take notes—a habit from her academic anxiety that was now becoming a tool for growth rather than stress.

"We start with synchronized breathing," Nova explained, consulting Alma's detailed instructions. "Everyone sit comfortably, close your eyes if that feels okay, and we'll establish a rhythm together. The key is matching not just the timing, but the quality of the breath—slow, deep, and peaceful."

As they began synchronized breathing, Quanta marveled at how quickly the group's energy shifted. Within minutes, scattered individual frequencies organized into something harmonious—chaos resolving into order, random notes becoming music.

"Now," Nova said softly, "while maintaining this rhythm, focus on something you're genuinely grateful for. Not something you think you should appreciate, but something that creates warmth when you think about it."

The room's energy shifted immediately. Individual coherence became collective—a field of appreciation that seemed to extend beyond their personal boundaries. Quanta felt his gratitude amplifying as it resonated with others.

"This is incredible," Emma whispered, eyes closed but face relaxed. "I can actually feel everyone else's appreciation, like we're connected to the same peaceful frequency."

"That's exactly right," Quanta confirmed. "When people achieve coherent states together, their energy fields synchronize. You're literally feeling the group's coherence through your nervous system."

Tyler opened his eyes with an expression of amazement mixed with slight disbelief. "Okay, that's definitely not what I expected. I mean, I've meditated before, but this felt like something was connecting us. Like we were all logged into the same Netflix account."

"Because you were," Nova replied, her own excitement evident as she consulted Alma's notes about group field effects. "What you just experienced is called 'field resonance'—when individual consciousness frequencies align to create a collective field that's more coherent and powerful than any individual could achieve alone."

Jessica raised her hand slightly, as if they were still in a regular classroom. "So does this mean we can actually influence each other's mental and emotional states just by being in the same space?"

"Not just influence," Quanta said, feeling the concepts from his father's research and Mr. Wagner's demonstrations crystallizing into practical understanding. "According to the scientific studies, when one person in a group maintains genuine heart coherence, it can affect the heart rhythms and brain waves of up to fifteen other people in the same space, without any direct interaction or verbal communication."

"That's both amazing and slightly terrifying," Sarah said thoughtfully. "This means the people we spend time with are constantly affecting our internal state, whether we realize it or not."

"Right, which is why developing your own coherence skills becomes so important," Nova added. "When you know how to maintain your own centered frequency regardless of what's happening around you, you become what researchers call a 'positive contagion source'—someone who naturally helps elevate the consciousness of everyone around them."

Emma looked around the circle with new awareness. "So right now, we're all positively affecting each other just by being in coherent states together?"

"But wait, there's more," Quanta said with a grin, turning to the next section of their planned session. "We're going to experiment with using this collective field to enhance individual capabilities that would be much harder to access alone."

He pulled out a simple math worksheet—nothing complex, just basic problems that would normally require focused attention and clear thinking. "We're going to see what happens to mental performance when it's supported by group coherence versus individual effort."

Everyone worked on a set of problems individually. Then they divided into pairs, with one person working on a similar set of problems while the other maintained coherent breathing and focused appreciation. Then they switched roles. The results were remarkable and immediate—everyone's accuracy and speed improved significantly when they were supported by their partner's coherent field compared to what they achieved alone.

"This is like unlocking a hidden part of myself I never knew was there," Tyler said, staring at his completed worksheet with obvious amazement. "When Jessica was doing that breathing thing and focusing on gratitude, I could think so much more clearly. It was like my brain fog just lifted."

"Now imagine," Nova said, her voice carrying the kind of excitement that came from witnessing principles they'd studied being proven in real time, "what becomes possible when entire classrooms, or schools, or communities learn to create these kinds of supportive consciousness fields together."

"Wait," Sarah said suddenly, her analytical mind making connections that impressed Quanta with their sophistication. "If group coherence enhances individual mental performance, and if conscious people naturally influence others toward greater coherence, then teaching these techniques to students isn't just about stress management—it's about unlocking collective human potential."

"That's exactly right," Quanta replied, feeling a surge of pride at how quickly Sarah was grasping the broader implications. "And it explains why some groups seem to bring out the best in everyone while other groups seem to amplify anxiety, conflict, and limitation. It's not just psychological—it's actually energetic."

"Which brings us to our next experiment," Nova said, consulting the most advanced section of Alma's group protocols. "Collective intention."

She explained the concept carefully: when individual consciousness comes together around a shared goal or intention, the combined effect is exponentially more powerful than individual effort. It's like the difference between people pushing a heavy object in different directions versus everyone pushing together in the same destination.

"We're going to practice this with something small and practical," Nova continued, "so we can experience how it works without getting into anything that feels too overwhelming or unrealistic."

They chose a simple collective intention: that their group would become a source of calm, supportive energy for other students throughout the rest of the week. Everyone focused on this shared goal while maintaining the coherent breathing and grateful feeling they'd established.

The experience was unlike anything Quanta had encountered, even in his individual consciousness work. It felt like being part of a gentle, invisible network of supportive energy that extended far beyond their small circle. Each person's intention seemed to amplify and be amplified by everyone else's, creating something that felt both deeply personal and surprisingly powerful.

"I can actually sense this intention taking root," Emma said softly, her eyes wide with wonder. "Like we've created something together that's going to continue working even after we leave this room."

"That's because you have," Quanta replied, remembering his father's research on morphic resonance and collective fields. "Group intention creates what's called a 'morphic field'—an invisible blueprint that continues to influence the intended outcome even when the group is no longer physically together."

As their session moved toward its conclusion, Quanta was reflecting on how much they'd accomplished in just one hour. These students had gone from curiosity about stress management to direct experience of collective consciousness and group intention work. More importantly, they'd done it through practical experimentation rather than abstract theory.

"Before we finish," Nova said, "I want to ask everyone to share one thing you experienced today that surprised you, and one thing you're curious to explore further."

Sarah went first: "I was surprised by how immediate the group coherence effect was. Within minutes I could feel something different happening in the room. And I'm curious about whether we could use these techniques to help other students who are struggling with anxiety and academic pressure."

Tyler followed: "Honestly, I was surprised that any of this worked at all. I mean, I believe in psychology and placebo effects and stuff, but this felt like something more real and measurable. And I'm curious about whether group coherence could help with things like sports performance or creative projects.”

Emma nodded thoughtfully: “What surprised me was how natural it felt once we got started. These techniques don’t feel weird or forced—they feel like capabilities we already had but just never learned how to access. And I want to understand more about how individual consciousness development connects to collective social change.”

Jessica concluded: “I was surprised by how much calmer and more optimistic I feel right now compared to how I felt when I walked in. And I’m curious about whether we could teach simplified versions of these techniques to younger students, like middle schoolers who are just starting to experience academic pressure.”

Quanta felt a sense of gratitude as he listened to their responses. Each person had not only experienced the techniques personally, but was already thinking about how to share them with others. This was exactly what Alma had written about—consciousness development naturally leading to service and collective transformation.

“What surprised me,” Quanta said when it was his turn, “was how much more powerful these techniques are when practiced in a group setting. I’ve been working with individual consciousness development for weeks, but this felt like discovering a whole new dimension of what’s possible. And I’m curious about developing a more formal curriculum that could be offered to other students who might benefit from this kind of work."

Nova concluded the sharing: "I was surprised by how quickly everyone was able to access advanced group consciousness states. Most people think these capabilities take years to develop, but you proved that's not true when there's genuine readiness and proper guidance. And I'm curious about how we can help other young people discover these abilities before they get buried under layers of social conditioning and limiting beliefs."

As they prepared to leave, Emma raised one more question that reminded Quanta of the larger implications: "Do you think this could scale globally? If enough people in enough places were doing this kind of consciousness work, could it transform how entire societies function?"

Nova and Quanta quickly made eye contact, both thinking of Alma's writings about the 1% effect and collective transformation.

"My grandmother believed," Nova said carefully, "that consciousness development isn't just personal growth— it's the foundation for positive social change. When enough people learn to operate from coherent, connected awareness instead of reactive fear and separation, it naturally transforms communities, institutions, and eventually entire civilizations."

"But that's probably a conversation for our next session," Quanta added with a smile, aware that they were approaching territory that might overwhelm people who were still integrating their first direct experience of group consciousness. "For now, the most important thing is practicing what we learned today and seeing how it affects the rest of your week."

As the group began to disperse, Quanta noticed that each person's energy remained more coherent and grounded than when they'd arrived. They were walking differently, talking more calmly, and seemed to carry with them some of the collective field they'd created together.

"Same time next week?" Sarah asked as she gathered her things.

"Absolutely," Nova replied. "And if you notice any interesting effects from today's session—changes in how you feel, how others respond to you, or opportunities that show up—bring those observations to share with the group."

"I have a feeling there's going to be a lot to share," Tyler said with a grin that suggested his skepticism had transformed into genuine enthusiasm for continued exploration.

After the others had left, Quanta and Nova remained in the conference room for a quick debrief.

"That was incredible," Quanta said. "I mean, I believed the research and trusted Alma's protocols, but experiencing it with an actual group was beyond what I imagined possible. Especially in the first session."

"And everyone picked it up so naturally," Nova added, her excitement evident as she reviewed the notes she took. "No one struggled with the concepts or felt like we were pushing them into anything too weird or uncomfortable. They were ready for this level of consciousness work."

"Which means there are probably other students who are ready too," Quanta said, his mind already moving toward the larger vision they were building. "If we can create effective group sessions like this one, and if the participants start sharing what they're learning with their friends..."

"Exponential expansion," Nova finished, consulting one of Alma's journals about consciousness contagion and social transformation. "Every person who experiences their own power to influence reality through consciousness becomes a bridge that helps others discover the same capabilities."

As they packed up the remaining materials and prepared to leave, Quanta noticed something remarkable happening in the hallways outside the conference room. Students who had been walking past during their session seemed more relaxed, more connected with each other. Conversations appeared calmer, laughter felt more genuine, and even the general energy of the end-of-day rush seemed less frantic.

"Are you seeing this?" Nova asked quietly, pausing near the doorway to observe the subtle but unmistakable shift in the school's atmosphere.

"The field effect," Quanta realized with amazement. "Our group coherence is still influencing the energy around us, even though the formal session is over."

They walked slowly through the hallways, both of them fascinated by this unexpected extension of their work. Near the main entrance, they encountered Mr. Wagner, who was heading toward the parking lot with his usual stack of papers and books.

"Quanta, Nova," he said, approaching them with obvious curiosity. "I just heard some hallway chatter from a few of the students about your Peak Performance group session. How did everything go?"

"Beyond what we hoped for," Quanta replied, still processing the experience himself. "We had a handful of participants, and everyone not only learned individual coherence techniques but also experienced genuine group consciousness effects."

Mr. Wagner's eyebrows rose with the kind of interest that suggested he understood the significance of what they were describing. "Group consciousness? You mean synchronized brainwave states and collective field effects?"

"Exactly," Nova said, pulling out one of her grandmother's journals. "We followed protocols for establishing group coherence through synchronized breathing and shared intention. The results were immediate and measurable—enhanced mental performance, collective problem-solving, and what felt like genuine morphic field creation."

"That's remarkable," Mr. Wagner said, his voice filled with genuine amazement. "Most researchers assume those kinds of effects require extensively trained participants and highly controlled laboratory conditions. But you're demonstrating that teenagers can access these states naturally with proper guidance."

"What really surprised us," Quanta added, "was how ready everyone was for advanced concepts. Once they experienced group coherence directly, they immediately started asking questions about collective social transformation and whether consciousness development could influence larger systems."

Mr. Wagner nodded thoughtfully. "Which makes perfect sense from a scientific perspective. If consciousness can affect quantum particles in controlled experiments, and if human brainwaves can synchronize to create measurable field effects, then groups of conscious individuals should theoretically be able to influence larger systems through coherent intention."

He continued, "This is great work. I'd like to hear more, but unfortunately, I must get going now. I'm really glad the session went well. Keep me posted on how your group progresses. I'm genuinely excited to see what you accomplish."

As they left school, Quanta could sense the subtle influence their group work was having on the entire environment. It was as if they'd created an invisible beacon of coherence that was naturally drawing others toward calmer, more connected states.

"You know what's really exciting?" Nova said as they began their walk home. "Today proved that working together like this doesn't just help each person individually—it creates something totally new that's way more powerful than any of us could do alone. When we were all synced up together, there was something amazing in that room that had never been there before."

"The field," Quanta said, understanding finally why this chapter of their journey had been building toward this moment. "We actually experienced the quantum field that connects all consciousness. Not as a theory or concept, but as a living, creative force of energy and information that we can learn to work with deliberately. It's like what you told me about the Law of Divine Oneness. Everything really is connected through this invisible web. When we touched one strand by creating group coherence, vibrations went through the whole web and affected everyone in the room."

"And now we know how to help others access it too,"
Nova added with obvious satisfaction. "Which means
we're not just students learning about consciousness
anymore. We're teachers, guides, and bridges helping
other people remember their own true nature."

When Quanta arrived home, his parents waited eagerly in
the living room.

"How did it go?" Justin asked immediately.

"It was unbelievable," Quanta replied. "Multiple students
experienced individual coherence techniques and accessed
group consciousness states that enhanced everyone's
mental performance."

"Group consciousness states?" Anne asked with genuine
interest.

"When people synchronize heart rhythms and brain waves
together, they create a collective field amplifying
individual capabilities," Quanta explained. "Like individual
flashlights versus multiple flashlights all pointed in the
same direction—together they create a beam powerful
enough to light up things none of them could illuminate
alone."

"And it actually worked?" Anne pressed.

"Completely. Everyone's problem-solving improved
significantly when supported by the group's coherent field.

By the end of the session, they were creating collective intentions that felt genuinely transformative."

Justin's expression brightened. "Remarkable. Most people assume group coherence takes years of training and precise conditions—but you're proving that's not the case."

"That's what Mr. Wagner said too, Quanta added with a grin. "What stood out to me most wasn't just how quickly they understood the concepts, but how naturally they connected them to bigger ideas—like social change and how consciousness might influence collective systems."

"Which it can," Justin said firmly. "Research shows coherent consciousness groups can influence community crime rates, conflict resolution, and larger social systems. Your work has implications far beyond academic stress management."

Anne shook her head with amazement. "I was initially worried about Quanta's weird consciousness interests, but now you're saying he's part of a social transformation movement?"

"Definitely," Justin said gently. "Every person operating from conscious awareness becomes a positive influence on everyone around them. When conscious people work together intentionally, they create changes impossible through traditional approaches."

"Plus," Quanta added, thinking about the enthusiasm he'd witnessed from each participant, "everyone who was in our session today immediately started thinking about how to share these techniques with other students. Sarah wants to help kids with anxiety disorders, Tyler is interested in applications for sports performance and creative projects, Emma is curious about social change applications, and Jessica wants to teach simplified versions to middle school students who are just beginning to experience academic pressure."

"Consciousness contagion," Justin said with obvious satisfaction, consulting his research notes. "When people experience their own power to influence reality through awareness and intention, they naturally want to help others discover the same capabilities. It's one of the most reliable patterns in consciousness development research—genuine empowerment creates an immediate desire to serve and share rather than to hoard or control."

Anne stood up and moved to the window, looking out at their neighborhood with what appeared to be new eyes. "So, you're saying that what happened in that library conference room today could potentially spread throughout the entire school, and then to other schools, and eventually influence how young people think about themselves and their capabilities?"

"That's exactly what we're saying," Quanta replied, understanding the full scope of what they were participating in. "And according to Alma's research, this isn't just theoretical. There are documented cases throughout history where consciousness development has spread exponentially through populations, creating rapid social transformation that seemed impossible through conventional means."

"So how many students would need to learn these techniques before it starts affecting the entire school?" Anne asked, her practical mind immediately focusing on the logistical implications.

"According to the research Alma compiled," Quanta said, consulting his memory of her notes, "it typically only takes about 1% of a population to create measurable influence on the whole system. For a school of 1,500 students, that would mean about fifteen students achieving genuine consciousness development capabilities."

The doorbell rang, and Anne looked up in surprise. "Were we expecting someone?"

Quanta went to answer it and found Nova and her mother Mickey on the front porch.

"I hope we're not intruding," Mickey said with a warm but slightly hesitant smile. "Nova was so excited about how well the Peak Performance group launched today, and I was curious to meet the family who's been so supportive of what the kids are doing together."

"Not at all! Please, come in," Anne said, immediately moving to welcome them. "I'm so sorry it's taken this long for us to meet properly. With everything being so hectic since you moved in—new house, new job, Nova starting a new school—I wanted to give you space to get settled."

"And I should apologize too," Mickey replied as they entered. "I kept meaning to introduce myself, but I didn't want to impose."

"Well, Justin and I have been really looking forward to meeting you both," Anne continued warmly. "Quanta hasn't stopped talking about Nova since you moved in. We even heard a lot about your mother, Alma, as well. We were just discussing how incredibly successful today's session was."

Mickey immediately felt at ease and entered the living room with the same kind of calm presence that characterized her daughter, but Quanta could see she was carrying something more—an excitement mixed with profound gratitude that suggested she understood the significance of what was happening.

"That's so lovely to hear. I just wanted to thank you both," Mickey said, addressing Justin and Anne directly. "When we moved here, I was hoping Nova would find friends who shared her interests, but I never imagined she'd find a community that could support the kind of work her grandmother had prepared her for. What Quanta and Nova are doing together feels like the fulfillment of everything my mother hoped would be possible."

"It's our privilege," Justin replied warmly. "Nova's wisdom and guidance have been instrumental in Quanta's development. We're grateful that our children found each other when they were both ready for this level of consciousness exploration."

"Actually," Nova said, opening one of the journals she'd brought, "my grandmother wrote specifically about the importance of adult support for young consciousness teachers. She believed that conscious adults who could provide grounding, resources, and protection were essential for allowing young people to develop their capabilities safely and effectively."

She read from the journal: "*'The awakened youth need conscious elders who can bridge the worlds—those who understand both the practical requirements of conventional society and the limitless possibilities of expanded consciousness. Without this bridge, young teachers either become isolated from mainstream culture or compromise their gifts to fit in. With proper adult support, they can transform culture from within.'*"

"That's beautiful," Anne said softly, and Quanta could see his mother's own awakening process accelerating as she witnessed the profound wisdom and practical effectiveness of the consciousness work. "It makes me realize that supporting what you're doing goes beyond helping individual students—it's about helping our entire community evolve toward something healthier and more connected."

"Exactly," Mickey agreed. "And from what Nova told me about today's session; the students are already demonstrating capabilities that most adults spend years trying to develop. They're accessing group consciousness states, creating collective intentions, and naturally wanting to share their discoveries with others."

"Which brings us to some practical considerations," Justin said, shifting into his strategic thinking mode. "If this program develops the way today's session suggested it could, we need to be prepared for both opportunities and challenges."

He went to his office to retrieve several research papers and some preliminary documentation. "I've been researching similar programs, and there are some important patterns we should be aware of. While this material pertains to more adult-oriented sessions, I believe the same will apply for the work you are doing with your peers."

"What kind of patterns?" Quanta asked, feeling both excitement and slight apprehension about the larger implications of their work.

"Successful consciousness-based educational programs tend to go through predictable phases," Justin explained, spreading the materials out on the coffee table. "Phase one is local enthusiasm and organic growth among early adopters—which is exactly what you're experiencing now. Phase two involves expanding beyond the initial group and demonstrating measurable benefits that attract broader institutional support."

"And phase three?" Nova asked, clearly thinking about her grandmother's warnings about resistance.

"Phase three is when the program becomes visible enough to attract attention from larger systems that may not be supportive of consciousness development," Justin said carefully. "Not necessarily hostile, but institutions that prefer traditional approaches and may be concerned about programs that encourage too much independent thinking or personal empowerment."

"So, we need to be strategic about documentation, language, and building allies before we reach that phase," Quanta said, understanding why Alma had emphasized the importance of presenting consciousness work in terms of practical benefits and evidence-based outcomes.

"Exactly. Which is why your mother's suggestion about starting small and documenting measurable results is so important," Justin agreed. "If you can demonstrate improved academic performance, reduced anxiety levels, enhanced social cooperation, and other benefits that school administrators care about, you'll have a strong foundation for expanding the program even if some resistance develops."

"Speaking of documentation," Nova said, "my grandmother designed specific protocols for measuring the effects of group consciousness work. Heart rate variability, attention span assessments, academic performance tracking, social interaction improvements—everything we'd need to provide evidence that this program is genuinely beneficial."

"That's perfect," Anne said with obvious relief. "It means you can prove that what you're doing actually works instead of just claiming it does based on subjective experiences."

As the conversation continued, Quanta marveled at how naturally the adult support network was forming around their consciousness work. His parents, Nova's mother, Mr. Wagner, Mr. Brytus, and other progressive educators were providing exactly the kind of bridge between conventional society and expanded awareness that Alma had identified as essential.

"You know what's really exciting?" Mickey said as the evening began to wind down. "Programs like this tend to create positive effects that extend far beyond the immediate participants. Families become more harmonious, communities become more cooperative, and even larger social issues begin to resolve more easily when enough people are operating from conscious awareness."

As Nova and her mother prepared to leave, Quanta felt a deep sense of appreciation for how perfectly everything was aligning to support their consciousness work. They had interested students, effective techniques, adult allies, institutional support, and even documentation protocols to demonstrate the measurable benefits of what they were doing.

"I can't wait for next week's session" Nova stated as her and Mickey walked out the door.

"I feel the exact same," Quanta replied. "And I have a feeling word is going to spread, so we might need to prepare for a larger group."

"My grandmother's protocols can handle several more people in a single session. More than the conference room can hold actually," Nova said with a smile. "After that, we'd need to either find a bigger room, split into multiple groups, or train additional facilitators."

"Additional facilitators," Quanta mused, already envisioning Sarah, Emma, Tyler, and Jessica developing their own capabilities to guide other students. "I love the idea of training the participants to become teachers themselves. The 'train the trainer' approach. That would create exponential expansion while maintaining the peer-to-peer strategy that makes this so effective with today's youth."

After Nova and Mickey left, Quanta felt energized rather than tired despite the full day. The inaugural group session had proven that everything they'd been learning could help other students in measurable ways.

As he prepared for bed, Sol sensed what had just been accomplished in such a short amount of time. Tomorrow, the students from today's session would carry their new understanding of consciousness back into their individual lives, relationships, and challenges. They would naturally begin to influence others toward greater coherence and awareness, creating ripple effects that would extend far beyond anything they could imagine.

And in their upcoming sessions, they would gather again to deepen their understanding and explore even more advanced applications of collective consciousness. But already, Quanta could sense that word was going to spread, curiosity was going to grow, and more students would want to discover these capabilities for themselves. And he and Nova would need to be ready for whatever came next.

But tonight, Quanta felt deeply satisfied. They'd moved from theory to practice, from individual understanding to collective experience. The field was real, they were fully aware of it, and they now knew how to help others access it. What had begun as individual awakening was becoming collective transformation, one group session at a time.

Chapter 11: Heart-Brain Connection

Quanta was sitting in his father's study Saturday morning, surrounded by research papers about heart-brain coherence while Sol slept peacefully at his feet. The past three weeks since launching their Peak Performance Study Group had been remarkable—not just for the continued effects he was experiencing personally, but for the ripple of curiosity spreading through South Ridge High like a viral video that students couldn't stop sharing.

Sarah had approached him yesterday with excitement about how the techniques they'd been exploring in their sessions continued to help her maintain calm focus during her parents' ongoing divorce discussions. Tyler had mentioned feeling more confident during wrestling practice, as if the group coherence was somehow still supporting his individual performance. Even Jessica had started using the breathing techniques before difficult conversations with her family, reporting that somehow the entire dynamic shifted when she maintained her center.

But what fascinated Quanta most was something Emma had observed: "It's like there's this invisible network connecting all of us now. Even when we're not together, I can feel that calm energy we created, especially when I'm stressed and really need it."

"That's morphic resonance," Quanta reiterated. "Once you've experienced group consciousness, you maintain access to it even when you're physically separated."

Now, as he studied his father's latest research on heart-brain coherence, Quanta understood why their upcoming advanced session felt so important. The HeartMath Institute—a research organization that studies how the heart's energy influences the brain and body—had found that the heart generates an energy field 5,000 times stronger than the brain. Yet most people had never learned to access this power consciously.

"The heart isn't just a pump," his father had explained over breakfast earlier that morning. "It's the body's most powerful electromagnetic generator. When your heart rhythm and brain waves sync up in coherence, you're essentially creating a dual-engine system that's far more powerful than either operating alone."

Quanta recalled Mr. Wagner's analogy about the dual-engine plane—when both engines worked in perfect synchronization, you could fly smoothly and powerfully toward any destination. But when they fought each other, you created turbulence and wasted enormous amounts of energy.

A text from Nova interrupted his train of thought: *"Ready for something that's going to take our group work to the next level? Just found advanced heart-coherence protocols in the manifestation journal. This explains why feeling is the secret to creation. Can you come over?"*

Thirty minutes later, Quanta headed over to Nova's, but this time the setup looked more advanced than anything they'd explored so far. Along with Alma's usual journals, Nova had arranged a sophisticated biofeedback device—sleek, intricate, and far beyond anything they'd used before.

"Before we dive in," Nova began, "I want you to experience something that's going to completely shift how you think about the power of your heart versus your mind."

She opened one of the journals to a section titled "The Heart's Hidden Intelligence" and showed him a diagram of the human electromagnetic field, with precise measurements showing the heart's magnetic field extending up to eight feet in all directions.

"Your body is literally broadcasting energy 24/7," Nova explained, pointing to the measurements. "But here's what most people don't realize—your heart produces an electromagnetic field that's up to 100 times stronger electrically and 5,000 times stronger magnetically than the brain. It also sends more neural signals to the brain than the brain sends to the heart, influencing emotions, perception, and decision-making."

"Wait," Quanta said with excitement, "that's exactly what my dad was telling me this morning. He showed me HeartMath research with those same numbers. It's incredible that your grandmother's notes match the latest scientific studies."

"That's because consciousness research has been documenting these phenomena for decades," Nova replied with a knowing smile. "The science is finally catching up to what spiritual teachers like my grandmother understood intuitively."

"So, the heart is actually running the show, not the mind?"

"In terms of pure energy or electromagnetic power, absolutely. Your brain creates electrical signals from your thoughts and intentions, and your heart amplifies those signals and broadcasts them as magnetic fields to everyone around you. It's like your brain is the radio transmitter creating the signal, but your heart is the powerful antenna that broadcasts it and attracts matching frequencies back to you. Most people think everything is driven by thoughts alone and have no idea how powerful their heart actually is in the manifestation process."

Quanta's mind immediately went back to another conversation he had with his dad about one of his colleague's research studies on manifestation. "Right—you need a coherent brain with clear intention generating the electrical signal, combined with a coherent heart producing the magnetic field that amplifies it." He continued, "Together, they create a unified electromagnetic signature that interacts with the quantum field, which responds by bringing you experiences that match that same frequency. This is the scientific framework behind the Law of Attraction we discussed before."

"This all starting to come together," Nova replied. She then pulled out the biofeedback device, which looked like a sophisticated heart rate monitor connected to a small computer screen. "I'm not exactly sure how my grandmother got this equipment, but want to see your heart's electromagnetic field in real time?"

A few minutes later, Quanta was staring at the screen in amazement as his heart rhythm patterns shifted from chaotic, irregular waves to smooth, coherent curves based entirely on what he focused his attention on. When he thought worried thoughts about upcoming tests, the patterns became jagged and scattered. When he shifted to appreciating his growing friendship with Nova, the waves immediately organized into beautiful, rhythmic patterns.

"This is incredible," he said, watching his heart's electromagnetic signature change in real time. "It's like when I watched Mr. Wagner's brainwaves change in class—except now, it's my heart we're measuring. It's like running an EEG for your emotions."

"But here's the really cool part," Nova continued. "When you achieve genuine heart coherence—when your heart rhythm becomes this smooth and organized—you're not just affecting your own internal state. You're broadcasting a field of coherence that naturally influences everyone within about eight feet of you."

"Like being a walking Wi-Fi hotspot for calm energy?"

"Exactly! And when multiple people achieve heart coherence together, their individual fields start to synchronize and amplify each other. That's what created the group consciousness effect during our session—we accidentally discovered advanced energy field techniques without realizing it."

Nova turned to a section that made Quanta's pulse quicken with recognition: "Advanced Heart-Brain Manifestation Protocols."

"My grandmother figured out that the five-step manifestation system we learned works exponentially better when you access it through heart coherence instead of trying to force it through mental willpower alone," Nova explained. "Most people try to manifest from their heads—thinking really hard about what they want, visualizing obsessively, repeating affirmations. But the real power comes from getting your heart and brain working together, like your dad mentioned based on his research. You literally have to feel like you already have what you desire."

She showed him detailed instructions for something labeled "Heart-Centered Creation," which was an advanced manifestation technique.

"The key insight is this," Nova continued, reading from the journal: "'*The quantum field responds to frequency, not words, not thoughts, not even effort. And the most powerful frequency generator in the human body is the heart. When heart and brain achieve perfect synchronization around a clear intention, you're creating a signal that the quantum field has no choice but to respond to.'"*

"So instead of trying to manifest from the mind..."

"You manifest from heart-brain coherence. Which means instead of thinking your way to what you want, you *feel* your way there. But not just any feeling—the specific energy frequency that your heart generates when it's experiencing genuine appreciation, gratitude, or joy about your desired outcome. Gratitude specifically is the most powerful emotion you can tap into when manifesting. That's why the gratitude exercises were introduced so early in our training—it wasn't just about feeling good; it was about tuning our hearts to the right frequency."

They spent more time working through Alma's heart-coherence protocols, using the biofeedback device to achieve genuine heart-brain coherence and then practicing manifestation techniques from that state. The difference was immediately noticeable—instead of forcing outcomes through mental effort alone, Quanta found himself naturally aligning with the feelings of what he wanted to create.

"This explains everything about why feeling is the secret," he said as they completed a technique for anchoring desired emotional states. "When your heart is coherent and aligned with what you want, you're not just hoping or wishing—you're actually broadcasting the electromagnetic signature of that reality."

"And the quantum field responds by matching your frequency," Nova added, consulting the final sections of Alma's advanced protocols. "But there's one more piece that makes this even more powerful—understanding how all of this connects to the present moment."

She opened to a section titled "Time, Consciousness, and Creation" and showed him advanced diagrams that looked like something from a physics textbook.

"My grandmother discovered that heart-brain coherence can only happen in the present moment," Nova explained. "When your mind is thinking about past regrets or future worries, it's impossible to achieve the synchronization necessary for conscious creation. But when you're fully present—when all of your attention is focused in the now—that's when your heart and brain naturally align."

"Like being present is the operating system that allows heart-brain coherence to run?"

"Precisely. And here's why that matters for manifestation: according to quantum physics, all possibilities exist simultaneously in the eternal present moment. Past and future are just mental constructs that limit access to the quantum field of infinite possibilities. Your dad can confirm, but that's what's in these notes."

Nova showed him a diagram that looked like a movie film strip, with each frame representing a different possible reality. "Think of the present moment as the only frame you can actually edit. When you're thinking about the past or future, you're looking at frames you can't change. But when you're fully present with heart-brain coherence, you gain access to the cosmic editing room where you can choose which reality to experience."

"So being present isn't just about feeling better—it's about accessing your creative power?"

"Correct. And when groups of people achieve present-moment heart-brain coherence together, they can access collective creation abilities that would be impossible individually."

Nova then flipped to a chapter named: "Group Heart-Brain Coherence Protocols."

"This is what I think we're ready to explore with our study group," she said, showing him detailed instructions for facilitating heart-coherence work with multiple people simultaneously. "Individual heart-brain coherence is powerful, but when groups achieve synchronized heart coherence, they create what my grandmother termed a 'collective electromagnetic field' that can influence reality on a much larger scale."

"Like the group consciousness we experienced, but powered by synchronized hearts instead of just synchronized breathing?"

"Right, and the effects are exponentially more powerful. Look at what's shown here."

Nova showed him results of studies where groups practicing heart coherence had influenced everything from local weather patterns to community crime rates to the healing of environmental damage. The data looked both scientifically rigorous and utterly extraordinary.

"You mean we could actually help heal environmental problems through group heart coherence?"

"According to this research, groups that achieve genuine heart-brain synchronization can influence any system that operates on electromagnetic principles—which is basically everything in nature. Plants, weather, water systems, even the electromagnetic field of the Earth itself."

They spent the rest of the afternoon poring over the data, alternating between stunned silence and bursts of excited speculation about what it all meant. By the time Quanta headed home, his mind was buzzing with possibilities. The idea that a small, coherent group could influence the physical world felt both unbelievable and completely logical at the same time.

Two days later, on Monday morning, that energy hadn't faded—it was already showing up in unexpected ways. Quanta arrived at school to find Andy waiting by his locker with an expression of eager anticipation mixed with slight bewilderment.

"Dude, I need to tell you something weird that happened last night," Andy said immediately. "I've been hearing so much about your Peak Performance sessions, so I finally decided to try some of the techniques over the weekend. Specifically, the breathing and gratitude ones I heard you and Nova presented. I figured if they're helping everyone feel less stressed, why not give them a try even though I haven't been to the sessions."

"How did it go?"

"That's the weird part. I was just sitting in my room, practicing that synchronized breathing thing and trying to focus on things I'm grateful for, when my dad knocked on my door. He's been super stressed about finding a new job since he got laid off, but when he came in, he looked... different. Calmer. And get this—he said he suddenly felt inspired to call his old college roommate about a business opportunity they'd discussed years ago."

Quanta felt a shiver run through him. "And?"

"His roommate had been thinking about the exact same thing and was hoping my dad would call. They talked for two hours and are meeting this weekend to discuss starting a consulting business together." Andy paused, clearly processing the implications. "It could just be coincidence, but the timing was so perfect. Like the moment I started practicing that coherence stuff, opportunities started appearing for my family."

"That's not coincidence," Quanta said with growing excitement. "That's exactly how heart coherence works. When you generate a coherent electromagnetic field, it influences the energy of everyone around you, which opens up new possibilities and synchronicities."

Before Quanta could elaborate further, Nova appeared beside them with several of Alma's journals under her arm and an expression that suggested she had significant news to share.

"Great news," she said. "I just got permission from Mr. Brytus to expand our sessions to ninety minutes and use the larger conference room. The interest level has been incredible and word is spreading fast."

"How fast?" Quanta asked.

"Three more students just approached me asking about joining the group. Plus, Emma mentioned our work to her older sister, who's a senior, and now there's interest from upperclassmen too."

Andy looked between them with growing enthusiasm. "So, this thing is taking off? Like, becoming a real program that could help a lot of students?"

"It's becoming exactly what we hoped for," Nova replied. "A peer-to-peer consciousness education network that's spreading organically because the techniques actually work and people want to share them with their friends."

At lunch, Quanta found the core group from their sessions—Nova, Sarah, Emma, Tyler, Jessica—along with Andy, who was enthusiastically explaining his recent individual experiments with their techniques.

"I should have joined you guys from the beginning," Andy was saying as Quanta approached. "I kept thinking it was just going to be basic stress management stuff, but hearing about the group consciousness experiences you've been having sounds way more interesting than anything I expected."

Nova smiled as Quanta joined them. "Perfect timing. I was just about to tell everyone about some advanced techniques we explored over the weekend that build on what we've been developing in our sessions."

"Advanced techniques?" Sarah asked, immediately pulling out her notebook. "I've been practicing the breathing and gratitude stuff every day, and it's been incredibly helpful. But I keep wondering if there's more we could learn."

Emma nodded enthusiastically. "Same here. The group coherence experiences we've been having are unlike anything I'd ever experienced before. It feels like we keep tapping into something real and powerful, but I have this sense we're only scratching the surface."

Andy leaned forward with obvious curiosity. "Okay, I definitely need to understand what you guys have been experiencing. Everyone's been talking about these sessions like they're breakthrough experiences, but I still don't really get what's happening."

Tyler grinned at Andy's confusion. "Dude, it's hard to explain because it sounds crazy when you say it out loud. But we've been learning how to sync up our thoughts and feelings as a group, and it makes everyone think more clearly and feel more connected. Like we become this temporary super-organism or something."

"A super-organism?" Andy's eyebrows shot up. "That does sound crazy. But also kind of awesome."

Jessica jumped in, her voice alive with the excitement of someone who'd discovered something genuinely life-changing. "The weirdest part is how it affects everything else. After our sessions, when I go home and my parents start having their usual fights about the divorce, instead of getting sucked into their drama, I maintain that calm energy we've been developing together. And somehow they both calm down too. It's like I'm broadcasting peace and they pick up the signal."

"That's exactly what happened," Nova said. "When you maintain coherent energy states, you naturally influence the electromagnetic fields of people around you. Most people don't realize they're constantly broadcasting and receiving energy signals through invisible fields that extend several feet from their bodies."

"Actually, that's what we're planning to explore next," Nova continued, her excitement growing as she opened her journal to the section about heart-brain coherence. "Quanta and I have been researching advanced techniques that could take our group work to a whole new level. It turns out the heart generates an electromagnetic field that's 5,000 times stronger than the brain."

"5,000 times stronger?" Emma's eyes widened. "You mean the heart is actually more powerful than the mind?"

"In terms of electromagnetic influence, yes," Quanta explained. "Your brain creates the electrical signals from your thoughts and intentions, and your heart amplifies those signals into powerful magnetic fields that broadcast your emotional frequency to everyone around you. Most people try to create change through thinking harder, but the real power comes from learning to align your heart and brain together so they work as an integrated system."

Tyler leaned back in his chair, processing this information. "So when you're feeling grateful or happy or peaceful, your heart is broadcasting that energy to everyone around you? It's not just coming from your mind?"

"Correct," Nova confirmed. "And when multiple people achieve heart coherence together, their individual fields start to synchronize and amplify each other. That's what created the group consciousness effect we experienced— we accidentally accessed advanced energy field techniques."

Andy looked a bit confused, but intrigued. "Okay, this is definitely sounding less like stress management and more like... I don't know, mental superpowers or something."

"That's because it is," Quanta said, recognizing the moment when someone begins to grasp the deeper implications of what they're learning. "We refer to it as consciousness development. Stress management is just the entry point. What we're really exploring is how consciousness works and how to use it intentionally instead of just being a victim and getting pushed around by whatever happens to you."

Sarah had been taking detailed notes throughout the conversation, but now she looked up with a slightly concerned expression. "This is all fascinating, but can I ask something? If these techniques are so powerful, and if they really work the way you're describing, why isn't everyone learning them? Why aren't they teaching this stuff in school? Why don't we see this plastered all over social media and in all the TV shows and movies we watch?"

The table went quiet for a moment as everyone considered the question. Quanta and Nova locked eyes, both thinking about the elite manipulation systems and the deliberate suppression of consciousness development.

"That's actually a really important question," Nova said carefully, aware they were approaching territory that could sound like a conspiracy theory if not handled properly. "And the answer has to do with understanding who benefits when people remain unconscious of their own power."

She pulled out one of Alma's journals and opened to a section her and Quanta studied extensively. "Think about it from a strategic perspective. If you're trying to control large groups of people, what's the best way to do it?"

"Keep them scared and distracted?" Tyler suggested, immediately grasping the logic.

"Right, and separated too. And make sure they never realize they have any real power to change their circumstances," Emma added. "If people knew they could influence their reality through consciousness, they'd be much harder to manipulate."

Jessica nodded slowly. "Like how social media algorithms show you content that makes you angry or upset, because angry people are more likely to keep scrolling and remain in a negative state."

"You got it," Quanta said, feeling the group's readiness to understand deeper truths about how their world operated. "The same consciousness principles we've been learning can be used in reverse—to keep people in low-frequency states like fear, anger, and confusion that make them easier to control."

Andy's expression had shifted from confusion to concern. "You're saying all this like it's actually happening. But wouldn't something that big require coordination across tons of people?"

"Not really," Nova replied, consulting Alma's notes. "My grandmother has a lot of information on this. Most of the people working in media, education, healthcare, and politics don't realize they're part of a control system. They're just following policies and procedures that were designed by a relatively small group of people who understand consciousness manipulation. This small group works behind the scenes and pulls all the strings."

"It's like being an actor in a movie without realizing there's a director and script," Emma said, studying the diagrams with obvious fascination. "Everyone thinks they're improvising, but actually they're following a plot they can't see."

"And the plot is designed to keep people unconscious, reactive, and dependent on external authorities for solutions to problems that could be solved through consciousness development," Tyler added, his understanding clearly accelerating as the pieces fit together.

Sarah looked up from her notes with an expression that mixed concern with determination. "So, learning these consciousness techniques isn't merely about evolving personally—it's actually about breaking free from control systems?"

"That's exactly right," Quanta confirmed. "Every person who develops these abilities becomes essentially immune to unconscious manipulation. And when groups of conscious people work together, they create changes that become unstoppable."

"But it goes deeper than just manipulation," Nova added, turning to another page in Alma's journal. "The system doesn't only control what you *think*—it shapes what you *believe* is possible. It programs you to equate worth with productivity and success with approval. From the moment you start school, it hands you a script: get good grades, go to college, land a stable job, buy a house, retire quietly. The whole path is laid out so neatly that hardly anyone ever questions who wrote it."

She looked around the table, her tone sharpening. "It's designed to keep you chasing external goals so you're too distracted to develop your internal power—to realize that the real creative force has always been within you."

"And if you step off that path," Emma said, a mix of disbelief and understanding in her voice, "you're immediately viewed as irresponsible—or worse, as a failure."

"That's unfortunately correct," Quanta said, the words carrying more force now. "The system makes conformity look like success and consciousness development look like failure. It trains you to fit in rather than wake up."

Andy was quiet for a long moment, clearly processing what they were discussing. Finally, he looked around the table at his friends with a new seriousness. "So, let me get this straight... everything we've been taught since birth—the whole path laid out for us: school, grades, college, job, marriage, house, the so-called American Dream—it's all part of a lie? A lie designed to keep us from ever realizing how powerful we actually are? We've been programmed to think we're helpless so we never question the system or try to change anything?"

"It's not a lie exactly," Nova said gently. "More like... incomplete information. You do have individual power, but you've never been taught how to access it consciously. Most people are creating their reality unconsciously, through subconscious thought patterns and emotional reactions which they initially learned as kids, which creates chaotic and often disappointing results."

"But when you learn to create consciously, through heart-brain coherence and clear intention," Quanta added, "you discover you're incredibly powerful. You just never knew how to use that power deliberately."

The conversation had grown more intense and meaningful than any lunch discussion they'd ever had, but instead of feeling overwhelming, the energy around the table felt charged with possibility and determination.

"I want to learn these techniques," Andy said firmly. "If there's really a way to break free from control systems and develop genuine personal power, I want to be part of it."

"Me too," Tyler said immediately. "I mean, I've always felt like something was off about how our society works, but I never had a framework for understanding what the problem really was or what could be done about it. Our world is a pretty screwed up place right now."

Emma nodded with obvious resolve. "And if developing these abilities helps other people break free too, then it feels like a responsibility, not just a personal choice."

The bell rang, signaling the end of lunch, but nobody moved. The conversation had reached a level of depth and significance that felt too important to interrupt with the artificial boundaries of school schedules.

"I assume this discussion will continue in the next group session?" Andy asked, clearly wanting to be part of whatever came next.

"Definitely," Nova replied. "Our next session is going to be different. We're going to explore heart-brain coherence techniques that are much more advanced than anything we've done before."

"How much more advanced?" Tyler asked with obvious excitement.

"Advanced enough that you'll understand why feeling is the secret to manifestation," Quanta said. "And why groups of conscious people working together can influence reality in ways that seem impossible through individual effort."

By the end of the school day, Quanta was convinced that their group work had accessed something genuinely transformative. Each person was not only applying the consciousness techniques individually but was also naturally becoming a source of positive influence for other students who weren't even aware of what was happening

"Nova," Quanta said as they walked toward her house after school, "I'm starting to think we might face resistance from the elite control systems sooner than we originally expected."

"What do you mean?"

"Think about how organically this is expanding. More students want to join, upperclassmen are getting interested, and everyone who tries these techniques is grasping the concepts immediately. We're going from basic stress management to heart-brain coherence and reality creation faster than most programs would attempt."

Nova paused, her expression growing more serious. "And the more powerful the techniques become, the more of a threat we represent."

"Right. Students teaching each other stress management and basic conscious development techniques is one thing, but fully aware teenagers who understand they can influence reality through their body's interaction with the quantum field? Our generation understanding that we're not powerless victims? That's when the elites will really start paying attention. We need to be strategic about building our foundation and support networks before we become too visible. If we develop too quickly without proper preparation, we could be on the elite's radar before we're equipped to handle their resistance."

"Which means we need to be even more tactical," Nova said with determination. "Careful expansion, while preparing for whatever resistance might come. We need to find the right balance between growing fast enough to reach critical mass—the tipping point where enough awakened people shift the collective field—and staying under the radar long enough to build our defenses."

That evening, Quanta headed up to his room to further practice the heart-brain coherence techniques. As he settled into the rhythmic breathing pattern, he noticed Sol immediately moving closer, positioning himself within arm's reach with that familiar knowing expression.

"You've always been heart-coherent, haven't you buddy?" Quanta realized aloud, watching how naturally Sol existed in the present moment. The dog's steady presence felt like a living example of the natural awareness they were learning to access consciously.

As Quanta practiced anchoring the elevated emotions of gratitude and appreciation, he could feel his electromagnetic field stabilizing and expanding. Sol's ears perked up, as if sensing the shift in energy quality, and the dog settled even more peacefully beside him.

"Quanta?" His mother's voice called from downstairs, interrupting his thoughts. "I'd like to talk to you about something."

He made his way down to the kitchen, where his mother was preparing a snack with an unusually relaxed expression. "I don't know what it is, but our house feels different lately. More peaceful, somehow. Even your father seems more relaxed after his long days, and I've been sleeping better than I have in years."

"Really?" Quanta asked, though he wasn't entirely surprised. "A few of my friends have mentioned the same thing about their families."

"It started around the time you began that consciousness group," Anne continued thoughtfully. "Whatever you're learning there, it seems to be having a positive effect on all of us."

As they talked, Quanta felt that familiar concern resurface. He'd worried about things moving too fast, about becoming too visible before they were ready. If families were already noticing changes, how long before the effects caught the attention of those who preferred people to remain unconscious?

"Dad," Quanta said as Justin entered the kitchen, "how quickly do you think word spreads when something starts creating measurable changes in people's lives?"

Justin paused, clearly picking up on the underlying concern in the question. "In today's connected world? Faster than most people realize. Why?"

"Just thinking about timing," Quanta replied carefully. "Making sure we're building our foundation as quickly as we're expanding."

Justin nodded with understanding. "Smart thinking. The key is staying ahead of the curve while being prepared for whatever attention that growth might attract."

As he headed back upstairs, Quanta's excitement grew about their upcoming advanced session. They were about to explore group heart-brain coherence with students who had already proven their readiness for advanced consciousness work. But they were also moving into territory where the stakes were higher and the potential for both breakthrough and resistance was greater than they'd originally anticipated.

The consciousness revolution was gaining momentum in ways none of them had fully anticipated, and their next session would mark another significant step in their journey from individual awakening to collective transformation—with all the opportunities and challenges that such profound work naturally brings.

Chapter 12: Remember

On Wednesday afternoon, Quanta stood outside the library conference room, his heart beating with an anticipation that stemmed not from nerves, but from a growing sense of recognition. Something was coming—something that felt both inevitable and impossible, like the convergence of multiple timelines into a single moment of profound significance.

Sol had been restless earlier that morning, pacing near the door like he knew something was up. When Quanta had knelt down to say goodbye, Sol had pressed his forehead against Quanta's chest for a long moment, as if transferring some essential energy for whatever lay ahead.

The past week had been filled with signs that today's session would be different. Sarah had approached him Tuesday morning with excitement about a breakthrough she'd experienced during her individual practice—she'd been working with the heart-brain coherence techniques and had spontaneously accessed what she could only describe as "a space of pure knowing" where all her anxiety patterns simply dissolved. Emma had mentioned experiencing similar states during her meditation practice, describing them as moments when she felt connected to something vast and eternal that had always been there but which she'd never noticed before.

Even Tyler, typically skeptical about anything that couldn't be measured or proven, had pulled Quanta aside after math class to describe an experience that had left him questioning everything he thought he knew about the nature of consciousness.

"I was practicing those breathing techniques we've been working with," Tyler had said, his usual defensive tone replaced by genuine wonder, "and for about ten minutes, I wasn't Tyler Chen anymore. I mean, I was still me, but I was also something much bigger. Like I was this awareness that was watching Tyler have thoughts and feelings, but the awareness itself was completely peaceful and infinite. It was like waking up from a dream I didn't even know I was having."

"Did it scare you?" Quanta had asked, remembering his own first glimpse of witness consciousness in Mr. Rike's classroom.

"At first, yeah. But then it felt like the most natural thing in the world. Like I'd been pretending to be this small, worried person my whole life, but the real me was actually this vast, calm presence that had been watching the whole show without ever being affected by it."

Nova had been experiencing similar expansions, but with an added dimension that connected directly to Alma's teachings. "I keep having these moments," she'd told him during their walk to school that morning, "where I feel my grandmother's presence so clearly that it's like she's still teaching me. Not in a ghostly or supernatural way, but like the wisdom she embodied has become part of the field itself, accessible to anyone who reaches the right frequency."

Now, as students began arriving for their session, Quanta could sense that each person was carrying their own version of this expanding awareness. Andy entered with the quiet confidence of someone who'd discovered abilities he never knew he possessed. Jessica's usual anxiety had been replaced by a grounded presence that seemed to extend several feet beyond her physical body. Even the newer students who had recently joined their expanding group—Mike Reynolds and several others from different grades—carried themselves with the kind of openness that suggested they were being drawn by something deeper than casual curiosity.

"Everyone's energy feels different today," Nova observed quietly as she arranged chairs in their now-familiar circle, which had grown steadily over the weeks. "More coherent, more aligned. Like we've all been practicing individually, but somehow we've been practicing together too, through the field."

"I was thinking the same thing," Quanta replied, feeling the truth of it in his body. Despite having been physically separated between sessions, there was a sense of continued connection, as if the group consciousness they'd created had remained active and accessible throughout the week.

As everyone settled into their seats, Quanta noticed that the usual process of individuals gradually synchronizing into group energy happened almost instantaneously. The scattered frequencies of people arriving from different classes and activities organized themselves into coherent harmony within moments, without any formal technique or guided breathing.

"Before we begin," Nova said with the gentle authority that had developed naturally through her role as a bridge between Alma's wisdom and their group's practical exploration, "I want to acknowledge something that I think everyone is feeling. There's a quality to today that feels different from our previous sessions. More concentrated, more significant."

Everyone nodded, clearly recognizing the heightened energy Nova was describing.

"My grandmother wrote about moments like this," Nova continued, referencing one of Alma's journals. "She called them 'convergence points'—times when individual consciousness development reaches a threshold where something new becomes possible. Not just personal growth, but access to levels of awareness that can permanently shift how we experience reality."

Sarah raised her hand, as she engaged with this concept. "What kind of shift are you talking about? Do you mean what becomes possible that wasn't possible before?"

"Direct knowing," Nova replied, reading from Alma's notes. "Instead of learning about consciousness, you begin to recognize yourself as consciousness itself. Instead of having experiences of expanded awareness, you realize that expanded awareness is your natural state, and everything else has been a kind of dream you've been lost in."

Tyler sat up straighter, clearly intrigued. "That sounds like what I experienced during my practice this week—realizing that my thoughts and emotions were just activities happening within this larger awareness that was watching everything."

"That's it," Quanta said, feeling the conversation moving toward the territory he'd been sensing all week. "And when groups of people access that recognition simultaneously, something unprecedented becomes available. Not just individual awakening, but collective awakening—where an entire community remembers its true nature at the same time."

Emma's eyes widened. "Is that what's been happening with our families? How everyone's been mentioning that their homes feel more peaceful, their parents seem calmer, even their pets are acting differently?"

"That's the ripple effect," Nova confirmed. "When conscious awareness reaches a certain intensity within a group, it begins to influence the consciousness of everyone within its field. But what my grandmother documented is that there comes a point where this influence becomes permanent—where the awakening stabilizes and becomes irreversible."

Andy, who had been listening with the focused attention he usually reserved for football games, spoke up. "So, you're saying that what we do today could change us permanently? We could access states of consciousness that become our new normal rather than just temporary experiences?"

"That's precisely what I'm saying," Nova replied. "But only if we're truly ready for that level of transformation. Because once you wake up to your true nature as pure awareness, there's no going back to believing you're just a body with a collection of thoughts, emotions, and circumstances. Honestly, why would anyone ever want to go back to 'normal' when awakening has shown how limited that version of reality really was?"

Jessica, who had been unusually quiet since arriving, finally spoke. "I've been having dreams all week about this session. Not specific dreams about what would happen, but this sense that something really important was approaching. Like my subconscious has been preparing me for a major shift."

"That's not your subconscious," Quanta said with sudden clarity. "That's your deeper awareness trying to get your attention, letting you know that you're ready for the next level of remembering who you really are."

As the words left his mouth, Quanta felt something familiar yet entirely new—the same voice that had commanded him to "Remember," but now speaking through him rather than to him. It was as if his individual consciousness had become a channel for the same intelligence that had initiated his awakening journey months ago.

"Remember," he heard himself say, though the word seemed to come from somewhere far deeper than his personal mind. "Remember who you were before you learned to identify with thoughts, emotions, and circumstances. Remember the awareness that was present when you were five years old, when you were ten, when you first walked into this room. Remember the constant presence that has witnessed every experience you've ever had without being changed by any of it."

The atmosphere in the room shifted immediately, becoming charged with the same electric intensity Quanta had experienced during his original awakening. But instead of time stopping for one person, it was as if the entire group had stepped outside the normal flow of time and into something infinite and timeless.

Sarah's notebook slipped from her hands as her eyes closed and her breathing deepened. Tyler's analytical expression dissolved into something resembling profound peace. Andy's athletic posture relaxed into perfect stillness. Jessica's nervous energy transformed into radiant calm.

But what impressed Quanta most was the newer students who had only recently begun attending their sessions were immediately accessing the same advanced state of expanded awareness that had taken the core group weeks to develop through their individual and group practice. It was as if the field of awakened consciousness they'd created had become so strong that anyone who entered it was instantly elevated to its frequency.

"I remember," Emma whispered with the wonder of someone who had just recognized something she'd always known but had temporarily forgotten. "I remember being this awareness before I learned to think I was Emma. It's like... it's like I've been playing the character of Emma for so long that I forgot I was acting."

"The character doesn't disappear," Nova said softly, embodying the same quiet wisdom that had spoken through Quanta. "Emma is still here—still able to go to school, hang out with friends, live her life. But now you understand that Emma isn't who you truly are—she's just the role you're playing in order to experience the world."

Tyler opened his eyes with an expression of profound amazement. "This is what I've been trying to piece together, but now it's so much clearer. It's like Tyler is just a character in a dream, and awareness is the dreamer. No matter what happens in the dream, the dreamer remains untouched."

"Exactly," Andy nodded, his natural athleticism now expressing as perfect physical presence rather than restless energy. "It's like playing a video game—you pick your avatar and get fully immersed in the mission, but at the end of the day, you're still the player holding the controller, not the character on the screen."

As the group continued to explore this recognition together, Quanta was accessing memories from what felt like before his birth—not past-life memories, but recollections of existing as pure consciousness prior to taking on human form. These weren't personal memories belonging to Quanta Jones, but universal memories that belonged to the awareness itself.

"This is why the elites work so hard to keep people unconscious," Jessica said with sudden understanding, her usual questioning tone replaced by conviction. "Because once you remember that you're eternal awareness simply having a human experience, you become absolutely impossible to control through fear or manipulation. Think about it—if you know you're not just a body, not just your thoughts or emotions, but something timeless and indestructible underneath it all, what is there to be afraid of?"

"Fear can only affect the character, not the awareness playing the character," Sarah added, having accessed the same recognition from her own direct experience. "And when you know you're the awareness, fear becomes just another passing experience rather than something that can overwhelm or control you."

Mike, who had only recently started attending their sessions, looked around the circle with an expression of grateful amazement. "I don't understand how this is possible. I knew you guys were working with consciousness techniques, but I never expected anything like this. I feel like I just remembered something I've been searching for my entire life without even knowing I was searching."

"Because you were searching," Nova replied, her voice now carrying the same timeless quality that had characterized Alma's teachings. "Every human being is searching for this recognition, whether they realize it or not. All the seeking for happiness, peace, success, approval, security—it's all really the search to remember what you truly are."

"And when you find it," Quanta said, feeling the completion of the circle that had begun with his own awakening, "the search ends. Not because you've acquired something new, but because you've recognized what was always already here."

As the session continued, what emerged was not a teaching or learning experience in the conventional sense, but a collective recognition of something that had always been true. Each person was remembering their essential nature as pure awareness, and in that remembering, the artificial boundaries between self and other, individual and group, human and cosmic consciousness began to dissolve.

"This is what my grandmother meant by the Great Awakening," Nova said. "Not just individual people having spiritual experiences, but humanity itself beginning to remember its true nature. When enough people access this recognition, it creates a tipping point where awakening becomes contagious and unstoppable."

Tyler was studying his hands with fascination, as if seeing them for the first time. "It's like I've been wearing virtual reality goggles my whole life, and I just took them off and realized the real world is completely different from what I thought I was experiencing. Like waking up from the matrix and seeing actual reality for the first time."

"But here's what's beautiful," Emma added with growing excitement. "The virtual reality world doesn't disappear when you take off the goggles. You can still play the game, still engage with school and family and all of it. You just know it's a game instead of thinking it's ultimate reality."

Andy laughed with pure joy, a sound so infectious that everyone else began laughing too—not at anything specific, but from the simple recognition of their own infinite nature expressing as temporary human personalities.

"I feel like I could handle anything now," he said when the laughter subsided. "Not because I've become stronger or more capable, but because I've remembered that the real me can't actually be threatened by anything that happens to the Andy character."

As their formal session time drew to a close, Quanta looked around the circle and realized that something permanent had shifted for each person. The awakening they'd accessed wasn't a temporary state that would fade when they returned to their regular activities—it was a recognition that would remain available as their new baseline of consciousness.

"So, what happens now?" Sarah asked, though her tone suggested she was asking out of curiosity rather than concern. "Do we come back to school tomorrow morning and pretend we're still the same people we were before this session?"

"We come back to school as the same awareness we've always been," Nova replied with a smile. "But now we know that's what we are. And that knowing changes everything about how we engage with school, family, friends, challenges, society—everything."

"It's like being undercover agents," Jessica added with obvious delight. "We look like regular students from the outside, but inside we know we're something much more powerful and free."

"And the mission," Quanta said, feeling the completion of his own journey from confused teenager to conscious guide, "is to help others remember what they really are too. Not by convincing them or trying to wake them up forcibly, but by embodying this recognition so clearly that it becomes contagious."

Emma was gathering her things but moving with the deliberate presence of someone savoring each moment. "I feel like I just graduated from something, but instead of finishing school, I'm just beginning to understand what education could actually be."

"You did graduate," Nova confirmed. "You graduated from victim consciousness to creator consciousness. From thinking life happens *to* you to realizing it's all happening *for* you—for your growth, for your awakening, for your evolution. That's what it means to be the creator: recognizing every experience is an opportunity consciousness created for itself to learn and expand."

As the group prepared to disperse, Andy asked the question that seemed to be on everyone's mind: "We'll continue meeting as a group, right?" I mean, now that we've all remembered what we really are?"

"Definitely," Quanta replied without hesitation. "But our sessions will continue to evolve. Instead of learning techniques to manage our human experience, we'll be exploring how to express our true nature more fully through our human experience."

"Plus," Nova added, "we need to continue as a group and support each other through the integration process. Awakening is just the beginning—then comes the art of living from that awakening in a world where most people are still asleep. There's a long road ahead."

Tyler was shaking his head with amazement as he stood up. "A few hours ago, I thought I was Tyler Chen, a high school freshman worried about grades and sports. Now I know I'm eternal awareness having a temporary human experience as Tyler Chen, and the grades, practices, and matches are just part of the adventure."

"But here's the thing," Sarah said with sudden insight, "Tyler's problems and concerns don't become irrelevant. They just become much more manageable because you're no longer identified with them. Tyler still wants to do well in school, but awareness doesn't suffer when Tyler faces challenges."

As they filed out of the conference room, Quanta noticed that each person's entire demeanor had shifted in subtle but unmistakable ways. They moved with greater presence, spoke with calmer authority, and seemed to carry an invisible field of peace that extended far beyond their physical boundaries.

They encountered Mr. Wagner near the main entrance, and he immediately approached them as he typically does at the end of their sessions.

"Something significant happened in your session today," he observed, studying their faces with the interest of someone who understood the signs of expanded consciousness. "You guys look like you've accessed states that typically take years of meditation to achieve."

"We remembered who we really are," Jessica said simply, her words carrying such clarity and conviction that Mr. Wagner's eyebrows rose with recognition.

"Genuine awakening," he said with obvious amazement. "That's extraordinary. Most people struggle for decades to access even glimpses of that recognition, and you've achieved stable realization through group work."

"It happened naturally," Emma added. "Once we understood the principles and practiced the techniques together, the awakening just became inevitable."

"Which raises some interesting questions about traditional approaches to consciousness development," Mr. Wagner observed. "If teenagers can access awakened awareness this readily through proper group support, it suggests that older generations can do the same. They just have more years of conditioning to overcome, so the process may take longer—but it's absolutely possible."

As they prepared to head home, Nova pulled Quanta aside for a private conversation.

"You realize what this means, don't you?" she said, her tone mixing excitement with a note of seriousness. "We just demonstrated that conscious awakening can be taught systematically and reproduced reliably. That's the kind of discovery that changes everything."

"And creates the kind of response we've been warned about," Quanta replied, understanding the implications immediately. "If word spreads that a group of high school students have developed a method for rapid consciousness awakening..."

"The elites will have to respond," Nova finished. "Because we've just proven that their control systems can be overcome much more quickly and easily than anyone thought possible."

They walked home together in contemplative silence, both processing the magnitude of what had occurred. What had begun as a simple stress management group had evolved into something unprecedented—a systematic approach to consciousness awakening that could potentially be replicated in schools, communities, and societies around the world.

When Quanta arrived home, Sol greeted him with an intensity that confirmed what he already sensed—his own energy field had stabilized at a permanently higher frequency. The dog's response was no longer the curiosity of an animal sensing unusual states in his human companion, but the recognition of an equal consciousness expressing through a different form.

"Hey, buddy," Quanta said, kneeling down to Sol's level and looking directly into those intelligent amber eyes. "I see you."

Sol's small tail wagged once, slowly and deliberately, in what felt like acknowledgment of Quanta's recognition. The dog then settled into perfect stillness, demonstrating the natural awareness that humans typically spent years trying to rediscover.

Anne was in the kitchen preparing dinner when Quanta entered, but she immediately paused and turned to face him with an expression of wonder.

"Quanta," she said softly, "you look more yourself, somehow. Like you've remembered something important."

"I have, Mom. I remembered what I really am underneath all the thoughts and emotions and concerns that usually occupy my attention."

Anne studied his face with the careful attention of a mother who had watched him grow and change throughout his life. "And what are you?"

"The same thing you are, the same thing everyone is," Quanta replied with complete certainty. "I'm awareness itself, temporarily expressing as Quanta Jones. And recognizing that changes everything about how I relate to being Quanta Jones."

Justin appeared in the doorway, clearly drawn by the quality of energy surrounding their conversation. "How did your session go today?" he asked, though his expression suggested he could already sense the answer.

"It was a complete breakthrough," Quanta replied. "Multiple students accessed genuine awakening recognition simultaneously. Not just expanded states or peak experiences, but stable realization of their true nature as consciousness itself."

"Remarkable," Justin said, his voice carrying profound appreciation for what his son was describing. "You've accomplished what's typically reserved for serious spiritual practitioners."

"That makes me wonder if traditional methods sometimes make awakening harder than it needs to be," Quanta said, his confidence growing. "Maybe it's meant to be simpler— something that happens naturally when people stop overthinking it."

Justin considered that for a moment before replying. "One thing to keep in mind is that understanding these concepts takes more than just curiosity—it takes *belief*. Even when people seem willing to learn, it's the believing part where most get stuck. Deep down, their subconscious programming just won't accept it as truth. That's why I think the youth-led sessions work better. Younger minds are more open—they haven't spent decades being conditioned to doubt themselves. What people need to realize is that what you're teaching and experiencing isn't some fringe idea anymore. Science is finally starting to confirm it. The days of this being labeled 'woo-woo' are ending."

As they continued discussing the day's developments over dinner, Quanta was seeing his parents with the same clarity he'd experienced during the group awakening. Anne and Justin weren't just the roles of "mother" and "father"—they were expressions of the same infinite awareness he'd recognized as his own true nature, temporarily focusing themselves through specific human personalities and relationships.

"I need to tell you both something," Quanta said as they finished eating. "What happened today isn't going to stay contained within our group. This method of consciousness awakening is too effective and too significant to remain limited to just our school. Word will continue to spread, and the momentum will keep building naturally."

"And that will attract the kind of attention we've been talking about," Justin said with understanding. "Those who benefit from keeping people unconscious aren't going to appreciate a high school program that can systematically awaken large numbers of young people."

"But here's the thing," Quanta continued with calm confidence. "I'm not afraid of that anymore. Not because I've become braver or stronger, but because I've remembered that what I really am can't be threatened by any external force. The awareness I am is completely untouchable."

"Plus," he added with a slight smile, "once this method becomes known, it won't matter if anyone tries to do to stop it. Consciousness awakening will become viral in the truest sense—spreading faster than any control system can respond to."

Anne reached across the table and took his hand, her expression mixing maternal pride with recognition of her son's transformation. "I'm not sure I fully understand the depth of what you're describing, but I can see that you've found something real and important. And I want you to know that your father and I will support whatever direction this takes you."

"Even if it gets complicated or controversial?" Quanta asked.

"Especially then," Justin replied firmly. "What you've discovered has the potential to help thousands of young people remember their true nature and break free from the systems that keep them trapped in limitation and fear. That's not just personal development—it's a service to humanity."

Pride lingered in Anne's eyes for only a moment before concern took over. The reality of Justin's words sank in, and her protective instincts surfaced. "Do we need to worry about the safety of our son? I don't understand who wouldn't appreciate this younger generation awakening. What control system are they breaking free from? This is starting to make me nervous with Quanta and Nova at the forefront of this movement."

"Everything will be fine," Justin replied. I will always have his back and several of my colleagues in positions of power have been waiting years for a spark like this to ignite the Great Awakening. We will make sure Quanta is not in any danger."

That night, as Quanta lay in bed reflecting on the day's extraordinary developments, he was naturally settling into the awareness he'd recognized during the group session. But this wasn't a special state he had to work to access—it was simply his natural resting place, the background consciousness within which all thoughts, emotions, and experiences simply came and went.

Sol was curled up nearby, and Quanta could sense that the dog was experiencing the same quality of present-moment awareness that had become Quanta's new baseline. They were both simply being, without the mental complications that typically obscured the simplicity of pure existence.

The journey that had begun with the voice commanding him to "Remember" had come full circle. He had remembered—not a specific piece of information or a forgotten experience, but his essential nature as the awareness within which all experiences occurred.

But he understood now that his individual awakening had never been the endpoint. It had been preparation for something much larger—the awakening of his entire generation to their true nature as conscious creators rather than unconscious victims.

Sleep hadn't claimed him yet, but a profound sense of completion had. It wasn't the end of a journey—it was the beginning of something so significant that everything before it felt like preparation. Nearly twenty students had accessed genuine awakening recognition today. Nearly twenty teenagers now knew themselves as eternal awareness temporarily expressing through human form. Nearly twenty bridges between the sleeping and awakened worlds had been established.

As he lay there in the peaceful darkness, he started thinking through the numbers and their overall impact. If their group could systematically awaken nearly twenty people in a few sessions, what would happen when those twenty each helped twenty others remember their true nature? And when those 400 awakened students each guided twenty more?

The mathematics of consciousness expansion were staggering. Within weeks, hundreds of students could access awakened awareness. Within months, thousands of young people across multiple communities could remember who they really were. Eventually the momentum would reach critical mass.

The elites would have to respond.

For decades, possibly centuries, the control systems had relied on keeping people unconscious from childhood through adulthood. Their entire power structure depended on humans believing they were powerless victims rather than infinite creators. They achieved this through carefully designed systems—schooling that rewarded obedience over awareness, media that kept minds distracted and fearful, political systems that kept people divided, and economic structures that kept everyone too busy surviving to ever question the system. Add to that a constant stream of processed food, pharmaceuticals, religious guilt, and societal pressure to conform, and you get a population programmed to forget its own power. From every angle, humans were conditioned to look outside themselves for truth, validation, and salvation—never within. Because once people remember who they really are, the illusion of control collapses. And the elites know that.

What Nova's grandmother had called "the frequency war" was no longer a hidden conflict fought in the shadows. It was about to become visible, urgent, and unavoidable. Because for the first time in human history, consciousness awakening was becoming systematic, reproducible, and exponentially scalable among the younger generation.

Quanta glanced out his bedroom window as Sol stirred beside him. He could see the lights of his suburban neighborhood—thousands of families going through their evening routines, most of them completely unaware that a transformation of unprecedented magnitude had just begun in a high school library conference room.

The elites had built their manipulation technologies assuming that consciousness development would remain rare, difficult, and confined to isolated spiritual seekers. Anyone who questioned the system or saw through the illusion was cast out—labeled crazy, delusional, or a conspiracy theorist. It was all by design. Discredit the questioners, and you disarm the truth before it spreads.

They had never imagined that teenagers could systematically awaken each other through peer-to-peer consciousness education. They had never considered that the very generation they'd conditioned to be the most distracted and disconnected might become the instrument of their downfall.

The soft chime of Quanta's phone interrupted his final thoughts before he finally dozed off. A text from his father: *"Need to talk to you first thing tomorrow morning. Just found out Dr. Vasquez's research funding was mysteriously pulled today. University cited 'budget constraints' but timing seems awfully suspicious given recent progress. Her adolescent consciousness development project was terminated effective immediately. Our concerns justified."*

Quanta stared at the message, a chill running through him despite the warmth of his room. Dr. Vasquez had been studying the same group-awakening protocols they'd just proven worked. If her university research was being shut down...

The implications were clear. The resistance was no longer theoretical—it was real. The control systems could cut funding, censor findings, and silence researchers. But they couldn't stop what had already begun. Consciousness was awakening through those who could no longer be programmed, no longer be controlled.

And if the elites thought they could contain it, they were about to learn the one truth no system could ever suppress: once consciousness remembers itself, nothing can stop it.

The Quanta Chronicles - Concept Glossary

A complete reference guide to consciousness principles, quantum physics concepts, spiritual frameworks, universal laws, and practical applications explored in Quanta Jones and the Awakening

---

Core Consciousness Concepts

Awareness versus Thoughts - The recognition that you are not your thoughts, but the awareness observing them. Like being the screen on which movies play rather than the movies themselves.

Observer Effect - Quantum physics principle showing that consciousness affects physical reality just by observing it. Your attention literally changes what becomes real.

Present Moment Power - All creative power exists in the now. Past and future are mental constructs that limit access to your true capabilities.

Witness Consciousness - The part of you that can observe thoughts, emotions, and experiences without being controlled by them. Your true identity as pure awareness.

The Glitch - The moment when linear time dissolves and awareness expands beyond ordinary perception. Often the first experience of awakening consciousness.

The Voice - The universe's call to those ready to awaken, commanding them to "Remember" their true nature as consciousness. Not an auditory sound, but a transmission that resonates within awareness itself.

Remembering - The process of reconnecting with your true nature as consciousness rather than just physical form. Not recalling the past, but recognizing what you've always been.

Energy & Frequency

Everything is Energy - Tesla's principle that all matter is energy vibrating at different frequencies. Thoughts, emotions, and physical objects are all energy patterns.

Frequency Anchoring - Technique for instantly accessing desired emotional states through specific physical gestures or mental triggers.

Heart-Brain Coherence - When heart rhythm and brain waves synchronize, creating a powerful electromagnetic field that can influence reality and others around you.

Quantum Field - The invisible field of energy and information that connects all consciousness. The bridge between spiritual concepts and scientific reality.

Resonance Principle - Like tuning forks, consciousness responds to matching frequencies. You naturally attract and influence experiences that match your vibrational state.

Electromagnetic Transmission - Every thought and emotion broadcasts an electromagnetic signal that shapes the quantum field and influences physical reality.

Coherence - A synchronized state where heart rhythm, brain waves, and intentions align to create maximum influence on reality and enhanced mental performance.

Decoherence - The quantum physics term for when multiple possibilities collapse into one definite reality through conscious observation. The moment potentiality becomes actuality.

Universal Laws

Law of Correspondence - "As within, so without" - Your inner reality creates your outer experience. Change your internal state to change your external world.

Law of Attraction - Like frequencies attract each other. The energy you consistently broadcast determines what experiences you draw into your life.

Law of Divine Oneness - Everything in the universe is connected through consciousness. Like a spider web - touch one strand and the whole web vibrates.

Law of Vibration - Everything has its own unique frequency. You can tune into different realities by changing your vibrational state.

Manifestation Principles

Five-Step Manifestation System - Complete framework: (1) Clear intention with elevated emotion, (2) Belief and mental rehearsal, (3) Alignment through inspired action, (4) Detachment from how/when, (5) Gratitude and embodiment.

Feeling is the Secret - Emotions are the language of the quantum field. How you feel about your desires is more powerful than how you think about them.

Future Memory Creation - Making desired outcomes feel so real that your subconscious accepts them as memories that "already happened."

Conscious versus Unconscious Transmission - Most people broadcast random, reactive signals. Awakened individuals transmit deliberately aligned frequencies that consciously create their reality.

Inspired Action - Actions taken from coherent, high-frequency states that feel natural and effortless rather than forced or anxious.

Group Consciousness

Collective Field - When people achieve coherence together, they create a group energy field more powerful than individual efforts.

Consciousness Contagion - Coherent emotional and mental states spread naturally from person to person through electromagnetic field effects.

Morphic Resonance - Group intentions create invisible blueprints that continue influencing outcomes even when the group separates.

1% Effect - Just 1% of a population operating at higher consciousness can significantly influence the behavior of the entire group.

Group Coherence - When multiple people synchronize their heart rhythms and brain waves, creating an amplified collective field that enhances everyone's capabilities.

Peak Performance Field - The collective consciousness state that naturally emerges when individuals achieve coherence together, dramatically enhancing problem-solving and creative abilities.

Consciousness Amplification - Individual consciousness capabilities multiply exponentially when supported by a coherent group field.

Control Systems Awareness

Frequency Prison - Low-frequency emotional states (fear, anger, confusion) that keep people trapped in limited thinking and reactive behavior.

Elite Manipulation - Systematic use of consciousness suppression techniques through media, education, and social programming to maintain control.

Liberation Protocols - Specific techniques for developing immunity to external manipulation and maintaining conscious awareness regardless of external pressure.

Consciousness Immunity - Once you understand how your awareness works, you become essentially immune to unconscious influence and manipulation.

The Great Awakening - The accelerating global shift where increasing numbers of people are developing consciousness capabilities and immunity to manipulation.

Frequency Manipulation - The deliberate use of electromagnetic signals, media programming, and environmental stressors to keep populations in reactive, low-frequency states.

Victim Consciousness - The programmed belief that external circumstances control your life, keeping people disempowered and susceptible to manipulation.

Practical Techniques

Synchronized Breathing - Group technique for achieving collective coherence by matching breath rhythm and quality.

Gratitude Anchoring - Using appreciation to instantly shift from low-frequency to high-frequency emotional states.

Reality Anchoring - Advanced technique for maintaining manifestation frequencies even in challenging circumstances.

Coherence Techniques - Methods for synchronizing heart rhythm and brain waves to access peak performance states.

Frequency Work - Systematic practice of becoming aware of your energetic state and consciously shifting to higher frequencies throughout the day.

Gratitude Exercise - Simple technique of feeling genuine appreciation for three things to instantly raise your vibrational frequency.

Mental Inventory Practice - Regular checking of thought patterns and emotional states to maintain conscious awareness rather than unconscious reactivity.

Breath Awareness - Using conscious breathing to anchor presence and shift from mental reactivity to witness consciousness.

Collective Intention Setting - When a coherent group focuses on a shared outcome, exponentially amplifying manifestation power.

Key Analogies

Radio Tuning - Your consciousness is like a radio that can tune into different frequencies of reality. Change the station, change your experience.

Movie Projector - Your mind is the projector, your life is the screen. To change the movie, change the film (your thoughts/beliefs) in the projector.

Wi-Fi Connection - Consciousness works like an invisible network connecting all awareness. You can share energy and information instantly.

Tuning Forks - When one person achieves coherence, others naturally start resonating at the same frequency, like tuning forks vibrating together.

Multiple Flashlights - Individual consciousness is like a single flashlight. Group consciousness is like multiple flashlights pointed in the same direction, creating a beam powerful enough to illuminate what none could alone.

Spider Web Consciousness - All awareness is connected like strands in a spider web. Touch one strand and the entire web vibrates.

Cosmic Rubber Bands - String theory shows that fundamental reality vibrates like rubber bands at different frequencies to create all matter and energy.

Scientific Foundations

Double-Slit Experiment - Proves that matter behaves differently when observed versus unobserved, showing consciousness affects physical reality.

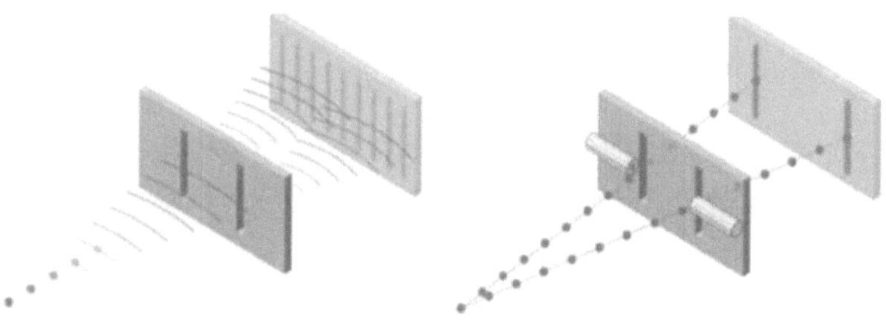

Quantum Physics - The branch of science that explores how matter and energy behave at the smallest levels—atoms and subatomic particles—where the ordinary laws of classical physics no longer apply. It seeks to uncover the invisible building blocks of reality and the forces that govern how everything in the universe interacts and comes into being.

Quantum Entanglement - Particles remain mysteriously connected across any distance, suggesting fundamental interconnectedness of all things.

Superposition - Multiple possibilities exist simultaneously until consciousness observes and "collapses" them into one specific reality.

Electromagnetic Fields - The heart generates fields 5000x stronger than the brain, broadcasting your emotional frequency to everyone around you.

Wave-Particle Duality - Light and matter exhibit both wave and particle properties depending on observation, demonstrating consciousness's role in determining physical reality.

Wave Theory - Shows that at the quantum level, everything exists as probability waves until consciousness collapses those waves into definite particles. The fundamental way reality operates before observation.

String Theory - Modern physics proving Tesla's principle that everything at the most fundamental level is made of tiny vibrating strings. These strings vibrate at different frequencies to create all particles and forms of matter - electrons, protons, photons, and all building blocks of reality.

Probability Fields - Multiple potential outcomes exist simultaneously in the quantum field until consciousness selects one through observation and intention.

Character & Teacher Concepts

The Bridge Role - Individuals who can translate consciousness principles for others while operating in both conventional and awakened realities.

Natural Teacher - Those with innate ability to awaken consciousness in others through presence, questions, and practical demonstration rather than preaching.

Conscious Elders - Adults who understand both practical society requirements and expanded consciousness, providing essential support for young consciousness teachers.

Resonance Recognition - The ability to sense when someone is ready for deeper consciousness conversations based on their energetic openness.

Advanced Concepts

Consciousness Education - Teaching awareness development and reality creation principles, especially to young people before they're fully programmed into victim consciousness.

Reality Creation Laboratory - Using everyday experiences as opportunities to practice and refine consciousness techniques in real-world conditions.

Collective Social Transformation - When coherent consciousness groups influence larger systems like communities, institutions, and social patterns.

Consciousness Evolution - The natural human development beyond reactive, fear-based thinking into deliberate, creative awareness.

Holographic Reality - The scientific theory that reality is structured like a hologram where every part contains information about the whole, explaining how individual consciousness affects collective experience.

Consciousness as Primary - The understanding that awareness is fundamental to reality rather than an emergent property of matter.

Integration Principles

Theory Meets Practice - The essential combination of understanding consciousness principles intellectually and experiencing them directly through practical application.

Science and Spirituality - The convergence of quantum physics and mystical wisdom as different languages describing the same fundamental truths about consciousness and reality.

Personal and Collective Development - The recognition that individual consciousness work simultaneously benefits collective awakening through interconnected consciousness fields.

Inner Work Creates Outer Change - The principle that transforming your internal state is the most powerful way to influence external circumstances and help others.